The reaper listened to the soft sounds of Roxanne disrobing.

The faucet cranked on, followed by the metallic hiss of the shower curtain being drawn. He pictured her standing beneath the spray, head tilted back as water cascaded down her body. Stripped, slick, slippery, and soft.

Before he understood the treachery of it, his imagination had placed him there with her, his body a dark shadow against the whiteness of hers, his hands big enough to span her waist, moving up to pull her yielding curves against the hard planes of his chest, fitting her to him.

Carnal. His own erotic thoughts stunned him. As much as violence made sense to the reaper, passion had completely bewildered him. He'd never understood the depth of emotion that drove humans to spend their lives together.

Until now.

THE FIVE DEATHS
OF
ROXANNE LOVE

ERIN QUINN

POCKET BOOKS

New York London Toronto Sydney New Delhi

Pocket Books
A Division of Simon & Schuster, Inc.
1230 Avenue of the Americas
New York, NY 10020

This book is a work of fiction. Any references to historical events, real people, or real places are used fictitiously. Other names, characters, places, and events are products of the author's imagination, and any resemblance to actual events or places or persons, living or dead, is entirely coincidental.

First Pocket Books paperback edition September 2013

POCKET and colophon are registered trademarks of Simon & Schuster, Inc.

For information about special discounts for bulk purchases, please contact Simon & Schuster Special Sales at 1-866-506-1949 or business@simonandschuster.com.

The Simon & Schuster Speakers Bureau can bring authors to your live event. For more information or to book an event, contact the Simon & Schuster Speakers Bureau at 1-866-248-3049 or visit our website at www.simonspeakers.com.

Designed by Lewelin Polanco

Manufactured in the United States of America

10 9 8 7 6 5 4 3 2 1

ISBN 978-1-4767-2747-9
ISBN 978-1-4767-2751-6 (ebook)

For my sister, who waves her magic wand and makes things beautiful. Love you, Berd.

—Smerd

ACKNOWLEDGMENTS

Thanks seems too small a word to say to Abby Zidle, whose incredibly intuitive edits reshaped this book into what it is, but I'm hoping if I shout it out really loud, maybe it will come close. Seriously, Abby. Thank you.

I required a lot of talking down on this book. Thank you to Paige Wheeler, Lynn Coulter, Calista Fox, Betty Grady, Kathryne Kennedy, and Kallie Owens for all of your support.

Special thanks go out to my wonderful family. Mom, I couldn't do it without you. Thank you for always being there with a dose of sanity and the occasional margarita. Rick, you'll always be my Spartacus. Kids, you make it all worthwhile.

Sylvia Day, thank you for taking time from your crazy (bestselling!!!) life to hold my hand, and tell me I could do it.

Jodi Springer and Rebecca Johnson, thank you for saving the day and being the best beta readers a writer ever had.

To the fine people of Arizona Mills mall and the Rainforest Café: I took unmentionable liberties with your Tempe establishments in this novel. Please forgive my overactive imagination and any alterations I made to your facilities in the name of fiction.

And last but never least, thank you to my readers. You know who you are—your emails and posts keep me at it. You will never know how grateful I am that you choose my books to read.

The reaper entered the room as Santo Castillo spun the cylinder of the revolver, took a deep swallow of Wild Turkey, then put the muzzle in his mouth. He pulled the trigger without hesitation. The hollow click that followed seemed to mock the shadowed silence.

Santo choked back a sob, dropped the gun on the low coffee table in front of him, and reached for his glass again. For a long moment he just sat there, shoulders hunched, silent, dry sobs wracking his body. A tall man, with broad shoulders and a heavy, muscular frame, he looked odd crying his dry tears. The reaper moved closer, perplexed by the duplicity of human emotion. The man wanted to die. He begged for death, yearned for it. And yet he fought it even now, when it was too late.

The reaper paused just behind him and blew a soft breath in his ear. Santo stiffened, lifted his head, and looked around uneasily.

Yes. I've come for you.

A shudder went through the human and he took another hasty drink, wincing as the burn of the alcohol slid down his throat.

A light hung just above the couch and coffee table where Santo wallowed in his misery. The reaper gave it a gentle nudge, making it sway back and forth, producing cadaverous shadows that slithered across the walls. The chain squeaked ever so slightly in a macabre overture to what would come. Santo's gaze darted warily around the room. His fear seasoned the air and the reaper breathed it in. Fear always honeyed the reaping.

He moved closer, trailing his fingers over Santo's broad shoulders, admiring the hard strength of him. Yes, he would be perfect.

Perfect, he whispered.

Santo jumped and spun in his seat, staring right through the reaper, seeing nothing but the queer boogeymen of his imagination. His anxious eyes grew hot with panic as he turned back around. The small hairs on his nape stood on end. Santo reached for his gun and fumbled, sending it in a tailspin across the table, knocking over a framed snapshot he'd propped in front of him—a silent witness to his madness. The gun skated off the smooth surface and hit the carpeted floor with a dull thud.

While Santo ducked down to retrieve it, the reaper righted the photo.

Visibly shaken, his pulse a staccato beat at his throat, Santo closed his eyes and rubbed the scruff of his beard. He mumbled something the reaper couldn't hear, but then again, he didn't need to hear it. They all prayed at this point.

After several deep breaths, Santo opened his eyes again and focused on the framed picture, once more positioned on the table. The image of a jubilant Santo with dark, sparkling eyes and a wide, dimpled smile looked back from the photograph. Wrapped around him from behind was a female with the same brown skin and velvety gaze. She laughed at the camera.

The reaper remembered her. He'd been the one to take her when her time had come. She and her baby had tasted of sweetness and light, and as he'd passed them through to their next destination, he'd been strangely moved by a sense of loss.

He frowned with distaste at the memory. He blamed another woman for the unwanted emotion. Roxanne Love. Before her, he'd never cared for the souls he'd reaped. Only that they'd abounded.

He watched Santo as the human scowled at the righted photograph. The reaper could see the memory of the last few moments replaying in Santo's mind, in his expression. The spinning gun careening toward the snapshot, the frame teetering, toppling over with a flat, cracking sound that had left a splinter in the glass at the bottom right corner. Santo's eyes shifted back and forth as he recounted each cause and effect in an attempt to rationalize how the frame could have come to be propped in front of him now, as if none of that had happened.

Santo shook his head in silent denial. Looking like the cop he'd been for the last twelve years, he narrowed his dark eyes and searched the room.

You know who I am. You invited me here.

The human's fear simmered to an erotic terror. He gave the gun in his hand a desperate look, took another drink, and shoved the muzzle in his mouth. The cruel click of the pulled trigger taunted him, as impotent as the dry tears.

He savored Santo's anguish. Few humans really desired death when they courted it in this manner. This one did, yet Santo felt he deserved the torture of the game he played. He owned a half-dozen guns that would have done the job quicker, but he endured the punishment of each deadly click. The torment of forcing himself to do it again and again.

The reaper knew Santo would keep pulling that trigger until the job was done. At 12:10 a.m., a clean shot would blow away the back of his skull and kill him instantly.

Or should.

For Santo Castillo, death would come, but not from a bullet. His beautiful face would remain intact, his gray matter safely stored in his cranium. The reaper had never taken a soul from a human that still lived, but he didn't hesitate to do it now. He needed a body for a day, maybe less. Just long enough to find the woman who'd escaped him. The woman whose soul he'd touched, held, and lost. Just long enough to reap her and return to the Beyond.

In less than twenty-four hours Roxanne Love would die once again. Only this time he'd be there, in flesh and spirit, to make sure she *stayed* dead.

As Santo put the gun in his mouth once more, the reaper sat down on the table in front of him and let himself be *seen*. For a single, glorious moment, Santo's terror swaddled them both, then the reaper took over and put an end to the human's misery.

(2)

Fifty-eight minutes before she died, Roxanne Love noticed three things. The stain on the ceiling, her brother's short fuse, and the tall stranger who quietly entered and sat in the back.

The stain had caught her eye earlier, and after that, she couldn't stop looking at it. A stain meant a leak and that meant a bill. Bad news all around. But worse than that, the black splotch crouching in the far corner like a fat spider gave her a bad case of the creeps, though she couldn't say just why. The crazy feeling stalked her as she served drinks to the two customers sitting at the bar of the pub she co-owned with her sister and brothers. She couldn't shake it.

Then the man came through the front door.

Six and a half feet tall, sporting the kind of muscle

that took work to build, he strode in like he was on a mission. He wore a black T-shirt beneath a weathered leather jacket that looked like it might have been brown at one time but had faded to a distressed shade of beige. Jeans hugged his long legs and a whole lot of masculine mojo followed him like fanfare.

He took a seat in the corner, seeming to pull all the shadows in around him. The observation was so strange that it made her pause.

"What can I get for you?" she asked, setting a cocktail napkin in front of him.

"Wild Turkey," he ordered in a smoky voice that teased her a step closer.

He was ridiculously attractive with all that dark, brooding attitude and he-man brawn. In contrast, he had the longest eyelashes she'd ever seen. Thick and black, they framed smoldering eyes the color of midnight.

"Please," he tacked on when she stood there staring.

Embarrassed, she asked, "Straight up or on the rocks?"

"In a glass," he answered with a bewildered frown.

She might have laughed if he hadn't seemed so serious.

"That's generally where we pour them," she said. "The floor is just too messy."

His startled expression became a slow grin that made her blush to her roots. He was *that* good-looking.

At the same time, a niggling sense of disquiet wormed its way into her addled brain.

"I'll be right back with your drink," she mumbled.

As she turned away, the stain caught her eye again and her unease tipped into foreboding. The power of the feeling on the heels of her embarrassment gave it a disproportionate weight that made it all the more disturbing. What the hell was wrong with her tonight?

She served the man's drink quickly, avoiding his eyes and returning to the safety of the bar like an awkward teenager with a really bad crush.

A minute later her twin brother pushed through the swinging door from the kitchen. "Eighty-six the meatloaf," Reece said, eyeing the deserted bar and tables. "We should just close up for the night."

"Ryan says not before midnight." Ryan was their older brother and the boss.

"Ryan says," Reece mocked.

He caught sight of the man sitting in the corner and paled.

"Who's that?" he demanded, turning his back as he filled his cup with ice and soda.

"A customer?" she answered.

He scowled at her. "I don't think so. He looks like a cop."

Surprised, Roxanne gave the man in question a glance. He didn't look like a cop to her, but he had this dark, sexy as sin, *if George Clooney were Latino* thing going on that lent him a mysterious, dangerous air. He'd walked in like he had a purpose, though. Now he sat cloaked in all that shadow and manliness. It was unnerving. *He* was unnerving. And he'd been watching her since he'd come in.

She knew because she'd been watching him back.

"What does it matter if he's a cop?" she asked Reece, trying not to look at the man again. "We're not breaking the law. We're serving food and drinks, just like it says we do on the front door. I've been checking IDs. Don't worry about him."

"I'm not worried," Reece snapped.

"Then why are you biting my head off?" She grabbed his sleeve when he would have turned away. "Seriously. What's up? What's the matter?"

Her brother glanced at the man again before he searched Roxanne's face as if seeking understanding. But she didn't get what he wanted her to understand. In all honesty, it had been a long time since she'd been on the same page with her twin. Not since the *accident*.

"Nothing's going on," Reece said at last. "I just want to get the fuck out of here."

With that, he filled his cup and went back to the kitchen. A few seconds later, she heard him slamming things around and cursing loud enough that Jim and Sal, regulars who could be found at their bar most any night, could hear him. The two men exchanged glances but said nothing. She felt bad for Manny, their dish-washer, who had to be stuck in the kitchen with Reece for the rest of the night.

She thought about following her brother and forc-ing him to talk to her, but what was the point? He'd either take his bad mood out on her or whine about having to work on Friday night, and she'd heard it all before. Love's had been opened by their grandparents back in the days when Mill Avenue had a producing flour mill and Tempe, Arizona, had been a sleepy town. When their father had died, the bar became theirs. It was a piece of their heritage that they all held on to, even though lately it felt more like labor than love.

With a frustrated sigh, she went back to work, but business was slow and her two customers had full drinks. She wiped the bar, forcing herself *not* to look at the man in the corner or the stain on the ceiling.

But she couldn't help it. Every few minutes she glanced up, eyeing the splotch balefully. Unable to shake the feeling that it was some kind of omen.

She couldn't stop peeping at the stranger in the back either. He sat alone, nursing his Wild Turkey, pretend-ing to mind his own business. But he was still watching her. She could feel it.

If he was a cop, why was he watching *her*?

And what did his presence have to do with Reece being strung so tight? The last time her brother had been such an ass-hat, bad things had happened. Things she didn't even like to remember. The thought of living through them again made her bones ache.

At last, she tossed her towel beneath the bar and decided to quit dancing around and just find out who the stranger was.

"How you doing over here?" she asked, approaching with an easy smile that felt utterly fake.

"I'm fine, thank you for asking," he answered.

His eyes held a bemused gleam as they made a lazy sweep of her hair and face. She caught herself smoothing her ponytail and tried not to look completely disconcerted by him. But it was harder than it should have been.

"I haven't seen you in here before," she said, pleased at how natural her voice sounded. It had just the right balance of warmth and inquisitiveness and none of the jittery nerves rioting inside her.

"It's my first visit."

She sensed that the innocuous statement held a double meaning she wasn't sharp enough to catch.

"Well, welcome to Love's. I'm Roxanne."

"I know. Roxanne Love."

He spoke her name in that husky tone, only now it held a note of satisfaction. As if finding her, recognizing her, had been a great feat that he'd accomplished against all odds.

Her smile faltered and she took a step back. The instinct was ingrained. It had been years since the media or the obsessed fanatics who'd stalked her in the past had caught her unaware, but she never fully let down her guard.

He smiled again. It seemed he couldn't help himself, and a dimple flashed from his cheek. "I've made you nervous."

"No," she lied, "but you have me at a disadvantage. I don't think we've met."

"Not formally."

Not at all. No way she would have forgotten him.

"I'm Detective Santo Castillo," he said, and Roxanne released her breath on a soft whoosh.

Okay, so not a stalker. That was good news. But Reece guessing he was a cop and then freaking out about it . . . not so great. Not when it made her think her brother must be guilty of something.

The detective leaned across the table and handed her his badge.

Wary, Roxanne studied the medal and verified that the picture matched the man before giving it back. But a bad feeling settled around her. Just like the damn stain, it began to spread. She glanced up again before she could stop herself. As if to confirm a relationship, the stain had grown bigger and somehow more threatening.

She swallowed and forced her attention back to Santo Castillo. His glass was almost empty. "Drinking on the job, Detective?" she asked, nodding at it.

"Off the clock."

"But not off duty?"

"What cop is ever off duty?"

She supposed he had a valid point, but she was getting too many mixed signals from him to know what to trust.

"So what brings you and your badge to Love's tonight?"

"Good food, fine brew, and great friends," he said, quoting the motto printed on the front window.

"So you're not looking for anyone?"

"Like?"

"I don't know. Outlaws."

"And if I am?" he asked.

She shrugged, glancing at the nearly deserted bar. "Good luck with that?"

A taut pause followed while he snared her gaze and held it prisoner.

"You seem a bit skittish, Roxanne."

She felt a bit skittish. Excited. Like she'd just raced down a long staircase and found that the last step dropped into nowhere.

She balanced on the edge, hyperaware of him. His size. His intensity. His *presence*. She didn't know if she wanted to bolt or move closer. He caught his bottom lip with his teeth and worried it for a moment, while his gaze delivered a message so *male* that she felt an instinctive, uncontrollable response.

He said very softly, "You have beautiful eyes. I didn't expect that."

"What?"

"It's the gold in the gray, I think. It's startling."

She didn't know what to say, so she stood there, speechless, mouth opened in surprise. She'd been told her eyes were pretty before—who hadn't?—but coming from him, it seemed to take a deeper meaning. She felt another hot blush creep up her throat.

"What do you mean, you didn't *expect* it?"

"I've been watching you."

"Yeah, I noticed that. Why?"

The question hung between them, filled with a weight she didn't quite fathom. He seemed to be sifting through his thoughts, examining and discarding responses. At last he said simply, "I find you intriguing."

"That sounds a little creepy considering you've never even met me before," she said.

He laughed, and the sound sent a trill down her spine. She didn't know if he was flirting with her or toying with her. Maybe it didn't matter. She was ill equipped to handle either one.

"You and your brother seem to be having a disagreement tonight," he said, switching the subject so unexpectedly that she had to scramble to keep up.

"I can't see how that's any of your business," she answered.

"Can't you? Why don't you have a seat? Let's talk about my business."

His eyes sparkled wickedly and the disquiet burrowing in the pit of her stomach spread its wings and became full-fledged anxiety. He was here to ask questions about Reece if she'd read the scenario correctly.

Reece? What did you do?

She needed to get back to the kitchen and find out what the hell was going on before the detective mind-melded her with another of those soul-searching looks and she said something stupid.

Roxanne pinned another fake smile in place and said, "Of course, Detective—"

"Santo. You can call me Santo."

Oh, I think not.

"Let me just check on things in the kitchen first," she said carefully. "We're about to close up for the night."

He glanced at his watch as if to confirm it and nodded. "By all means. Put your affairs in order."

A really weird way of saying *do what you need to do* that pinged her inner alarms. She wanted to ask what he meant by that, but she glanced up again and all other thoughts vanished as she sucked in a stunned breath.

In the time she'd been talking to him, the stain had spread to the edges of the ceiling. She could see it moving like a wave rushing the shore. The idea that it was alive and with purpose took root in some sequestered part of her psyche and began to grow. She imagined she could even smell it. Dank and sulfurous.

The detective pushed away from the table, staring up at it with sudden anger that was almost as confounding as the speed with which the stain had spread.

As if from a distance, she heard her two regulars, Jim and Sal, talking. Jim muttered, "You smell that? Toilets backed up, you think?"

"Must be," Sal agreed.

She jerked her gaze away and stared at the two men in shock. "Look," she said, her voice squeaking. She jabbed a finger at the ceiling.

They did, both of them coming to their feet as they stared at the seeping blackness overhead. "What the fuck *is* that?" Sal demanded.

"I don't know. It was just a spot earlier, but now—"

A loud buzzing spun them all around to face the front door and windows. The noise seemed to come from just outside. Droning and harsh, it grew in volume and intensity as they watched with mouths open and eyes wide.

Everyone except the detective.

He knew what was coming, knew what made that hideous, atonal sound. She could see it on his face. He scanned from the ceiling to the windows and back, eyes hard, brows pulled.

"What?" she breathed. "What is—"

The first of the bugs hit the window with a squelching pop, and Roxanne screamed, jumping back. Greenish-brown goo splattered out from the point of impact, but she barely had a moment to register it before more slammed into the glass. Hundreds of them peppered it like bullets, leaving behind a nauseating smear of guts and gore. Each impact sent her back another jerky step until she bumped into the bar.

"Why are they doing that?" she demanded to keep from screaming again. She wanted to cover her eyes and ears, but fear of *not* seeing kept her from doing either one.

"Fuck," Sal yelled. "Look at the ceiling."

She tore her gaze away only to see that the stain above had thickened into a slick black ooze. It looked like an upside-down oil spill on a choppy sea. Soon it would reach the bar and the kitchen. And the stench . . . Damp and foul. Rotten eggs in a steamy soup.

The blackness began to drip, and Roxanne fought down another scream.

"Reece! Reece, get out here!" she shouted instead, just as a loud crash came from the kitchen.

"*Reece!*"

Santo turned, his gaze unerringly finding hers. The look he gave her spoke volumes, but she couldn't understand what it meant. She couldn't understand what was happening. The bugs had completely obscured the windows, the live ones crawling over the splattered remains, trying to get in. She felt the blood drain from her face. Could they? Would they find a way?

It felt obscene and, at the same time, somehow biblical in a very not-okay way. Reece still hadn't appeared, but a cry came from the kitchen, followed by a loud bang.

"That's a gun," Sal said, jumping.

A gun?

Roxanne shoved her fear aside and raced to the swinging door, calling out her brother's name as she ran. She burst into the kitchen, aware of Santo a few steps behind.

What she saw brought her to a skidding stop. Santo took her hand and tried to pull her back, but when she refused to budge, he gave up and angled his body in front of hers. Even a man his size couldn't block out the horror, though.

The oily tide coated the ceiling and lapped against the walls in the kitchen, stark against the stainless steel and new paint.

The back door stood wide open to the October night. The same back door that Reece and their older brother, Ryan, fought about constantly. Ryan insisted that it remain locked after five. Reece complained that Ryan was a control freak who needed to get a life. *"What the fuck does he care if the back door is open? For Christ sake, let the slaves have some fresh air."*

The shelving that held pots and pans had been

knocked over, its contents scattered all around it. The dishwasher was sprawled beside the sink. She could only see his legs and feet, but she recognized the rolled-up jeans, bright yellow sneakers, and hem of his too-big Iron Man T-shirt bunched around his thighs. The black ooze splattered his inert form.

Flash, flash, flash. The images bombarded her so fast that she could barely focus on one before moving to another.

Reece stood in the doorway to the small office that was tucked between the walk-in refrigerator and the far wall, facing away from her. Through the big window that allowed an unobstructed view from the desk into the kitchen, she saw a man in front of the opened safe.

"You shot him. You fucking shot Manny," Reece shouted.

The man glanced over his shoulder at Reece, and Roxanne felt all the air leave her lungs. He wore a ski mask pulled down to hide his features, with black paint rimming his eyes. Only the whites and the pale blue irises could be seen. He'd sewn the mouth-hole closed with fat, ugly stitches so that not even his lips showed. He glanced past Reece to where Roxanne and the others now stood. Reece turned, too, and in the dread she saw on his face, Roxanne read so much more.

Reece knew this masked man. More than that, her brother had let him in.

Disbelief pierced her as the man spoke. His words

came disembodied from behind the stitched mask and all the more terrifying for those frigid eyes in their obsidian setting.

"Trust me, Reece."

He shot her twin brother before she could grasp what he meant to do. Roxanne screamed again, but fear had closed her throat and all that emerged was a strangled cry. The echo of the gunfire reverberated through the kitchen, and her brother fell to the hard, tiled floor, his blood spilling from a wound in his chest. Then the man with the ghastly mask spun and she looked into the pale eyes and knew that what lurked behind that frozen blue was not human.

Not human by any measure.

As if invited by the blood spurting from her brother's chest and the black gunk pooling on the floor, others began to pour in through the back door like roaches from a drain. Others. Not people but . . . She stared numbly, trying and failing to label what she saw. Whatever *they* were, they didn't wear masks. They didn't need to. Their appearance was hunched and gnarled, their skin so colorless it looked like paste. And their eyes . . . white except for the pinpoints of the pupils. White lanterns in the most gruesome faces she'd ever seen.

Santo jerked her away just as the man with the mask pulled the trigger two times in rapid succession and Sal and Jim hit the floor.

"No!" she cried as a hot spray splattered her skin. Santo was dragging her through the swinging doors when something slammed into her from behind and she stumbled. Excruciating pain exploded through her, and Santo was all that kept her from falling.

He shouted something, but she couldn't make out the words through the screeching agony. The pain became an entity that owned her.

She looked down to see that blood covered her pink Love's T-shirt and bubbled when she tried to suck in a breath. She'd been shot. Just like Reece . . . Her thoughts blurred and her knees gave.

Santo swept her into his arms as he raced across the dining room, charging into the bug-infested night. Roxanne felt herself slipping, *hurtling* toward a black unknown that felt ominously familiar. They'd met before, Roxanne and death, and she knew that in the darkness, she'd find someone waiting. He always waited, that nameless, faceless presence that welcomed and terrified her at once.

Santo called her name, and for a moment she was back with him, looking into his eyes, trying to read what she saw there. What did he have to do with all of this? In a sliver of lucidity, her mind connected a dot she didn't understand. Before she could decipher the hidden meaning, it was gone again.

She thought of her older brother and sister and

began to cry. Her eyes squeezed tight against the pain that throbbed from inside out.

She released one last wheezing breath.

And then, for the fourth time in her life, Roxanne Love died.

(3)

The reaper—*Santo* now, he reminded himself, while he remained in this world, his name was Santo Castillo—raced to the vehicle he'd taken from the human's garage with a feeling of panic as alien as it was unwanted. From inside the bar came sounds of chaos and carnage that assaulted his new senses. He tried to reconcile the riotous impressions into some kind of order. But he couldn't. What had just happened in there?

One of the creatures who'd spilled through the back door chased him out to the street but stopped short of crossing.

He looked over his shoulder as he ran with Roxanne's soft, defenseless body clutched tight to his chest and caught a flash of burning white eyes and long, curved canines. The creature snarled at him before it disappeared back into the restaurant, leaving him with the unsettling idea that he'd been spared.

He'd never seen anything like it before, couldn't hazard a guess about what manner of beast it was. But he'd seen cunning in those lantern eyes and he couldn't mistake the feeling burrowing deep inside him now. Fear.

Fear. In a reaper.

In his arms, Roxanne lay bloodied and completely still. Her heart had stopped beating. Her labored breath had fallen silent. Her skin had chilled.

Dead by any assessment, right on time.

Except he knew her lungs would fill again and those startling eyes would open. If he let them.

He'd come to reap her, after all.

He'd crossed from the Beyond, breaking the laws of the Otherworld to experience her death on both planes. He'd fantasized about it, waiting impatiently for the call that her time had arrived once again.

His plan had been simple. Fire for them both. End it all with flames that would destroy her human body at the same time it devoured the one he'd taken. It was easy. Clean. Irrevocable.

So why didn't he act?

Was it because he'd seen her now with human vision that discerned detail and dimension he'd never known as a reaper? Vision that perceived nuance and sensitivity? He'd watched the easy grace of her move-ments. Gazed spellbound at the way the light played off her creamy skin, glinted in the golds and rich browns of her hair. He'd caught her scent and it had twisted something inside him, making him want more.

Then she'd looked into his eyes and he'd felt . . . *alive*.

"Fuck," he muttered, liking the vulgar way the human word rolled off his tongue.

It made no sense, the knot of rage and uncertainty lodged just beneath his breastbone. Human emotions as invasive as a strangling vine. As dreaded as a reaper at a wedding.

Carefully, he settled Roxanne in the passenger seat of the vehicle, then shrugged out of his jacket and pulled it around her. She'd be cold when she came back.

He circled Santo's vehicle and got in on the other side. Gripping the steering wheel, he flexed his muscles, fighting the urge to strike out at something, anything. In those first few hours after he'd taken the human, he'd felt trapped by the awkward form, but now the flesh and bone he'd stolen no longer felt heavy and cumbersome. It felt strong, powerful. A finely tuned machine of mus-cle and will. Yet he was helpless to do anything but wait as he battled his doubt.

He curled his fist and gave in, slamming his knuck-les into the dash until pain cleared his head. He started the engine, tapping as seamlessly into Santo's driving skills as he had the rest of the man, and pulled away from the curb, foot heavy on the gas pedal as he left behind the pandemonium and bodies inside Love's.

Beside him, Roxanne's head lolled to the side.

He'd come to reap her.

He meant to do it still. Even now the reaper inside him felt tight with excitement, imagining her fear, treasuring her pain. But something had soured the pleasure he'd anticipated.

No, not something. Some*one*. Santo Castillo.

Perhaps if he hadn't taken Santo before his natural death, it would have been different. But in his effort to preserve the vessel, he'd inadvertently saved pieces of the man. And now those pieces bobbed in his bloodstream, pulsed through his heart. Sentiment. Memories. Convictions. Despair. Emotions . . . like grit beneath his skin.

And somehow that terrible miasma of emotion had mated with his own objective. Roxanne. Like a hook sunk deep in his cheek, the crippling feelings tried to steer him from his goal, the vestiges of Santo at the reins. Santo had been unable to save his wife, whose death had crippled and finally stolen his own desire to live. But this woman, *Roxanne,* he could help. This woman he thought he could save.

From Death himself.

The reaper clenched his jaw and shook his head. *No.*

He had come to reap her.

She belonged to *him,* this woman who'd slipped through his grasp like a wind, who'd engaged him in a predator's hunt, turning him into a stalking animal that needed to feed. Now was the time. Now was the chance.

And still he hesitated as Santo's emotions whispered through his subconscious, urging him to stop. To think. Why did this female hold such power over him? Why did she defy the natural order of life and death? Why did she return to the human world when she was meant to move on?

"Why do you live, Roxanne Love?"

It astounded him that he'd never thought to ask before. He'd been so focused on *how* that he'd never considered the bigger question. He'd attributed Roxanne's ability to escape her fate to some errant gene, some throwback trait. It happened. Some humans had special senses. Some could see the dead, some could see the future, and others still could move matter with their minds, start fires with a thought, heal sickness with a wish. No one understood why. In the grand scheme, what did *why* matter?

But once asked, he couldn't ignore the question.

Why? Why did *this* woman cheat death?

Curiosity filled him as he glanced at her lifeless form. Who was she? Why had having her become so vital to him? Important enough to drag him from his world to hers?

And what had drawn the Others? The very underbelly of the Beyond had been at her front door. The locusts, the scavenger demon who'd shot both her and her brother, the Black Tides of Abaddon . . .

He felt a chill go through his human body. In the Beyond, identity was a luxury afforded to the very few. God, of course, stood separate from the mass of His creations. Some angels bore names and reputations—usually the wrong kind for the wrong reasons—but not all did. Entire battalions of winged entities answered to *angel,* just as thousands of faceless, nameless entities called themselves *reaper*.

But even in the Beyond—or perhaps *especially* in the Beyond—anomalies existed. Lilith, Mammon, Beelzebub, Lucifer . . .

And Abaddon, a name most humans wouldn't recognize even though it was the very reason they feared death. A name that marked a place in hell all its own. Scavenger demons took delight in killing, in the terror that consumed their victims, but Abaddon had bathed in their blood. He'd been so cruel, so vicious that he'd been locked away, named for the place of destruction where he'd been banished.

What humans had never understood was that hell had been made for creatures of the Beyond, not for mortals. God would never send one of His beloved creations there, no matter how great the sin. But His army . . . His workers . . . His devoted servants . . . He expected more of them. Those who broke ranks found themselves alongside Lucifer, roasting under the seething displeasure of their maker.

He'd seen Abaddon's messengers and minions tonight and more, like the thing that had followed him. It had been unnatural, even for a creature from the Beyond. And what had been that building pressure he'd felt in Roxanne's last moments? The hot whip of wind that couldn't have existed?

Why had they let him leave with Roxanne? Did that mean she was not their target?

Though *he* was not her brother's reaper, the twins shared more than a birthday. Reece and Roxanne shared death days, too. Four of them, counting tonight.

He disliked the turn of his thoughts. Disliked that they led him away from the prize. And he fucking hated that he could feel the human urging them on.

Creatures of the Beyond had manifested in Roxanne's restaurant tonight. Now he couldn't just reap her and return home as if he hadn't seen it. Nor could he go back to the Beyond and report it. He shouldn't be here. If he was caught, he'd be banished to Abaddon.

Both demon and domain, Abaddon stood for and personified evil and darkness. Abaddon made hell look like paradise. If at all possible, the reaper—*Santo*, an irritated voice in his head reprimanded—would like to avoid it.

That left him one course of action. He couldn't reap

Roxanne Love. Not yet. Not until he understood what he'd seen tonight.

He scowled at the relief that flooded his system, wanting to purge the remnants of the human causing it. He consoled himself with the reminder. His goal had been delayed. Not changed. He'd waited for her before. He could wait again.

He didn't have a plan. Didn't know what the next step would be and certainly didn't like the ambiguity of allowing an unstable, suicidal cop to make the calls. But the reaper recognized danger when he saw it, and left without choices, he'd do what he had to do. And when it came time, he *would* reap Roxanne Love.

The pledge echoed in his head as he turned west and headed for the hotel he'd checked into the night before, using Santo's credit card to pay for the room. A few minutes later, he parked in the lot and shut off the engine. In the sudden quiet, he gazed at the unmoving woman sprawled on the seat, limp and unresponsive.

Her skin looked like pearl against the hue of his fingers. He brushed his knuckles over her cheek, fascinated by the contrast in their color, by the silken feel of her. He couldn't look away as he willed her to take a breath. To open her eyes.

She'd gone to the darkness without him there to meet her. Was she afraid? Did she search for him?

"Come back to me," he whispered.

Gently, he traced his fingertips along the curve of

her jaw, then the pad of his thumb across that full bottom lip. He leaned closer, his mouth a breath from hers, his hand gliding down her smooth throat to settle over her silent, unbeating heart.

"Come back," he murmured against her mouth.

Some part of him noted the irony of his actions. Death's kiss never restored a life, yet as he pressed his lips to hers, his senses awoke and ricocheted throughout him. He felt a jolt go through her body, racing like lightning across a stormy sky, a current that stretched from his touch to her absent soul.

Triumph welled up inside him as he felt her heart stutter and thump beneath his fingers. He stole her first shivering breath and replaced it with his own.

R oxanne regained consciousness by degrees, a part
of her unwilling to give up the embrace of oblivion. She recognized it—she'd been here before. Within
the layered darkness she'd find *him,* the one who always waited there. He'd comforted her as an infant,
wiped her tears as a child, and held her as a woman. He
needed her, desired her . . . and frightened her all at the
same time.

But now she was alone and that frightened her even
more. Where had he gone? Why wasn't he waiting?
What would she find here without him? She began to
search for him just as she felt the warmth on her cheek,
a caress against her throat. Lips pressed to hers. At
last. . . .

She opened her eyes with a soft gasp and found herself caught in the midnight depths of Santo Castillo's gaze. He leaned over her, one hand braced against the back of her seat, the other resting just above her heart. Within his stare she saw a tangle of emotions. Worry, relief, victory, suspicion. The mix was too complex for her to unravel.

"Welcome back," he said in that deep voice she'd already come to know.

He eased away and settled in his seat beside her, and immediately she missed his warmth. She wanted to follow him so she could huddle in it and let his heat sink into her bones. Disconcerted by the power of the yearning, she looked away and took stock of her surroundings. She sat in an unfamiliar SUV parked on the fringe of a half-empty lot, location unknown. The clock on the dash said 11:20. She had no idea how she'd gotten there.

"Where am I?" she asked.

He nodded at the building squatting near the edge of the blacktop. "That's my hotel."

She narrowed her eyes, trying to make sense of that answer. *His hotel?* Why was he staying in a hotel? And more important, why had he brought *her* here? She struggled to work it out, but a deep murk had veiled her thoughts, making it hard to distinguish one from the other. She'd been at work and he'd come in and then . . .

An avalanche of memory rumbled down on top of her. The bugs. The stench. The seeping stain and the . . . No. *No, no, no.* That hadn't been real. *Couldn't* be real. She knew from experience that dying brought with it a host of hallucinations. What she thought she'd seen could only be part imagination, part trauma. How many times had one doctor or another told her what a mysterious, indecipherable organ the brain was? How lack of oxygen could cause delusions? Her brain, after so many deaths, couldn't be trusted.

Stains did not come alive. Bugs didn't commit mass suicide by window for absolutely no reason. And whatever it was she thought had come through the back door—they *definitely* had to be a delusion.

But something *had* happened. A robbery. A shooting.

In her mind's eye she saw Manny's body on the floor. Manny, who washed dishes for a living and wouldn't hurt anyone. He was a special needs worker they'd hired six years ago. He'd been such a good employee that they'd made it a practice to hire other disabled workers, but Manny had been with them the longest. He was like family.

Who would shoot him? Was he okay? And what about the rest of them? Reece? Jim? Sal?

"Where is my brother?" she asked. "Is he alive?"

Santo cocked his head, as if weighing the validity of her query. The small questioning gesture set off a spark of panic.

"Your guess is as good as mine," he said after a moment.

Her *guess*? "What—"

"How much do you remember?" Santo went on. "Dying?"

The questions felt overwhelming. Answering them, impossible. She shifted, realizing only then that she wore his leather jacket. It was big and warm, the sleeves long enough to cover her hands. It held the scent of the man. Clean. Masculine. Distracting.

"Do you remember dying, Roxanne?" he repeated patiently.

"I remember being shot."

"Not the same thing," he replied.

His indifference stung, though there was nothing apathetic in his expression. His gaze was so intense that she *felt* it. She studied his face, trying to get a read on what he was thinking. He gazed back implacably. He could be plotting a revolution or thinking about cheese for all she could tell.

"Why am I not in a hospital?" she asked.

"It seemed unnecessary under the circumstances."

"Which are?"

"You can't die, Roxanne," he said as if speaking to a child.

"That's a lie. Of course I can."

His smile mocked her, but he didn't argue.

"Is that what this is about?"

"This?" he said.

"Yes. This." She moved her hand between them. "What am I doing here? Why did you come to Love's tonight?"

"I had questions. Now I have even more. Let's go upstairs and talk."

"Upstairs? You mean to your *room*?"

"Or we could stay here and have our discussion in the parking lot. It doesn't matter to me."

"What if I don't want to talk to you? What if I refuse?"

"You won't."

He opened his door and came around to the other side. She fumbled with the latch, intending to get out before he reached her, but the sleeves of his jacket got in her way and her body moved sluggishly, her limbs still numb. It would take time before she had the strength to do more than keep her wits about her. She certainly didn't have the defenses to spar—physically *or* mentally—with someone like Santo Castillo.

He opened her door without a word and slid one arm beneath her legs and the other around her back. His face was very close to hers, and his warmth felt like a balm to her frozen body.

"I could scream," she said.

"Go ahead."

"Someone will hear me and call the police," she warned.

"I am the police, remember?"

She eyed him, not in the least reassured.

"Relax, Roxanne," he said gently. "You haven't been abducted. I just want to talk, and I needed to get you someplace safe to do it. When we're done, I'll take you wherever you want to go. Hospital. Police station. Home. Your call."

When she remained stiff and silent, he leaned closer and his warm scent enveloped her.

"I showed you my badge. You can see it again if that would make you feel better."

Yes, he had shown it to her. She'd seen his picture and name on the ID. And, if any of her memory could be believed, he'd also put his body between her and a man with a gun. He'd tried to get her out of danger before it all went bad. But the bad had come too fast.

"Think about it," he said. "What you saw tonight. You have bigger things to fear than me." At her startled glance, he went on. "I don't care if the safe was open. That wasn't a robbery and you know it."

She swallowed, an instant replay flashing in her head and forcing her to call it a memory. The man with the mask . . . the chill of his eyes. The open safe. Her brother, shouting as the black stain washed the kitchen walls. The shot that killed him just as the back door opened.

She halted her thoughts before they turned the corner. Santo was right. Whatever had happened, robbery was only a small part of it.

In Love's kitchen, Santo had faced that terrifying unknown fearlessly. *That* memory she knew was real.

"I still don't see why you thought bringing me to your hotel was the best option."

"It's complicated."

He lifted her effortlessly and she settled against him without even a token resistance. Dying had a way of draining the reserves and she doubted she could walk just yet, let alone run or fight. Better to cooperate than reveal exactly how weak she was. Besides, she didn't feel threatened by him. Not now anyway.

All of those muscles she'd noted from a distance felt hard and unyielding up close. Her softer curves molded to them like she belonged there, in his arms. She stiffened, resisting the urge to give in to his strength. She needed to keep what little wits she possessed lined up and on alert.

The door closed with a soft *thunk* before he jangled the keys dangling from the hand that rested just beneath her breast.

"Lock it," he said.

The action felt bigger than it should, slipping the keys from his fingers and clicking the button on the fob until the alarm chirped, but he didn't seem to notice the tension that filled her as she did it.

He took the outdoor stairs up to the third floor,

managing to avoid running into anyone else on the way. Not a single witness was there to see Roxanne Love enter this man's hotel room.

Not just a man, a voice reassured her in her head. *A cop. Someone who protected you.*

Santo stopped in front of door number 311 and set her on her feet, but he kept his arms around her when she swayed, his hands strong and firm on her waist and as searing as an iron brand. He reached inside the jacket and his knuckles brushed the lower curve of her breast as he pulled out his wallet.

For a charged instant, his gaze tethered hers again, sharp with awareness.

Without a word, he removed his keycard and unlocked the door.

When he stood back, she understood that he was waiting for her to go first. For her consent. Entering implied a hell of a lot of trust and they both knew it. Dressed in her bloody T-shirt and jeans, swimming in his big leather jacket, she felt too vulnerable and scared to make such a big decision. How had she ended up here? How could she rewind the clock and find a different outcome?

He said nothing as she considered her options. It didn't take long. She could call his bluff and run . . . and probably fall on her face. Or she could believe the actions she'd seen so far. That he would help her. That he wouldn't have protected her in the bar only to hurt her now.

A bloated brown grasshopper landed by her feet. She jumped and Santo took the choice away from her. He stepped on the bug, wiped his shoe, and then pulled Roxanne into the room, shutting the door behind them.

Uncertainly, she watched him toss his keycard on the dresser with his wallet. For some reason, the casual discarding of those items spiked her unease. It was such a masculine, everyday thing to do, emptying pockets that way. It clashed with the extraordinary circumstances of her being there at all.

"Why didn't you take me home or to the station instead of here?" she asked belatedly as her few functioning brain cells woke up.

"You were in no shape to haul into the station."

He had that right. She still wasn't. She shuddered, thinking of all the people and questions she'd have had to face if he'd taken her there. Instead of Santo's eyes watching her come back from the dead, there would have been dozens of others, cameras recording each moment, microphones shoved in her face. Prying questions, prying eyes. She sucked in a shaky breath of gratitude that he'd saved her from having to face that again.

After the last time she and Reece had died, the media furor had transformed the miracle of their survival into something vile. For months reporters had stalked the entire family until Roxanne felt like the abomination they accused her of being.

"Why didn't you just take me home?" she asked suddenly.

His eyes glinted with amusement. "You might not have noticed, but you weren't breathing at the time and I don't know where you live."

Oh. Good point.

"Besides," he said, "you wouldn't be safe there."

Safe.

"Safe from what? What was . . . What *happened* tonight?"

"Sit down," Santo said as he went to look out the window.

A chair sat tucked up under a desk holding a lamp and a phone. Beside it a duffel bag with clothes in it sat on a luggage rack. Other than that, the only furnishings were a king-sized bed with a dated comforter and a nightstand. She eyed the chair, preferring to stay far away from the bed, but Santo took it before she could, spinning it around so he could face her. He sat with his knees spread and his forearms resting on them, watching her every move. Reluctantly, she perched on the edge of the mattress. Santo seemed to find her caution amusing.

"I'm not going to pounce on you."

"I didn't say you were."

She lifted her chin, hiding a wince. She could feel

her body healing, but that didn't mean it felt good. Every muscle ached, her chest and lungs burned with each breath. Even her skin hurt.

"Are you in pain?"

"I'll live," she said, trotting out the tired joke she and her family shared. Santo didn't smile. She didn't blame him.

"Are you in pain?" he repeated.

"I was shot, Santo. By someone who looked like he stepped out of a nightmare. Of course I'm in pain."

A flinty light flared in his eyes at that, as if the idea of her feeling pain upset the imperturbable man.

An uncomfortable silence followed her words, during which Santo subjected her to a scrutiny that made her want to squirm. She leveled her gaze back, trying to gauge his thoughts. But a layer of ice seemed to have formed beneath her skin, making her shiver. Thinking became that much more difficult.

"Why did you say it wasn't a robbery?" she asked, deciding that was as good a place as any to start.

Santo stood and peeled the covers back from the bed. Blood had soaked her sneakers and the legs of her jeans. In fact, she felt tacky with it and the smell was making her sick. He lifted each foot, removed her shoe and sock, then popped the buttons on her fly and yanked her pants down before she realized what he meant to do.

"Get in," he ordered, pointing at the bed.

All too aware of him watching her, she crawled beneath the covers. Gently, he tucked the blankets around her legs as she sat with the pillows propped behind her. She still wore his coat, but he didn't ask for it back and she didn't want to relinquish it, so she wrapped it tighter around her shaking body.

Instead of returning to his chair, Santo sat beside her on the bed, his hand finding her frozen feet beneath the blankets and covering them. Even through the layers, she felt his heat, felt the shock of his touch.

He hadn't answered her yet and she was about to ask again when he finally spoke, stunning her with his question.

"When did your brother make the deal with the demons?"

(5)

Roxanne stared at Santo until finally a strangled laugh burst from her lips. "*What?*"

"The black tide? The locusts? The *demons* in the kitchen? You didn't notice them?"

Her mouth was open. She shut it with a snap. He couldn't be serious. And yet he certainly looked it.

"Demons," she repeated.

He nodded, stoic.

"There's no such thing as demons."

"There's no such thing as miracles either. But I watched one tonight. A woman who was clearly dead suddenly took a breath."

Roxanne felt her face grow hot. "That's different."

"Is it? Four times you've died, Roxanne. And yet here you are."

"Last time I checked, that wasn't against the law."

"But dallying with demons . . ." He clicked his tongue. "That is."

"No one was *dallying* with any demons. Especially not my brother."

Santo said nothing to that. Just watched her with those eloquent eyes.

"There was a *man*," she said. "A man with a mask and he shot—" Her voice cracked and she took a breath to steady it. "He shot my brother and Manny. He shot Sal. And Jim. He shot them for no reason."

"And you," Santo said softly. "He shot you, too."

She looked up, hurt that he would speak it. "Yes. *He* did. A man with a mask. A sick, violent masked man."

Santo only continued to stare at her, and she forced herself not to look away. Some part of her braced for the punch line. He'd thrown the word *demon* out there so casually. And now he waited like a patient older sibling while she worked out the logistics of Santa Claus's run and realized that it had to be mom and dad under the tree.

Only instead of Santa, he was talking about demons. Tonight. In her family-owned restaurant, for God's sake.

"Roxanne, you have been saved by a higher power four times. How can you not believe in demons?"

"It's exactly that reason. There's no heaven or hell."

He raised his brows. "So billions and billions of people are wrong about that?"

"I just meant that *I've* never seen it. There's only the darkness."

He looked like he wanted to comment on that, but what she found in death was far too intimate a conversation to have with him, no matter how attractive or compelling he was.

"Do you know what they call me and my brother?" she blurted instead.

"Freaks?" he offered helpfully.

"Yes," she answered, as if it didn't wound. "Among other things. Like demon. Devil's Spawn. Possessed. Being an unexplained mystery isn't as fun as one might imagine." She paused, watching his fingers rub her feet. She doubted he even realized he was doing it. But Roxanne was very much aware of each touch. Too aware.

"After the last time," she went on in an unsteady voice, "we had to file seven restraining orders. Seven, because of the fanatics who followed us trying to exorcise our demons. More than a few of them assumed we'd need to be sacrificed for the good of the cause."

His eyes narrowed, but he said nothing.

"It only makes it worse that Reece and I are twins. Did you know that in some cultures, they believe twins are a curse? They think twins share one soul that's split in two, one half good, the other evil."

"Are you telling me you think your brother is evil?"

"No," she said angrily. "I'm saying, when faced with something they can't understand, people fear it. So when you tell me that you saw demons in my family's pub tonight, all I can say is, sorry. People see what they want to see."

"And you think I wanted to see demons?"

"I don't know what you want, Santo."

"You saw them coming in the door. You know they weren't human."

"I saw people in masks."

"Do you always lie when you don't like the truth?"

"Are you always so cruel when you question someone?"

That set him back. For a moment, he looked completely bewildered. "I'm cruel?" he said.

"Even if they did exist, how can you believe *my brother* would be making deals with demons? He was shot tonight. Just like me."

"He invited them into your kitchen. If you're going to play pretend, you should learn to be more convincing."

"Why are you so sure they were demons? They could have been some other monster."

"So you did see them."

She sighed. "I don't know what I saw."

She could feel his fixed stare, knew her answer hadn't satisfied him. But at least she'd given one. He'd sidestepped hers like a pro. How did he know any of this?

"Are you really a cop, Santo? Because I don't know too many police officers who'd be so quick to say demons were running around the college district."

He stood, picked up his badge, and tossed it to her. It bounced off the mattress and into her lap. She examined it again. The dates, the picture, the name. It all looked official and correct, like the real deal. But a badge didn't make him her savior.

"Whoa," she said, noting the embossed text circling the edges. "This says you're Flagstaff PD. Aren't you out of your jurisdiction or something?"

"Or something."

"What kind of something?"

"The kind that has to do with demons."

She laughed harshly. "Flagstaff PD has a demon department?"

"Don't get hung up on the label."

Her mouth had fallen open again. He was serious. He really believed those things she'd seen tonight were demons. Those and . . . what had he called them? The black tides? The locusts?

She peered into her memory, seeing it all clearly, letting it come even when it filled her with terror. What if he was right? What if her brain *wasn't* playing tricks? What if it had all been real? And if she accepted that, how could she *not* believe that the terrifying creatures that had come through the door were anything less than demons?

She swallowed hard. "What *should* I get hung up on, Santo? Why are you here? Why am I?"

Something unreadable moved behind his eyes. He was sifting his responses again, just as he'd done earlier. Weighing each word before offering it up. Did that mean he was lying? Or only being cautious? He turned his back before she could reach a decision.

"I was sent," he said in a dark voice. "To protect you."

"Why am I hearing conflict in your tone?"

He glanced at her and quickly away. "Because you're afraid of the truth."

"More like you're not telling it. There are too many holes in your *truth*."

"Like?"

"You were sent? From Flagstaff?"

"Yes."

"They sent you from *Flagstaff* to protect *me* from demons."

"Does it matter where I'm from?"

No, she supposed it didn't, but somehow she felt it should. Santo let out a deep breath and took her hands. His were square, strong, and a little rough. Man's hands. He rubbed her icy fingers and looked into her eyes.

"Regardless of what you think you saw tonight, can we agree that whoever—*whatever*—came through that door . . . They meant you harm?"

She nodded. Yep, they'd made that crystal clear.

He gave her a tight smile. "Can we agree that I don't?"

"The jury is still out on that."

"Come on, Roxanne. You would have bolted at the door if you really had doubts. I saw you think about it and change your mind."

Arguing that he'd pushed her in here would be immature and irrelevant. He was right. She'd already decided that she was coming inside when he'd forced her hand. She didn't know what had happened tonight, but Santo seemed to think he did, and right now it made sense to stick with him.

When she didn't speak, he released her hands and tipped her chin up. She hadn't realized just how close he was until she met his eyes, noting the flecks of onyx in the deep chocolate depths. She could see each individual eyelash framing them, and she felt lost as she stared back.

"I'm here to help you," he said.

"Why?" she asked.

"Because you're special. Surely you've figured that out?"

Special carried a lot of different meanings. Which one was he talking about?

"Because I'm still alive?"

"Because you keep cheating death."

His husky words sent a shiver down her spine. Is

that what she did? Cheat death? And what did it matter to *him*? This cop from Flagstaff who'd taken such an intense interest in her?

His gaze settled on her mouth and she felt tension go through him, sparking and sending a current across the small distance that separated them. Her own body seemed to be fine-tuned to his and awareness whispered across her skin. Her breath caught, and it lured him forward. Had she moved, too? She remembered a kiss pulling her from oblivion. Had he done that? Was he going to do it again?

Did she intend to let him?

There was something sinfully sensual about this man that urged her to say yes. A decidedly male light gleamed in the depths of his eyes and she knew he'd read her thoughts. A hot flush spread over her whole body. Not a blush, but a reaction she couldn't control.

Everything that made her female recognized its counterpart in him and responded to it, but there was a whole lot of unknown between point A and point B. Roxanne didn't trust a single hidden nuance.

Completely undone, she forced herself to look away as she searched for her voice. Santo spoke first, his tone low and unsteady, as if he, too, had been unraveled by that *moment* they'd shared.

"The Black Tides of Abaddon were at your shores tonight, Roxanne."

"The stain on the ceiling," she said.

"You know it was more than that. You *felt* it."

Yeah. She had.

"And when was the last time a swarm of locusts stopped by for cocktails?"

Um. Never.

"So why are you fighting the truth about what came through your door?"

Because the truth terrified her.

She cleared her throat, wanting to ease back and put some distance between the two of them. But the force of his presence and the dark seduction in his eyes kept her still.

"What is Abaddon?" she asked.

"What the devil has nightmares about."

The deadpan tone, the chilling image his words painted. It all congealed in her gut and made her feel queasy.

"Look at me, Roxanne."

His expression was serious. Intent. Sincere.

"If you let me, I'll help you figure things out. And if I'm right, I'll help you fight."

"Fight?"

He stared back, his silence an answer in itself.

Fight. He thought she was going to have to fight. Demons. Things so horrible the devil cowered from them. She wished she knew how to faint. Now would be a perfect time for some blessed unconsciousness.

"How do you know all of this, Santo? How do you know any of it?"

He studied her for a long, heavy moment and she had the sense of a sharp turn looming just ahead. One that came so fast, she had no hope of navigating it. When he spoke, his voice held a rough edge. "You're not the only one who knows death, Roxanne."

It took a few seconds before his words sunk in. "You've died before?" she asked. "When? How many times?"

He leaned in as if he, too, found talk of death so intimate it had to be hushed. "I have seen the darkness," he murmured, his breath a soft caress against her cheek.

"How many times?" she asked again.

"Enough to know what I'm talking about."

"I've never seen demons there," she said. "Not once."

"Are you alone then?"

"No. Someone waits for me. Does someone wait for you?"

She sensed his smile, though his expression remained grave. "Not always, but sometimes she's there."

She? An irrational, possessive feeling flooded her. Who was this *she*?

He'd moved closer and his features blurred, making her want to close her eyes. Making her want to surrender to the feelings coiling tight inside her.

"Sometimes she's there," he repeated. "But other times . . . it's just me. Alone, in the darkness."

"I was alone tonight," she murmured.

"So you know how vast it can be."

She nodded, and he tucked a strand of hair behind her ear, letting his fingers rest lightly against her throat.

"I have seen more than the darkness," he said in that honeyed voice. "I have seen the Beyond."

There it was again, that strange word choice, an uneven pause, an implied capitalization. "What does that mean?"

For an instant she thought he might disregard her question and do what it seemed they both longed for him to do. Her lips softened in response to that powerful gaze and her body listed closer to his.

A movement in the periphery of her vision broke the drugging spell he'd cast. She looked up, but only monochrome shades of dark waited in the corners. She could have sworn she'd seen something, though. *A flash of red and blue . . .*

"What's wrong?" he asked, leaning back and raking his fingers through his hair. His hand wasn't quite steady.

"I thought I saw something."

Immediately alert, he searched the corner where she stared. "Do you still see it?"

"No."

He stood and walked the perimeter before facing

The Five Deaths of Roxanne Love   55

her again just as her stomach gave a loud, hollow rumble. Her body desperately needed fuel and time to rejuvenate, but she was strung so tight she couldn't imagine letting down her guard to sleep. She needed to get in touch with her family, find out how Reece and the others were. She needed to clear her head and decide what came next.

"You're hungry?" he asked, surprised.

"And cold and tired," she answered. More than anything she wanted a hot shower, warm food, and a few hours of not being afraid.

Santo moved to the desk and opened a cracked, faux-leather-bound notebook before handing it to her. She saw he'd turned the page to a menu.

"They have room service here?" she said, stunned. The hotel had struck her as severely lacking in amenities.

"Not exactly. They have a desk clerk who'll pick up from the twenty-four-hour coffee shop next door. Don't expect gourmet cuisine."

She almost smiled, but her stomach growled again and the echo seemed to accentuate everything that was wrong with this scenario. She looked at the offerings listed on a plastic-covered page, but she felt awkward. She had no money on her, no purse, not even a cell phone. She didn't want to owe him anything more than she already did.

"Pick something or I'll pick it for you," he said in

a tone that made it clear he would also hold her down and shovel it into her mouth if she refused.

She could do without his high-handed attitude but not without the food. She felt weak as she stared at the menu, knowing she should order something mild. Bland.

"Turkey sandwich," she said with a sigh, closing the notebook. He reached for it and she pulled it back. "Make that a cheeseburger. And fries."

"Anything else?"

She studied the menu again, her gaze moving to desserts. "Brownie. No, apple pie. No, a brownie. And a diet soda. Thank you."

His mouth quirked. "Diet?"

She shrugged.

He set the menu by the phone and rummaged in his bag for a T-shirt, sweatpants, and some socks. He handed them to her.

"Take a hot shower or a bath if you want. I'll order."

"I need to call my brother or sister. Find out about Reece and the others."

"No," Santo answered.

"No?" For a moment she couldn't comprehend that he'd said it. "Why?"

"Whatever you want to call the *things* that came to your place tonight—they saw you. They know you got away. They'll be looking for you now."

She nodded, wishing he hadn't pointed that out.

"You don't want to bring anyone else into their spotlight."

"I'll make it a quick call. They'll be worried."

"Isn't that better than being endangered?"

"A phone call. Just to let them know I'm okay."

"And if someone is listening in?"

"That's a bit paranoid."

"Demons are treacherous creatures."

She had no response to that, so she didn't even try.

"It's safer if I let them know at the police station and they'll get in touch with your family for you."

That made sense, yet she didn't like the plan. She wanted to talk to Ryan. She needed to hear her older brother's voice.

"If this is going to work between us, you're going to have to trust me, Roxanne."

She let out a frustrated breath, catching her lip with her teeth as she considered her answer. "That's not so easy for me."

"Really? I never would have guessed."

He took her arm and pulled her up from the bed, turning her in the direction of the bathroom. She wore only her shirt, his jacket and her underwear, but he didn't look below her chin. She thought better of him for it.

"Go take your shower and I'll make the call."

Still she hesitated, wanting to insist he do it now, while she listened in. He waited, eyebrows raised, message clear. If she couldn't count on him to do even that, what was she still doing here?

"Don't forget to ask about my brother. And Manny. Jim. Sal."

"I won't."

She nodded, still reluctant to leave.

"I'll call, I'll ask. I promise."

With a mumbled thanks, she took the bundle of clothes and headed for the bathroom. Now that she'd made the decision, she wanted the shower as much as she needed some time apart from him to regroup.

Before she closed the door, she looked back and asked, "So what happens next? How long do you plan to keep me here?"

"You're not a prisoner," he said.

"Just a hostage?"

He gave her a lopsided grin that did funny things to her pulse. "Protected witness sounds better."

Yet as she closed the door behind her, she feared *fugitive* was probably more accurate.

(6)

The reaper—*Santo*—listened to the soft sounds of Roxanne disrobing. The whoosh of leather sliding down her arms as she peeled off his jacket. The rustle as she set it aside. She gave a sharp gasp after that. Had she pulled at her wound when she took off her shirt? Should he have helped her?

He pictured himself there, his dark fingers pushing the hem of her shirt up and over her breasts. They would be soft. He would be hard.

The faucet cranked on, followed by the metallic hiss of the shower curtain opening and closing again. The water sounded different when it hit her body. Welcoming. *Beguiling.* She'd be naked beneath it.

Carnal. His own erotic thoughts stunned him. As much as violence made sense to the reaper, passion had completely bewildered him. He'd never understood the depth of emotion that drove humans to spend their lives together.

Until now.

He ordered food for them both, so focused on the pitch of the spray that the desk clerk on the phone had to "sir" him twice to get a response. He finished speaking and hung up thinking about her skin, how smooth and slippery it might feel beneath his touch, his body a dark shadow against the whiteness of hers.

Everything here was a little more *real* than Santo had expected. Especially Roxanne.

He paused, surprised by the realization that he'd just referred to himself as Santo without having to think of it first. Conversely pleased and uneasy about the unintentional slip, he shook his head and returned to his thoughts.

He hadn't anticipated that his hunger for Roxanne would extend to the physical. He needed to reel in his imagination. He needed to keep his distance. Maintain perspective and control, all things the human Santo had lost.

The hopeless man, the broken vessel the reaper had taken over had been crippled by the death of his wife two years ago. Most humans would have healed and moved on after so much time. But for Santo, one loss followed another. After his wife came his mother and then his wife's godfather, whom he'd loved like the dad he'd never known. The never-ending grief had toppled him like a lightning-struck tree. He could feel the other man's pain even now, a pebble in his shoe that could be ignored but never really forgotten. Even when his thoughts centered on the naked woman in his shower.

He rubbed a hand over his face. His body was drawn tight as a bow and he had a bulge in his jeans that mocked his ambition of distance and control.

He still meant to reap Roxanne, to keep her with him forever. Becoming more embroiled in the human world would not serve that purpose. Best to shut down his rampant desires now. He pulled his gaze from the bathroom door. He needed to focus on his *brethren,* not Roxanne's enticing curves.

His little human might be in denial over what she'd seen tonight, but *he* had no doubts. The creatures at Love's had all been demons—even the one in the mask. Especially the one in the mask.

Santo recognized that one for what he was and what he had been once before: a reaper, like himself. A reaper who had been condemned to Abaddon because of his thirst for souls. Every reaper felt the craving for them, but only a few crossed sacred lines to quench it. The demon with the mask was one who did. A soul junkie.

Santo took a deep breath. Reaping held too much rapture and elation for it not to be addicting. It had to be that way. What else would keep reapers in their roles for eons upon eons? Without the exhilaration that came with dragging a soul into the Beyond, a reaper couldn't be controlled. The reward of the reaping kept them in line, yearning for the next time. For that fraction of a second when life intermingled with death as the last breath rattled out and the reaper took what remained. Inside him, he carried a small piece of every soul he'd taken.

Each time Roxanne died and returned to life, he collected a sliver of her soul and those small shards made him yearn for more of her. Always more. It's what had pulled him from the Beyond to take the rest.

But what had lured the demon who shot Roxanne here? After being condemned to Abaddon, how had he managed to breach the barriers of the Beyond and come to this world? The demon had been caught feasting on the living, driving them to their deaths by twisting their minds and bending their wills as he devoured their souls. In short, eating them alive.

The demon had been branded *scavenger* and sent to Abaddon. Once there, he should not have been able to escape. Not even Abaddon himself could escape. Yet here was one of his minions, on earth. He'd brought the black tides and locusts. He'd brought other creatures that Santo couldn't even identify. How? Why?

Santo shook his head and turned on the TV, scanning until he found a news station. The front doors of Love's filled the screen. In silence, he listened as a reporter described a bizarre robbery that had officials baffled. Witnesses—he hadn't realized there'd been any—claimed to have heard buzzing that sounded like bees or wasps. Some claimed there'd been a pack of wolves roaming the streets.

Wolves? Only if they came sized like a human.

The only fact that could be verified was that a robbery and shooting had taken place at Love's. The police seemed to believe that three to five people had been inside at the time. From the evidence left behind, all were feared dead.

But no bodies had been found. Not one.

Santo sat back. He'd expected the deaths, but what had they done with the bodies? Had the creatures like the one that followed them out devoured the flesh as the scavenger demon made a meal of the souls? A very real possibility, and yet . . .

He rolled his head back, trying to ease his tension and organize the disorder in his mind. But a traitorous part of him had never stopped listening to the shower or thinking of Roxanne naked beneath the spray. He was more than a human, *better* than a human, but he couldn't seem to quell his desire to open the door, to shed his clothing, to join her. . . .

Fuck.

The water in the bathroom turned off and Santo quieted his breath so he could hear. A few moments later, Roxanne emerged, a white towel wrapped around her brown hair and his T-shirt and sweatpants hanging on her small frame. She'd donned his jacket once more, but it hung open, and he saw the faint bounce of her breasts as she walked. A slicing tension went through him as he remembered how they'd felt when he'd held her in his arms.

As if hearing his thoughts, her startled gaze locked with his, layered grays and lightning gold mixed together. His chest grew tight, his lungs constricted.

A knock on the door freed him from the hold she seemed to have over him. Cursing beneath his breath, Santo opened it to the delivery boy who waited on the other side. The kid looked to be about eighteen, with black skin and a nametag proclaiming him Chidi. He gave Santo a bright, mischievous smile that made his eyes sparkle—as if he'd just heard a joke and could barely keep his laughter inside. Flashing white teeth, he stepped into the room and held up a bag of food and a cardboard tray with two cups.

"Good evening, sir, madam," he said in heavily accented English. "I am Chidi. I bring your dinner."

Roxanne smiled sweetly and thanked him.

Scowling, Santo took the bag and drinks and paid him. Before the boy knew what had happened, Santo had ushered the kid out the door and shut it. His last glimpse was of indignation on the young man's face at his abrupt ejection, and an inkling of embarrassment caught Santo by surprise. What did he care about this stranger and his feelings?

Frowning, he faced his room and the woman in his bed. *His* bed. There it was again, that possessive trill that seemed to pulse with his blood whenever he thought of her. She'd climbed beneath the covers again and watched him with that wariness that grated against his overwrought senses.

He wanted her to trust him. Another irony he couldn't escape.

"Did you get in touch with my brother and sister?" she asked. "Did you find out how everyone is? Are they okay?"

"Five people were shot, including you," he said without preamble. "That's all they know. They're not saying if the victims are dead or alive."

"Why?" she breathed.

"Because the bodies are gone."

Gone with the black tide and the demons, if lack of mention could be attributed.

"All of them? My brother, too?"

He nodded, hating the pain he saw in her expression.

"But . . . gone . . . where?"

"That's the question, isn't it?"

She waited for him to continue, but he wasn't sure where to go from there. He couldn't tell her the truth, and the way her eyes followed his every move said that he'd need to be very careful how he worded his lies.

"What do *you* think happened to them, Santo?" she asked. "Did the . . . demons take them?"

Ah. Now she was willing to call them by name. She must have done some heavy thinking in the shower.

Again the thought brought the visual. Creamy skin, slick as silk . . .

He cleared his throat. "I don't know why they would have taken them. Demons are interested in the soul. They have no use for the body."

She swallowed hard and took a drink of her soda. After a deep breath she asked, "How is my brother Ryan holding up? And Ruby? My sister?"

"I don't know. But the officer I talked to said he'd get word to them."

Her grateful expression made the lie taste like sludge. Annoyed, he looked away.

"What do they want us to do now?" she asked.

"Lay low. Wait for orders."

She tilted her head to the side, and a damp lock of hair brushed her shoulder. "Wait?"

He'd known she wouldn't like that, just as he knew that bringing her on board with his plans would be so much easier if she thought she'd made the decision herself.

"Do they—the officers you talked to—do they know what they're dealing with?"

"The same thing they deal with every day. A fucked-up world."

The bitter statement came from someplace deep and unexpected. The human. Again.

Roxanne nodded, muttering, "Fucked-up is right."

He kept quiet, counting the moments as she thought

through their situation and worried over the idea of waiting. At last, she asked the question he wanted to hear.

"What do *you* want us to do, Santo?"

"Find them. Your brother, your friends. The demons who took them."

She nodded without hesitation. "I like that plan better."

"I thought you would."

"So do you think we can? Find them?"

"I wouldn't be here if I didn't."

She smiled, and he felt the praise in it all the way to his toes. Exasperated with himself, he watched her tear open the wrapper around her burger and take a bite. She ate with gusto, pausing only to wipe her mouth. "I'm sorry," she said. "I'm starving."

A tiny barb lodged in his flesh. She'd been starving and he hadn't even known. He had no idea why that bothered him, but it did. Greatly.

He was hungry, too—another new sensation he didn't like. He'd taken her lead and ordered the same thing she had. The soft drink had a bittersweet flavor, but the cheeseburger tasted so good that he ate the whole thing. Afterwards, it felt like a lead ball had landed in his stomach. Roxanne stopped halfway, munched a few more fries, and devoured the brownie. He watched her as each chocolate bite found her lips. He couldn't help it.

When she looked up and caught him staring, she

blushed. She did that a lot and he suspected that he caused it. But he didn't know how to interpret the reaction. What did the color flooding her face signify? That his presence unbalanced her as much as hers did him? He hoped so, no matter how pointless that hope might be.

He stuffed their trash in the small can by the desk, leaving her drink on the bedside table.

"Get some rest," he said. "The sun will be up in a few hours. We'll figure out how to find your brother in the morning."

"I'm not tired. Let's figure it out now."

"Give me fifty jumping jacks and you have a deal."

She flopped back against the pillows and glared.

"You're exhausted. It's the middle of the night. We don't even know where to start."

She looked like she wanted to keep arguing, but he'd spoken the truth, and for all that she was stubborn, she was also smart enough to know it. "Do you think he could still be alive?" she asked.

"Your brother? Sure. He's a survivor, just like you." Hurt glimmered in her eyes, though he hadn't said it to injure her. "What's wrong?"

"It's just . . . he's alone this time."

"You think he's survived in the past because of you?" he asked curiously. "Do you *do* something that makes it happen?"

"Of course not. What could *I* do?" she asked in earnest, addressing a question that had puzzled him. She didn't know why she was special.

"Go to sleep, *angelita*. We'll talk about it in the morning."

"Don't call me that," she muttered, but she couldn't fight the pull of fatigue.

His jacket had bunched up around her and he eased it off, ignoring her protest as he spread it over her feet and pulled the covers up to her shoulders.

"Just a few hours?" she asked in a drifting voice.

"Just a few," he confirmed.

"Thank you, Santo."

He didn't understand the feelings her use of his name inspired—a name that didn't even belong to him but had somehow become as integral as the stolen body. But the emotions—at once fierce, tender, and possessive—raged within him, ruling him against his will.

Gently, he brushed his fingertips over her cheek, pushing a stray lock of hair behind her ear. Her skin felt like satin—just as he'd imagined. Captivated and mystified, he watched her sleep until finally, he eased back beside her, kicking off his shoes and arranging the extra pillows behind him.

He scanned the stations on the television for a while before the soft sounds of Roxanne's even breathing lulled him into a dreamless sleep beside the woman he intended to protect . . . right up until the moment he would reap her once and for all.

(7)

Roxanne woke up warm for the first time in what felt like forever. For a few peaceful minutes, she drifted between sleep and wakefulness. On some level, she was aware of the television flickering light into the dark. She shifted drowsily beneath her blankets, and something tightened around her, keeping her in place.

Her eyes snapped open, and instantly she remembered everything. With a soft gasp, she twisted to find Santo Castillo asleep behind her, his body curled around hers like a protective shield, one arm beneath her head, the other wrapped around her waist. He was still dressed, except for his shoes, and he lay on top of the covers, yet the intimacy of him holding her in his sleep reverberated through every nerve ending.

She tried to wiggle out of his grasp without waking

him, but a second later those long lashes lifted and his black eyes looked into hers, warm as velvet. Sleep had disoriented him—she could see it in his soft, unfocused gaze. As if it was the most natural thing in the world, he pulled her closer, and his heavy-lidded eyes heated, his stare moving over her face, then dropping lower to her breasts pressed against his chest.

Then suddenly he was wide awake, his expression surprised, as if he'd expected to find another woman in his arms. His wife, perhaps? He didn't wear a ring, but for all she knew, he was married. He jerked, coming upright and scooting back in the same shocked motion.

"I fell asleep," he said, scowling with accusation.

Roxanne nodded warily.

Santo cursed and swung his legs off the side of the bed, facing away with his forearms resting on his spread thighs. He rubbed the bristle on his cheeks and shook his head. Tension rippled through the muscles in his shoulders and back and curled his fingers into fists. She didn't know if that hostility was directed at her or himself. It didn't really matter when he was straining like a wild animal at the end of a leash.

From the start, he'd been this way. Hot, cold, tender, cruel. She didn't know how to deal with the mercurial swings of his moods—or the strange, unsettling feeling that *he* didn't either. He seemed perpetually disconcerted by the spectrum of his emotions—like a man who'd been in a deep freeze and who'd thawed to find everything intact when he'd expected fractured joints and missing pieces.

"Are you married?" she asked him.

"No," he said in a thick voice. "Not anymore."

He turned to face her and something flickered in the black depths of his eyes. It was gone in an instant, leaving her feeling oddly cheated.

He caught a strand of her hair between his fingers and his thumb and rubbed it with a look of absorption that echoed through her body. Then his hand was on her throat, then her jaw, cupping her head as he pulled her in.

There were a thousand reasons she should resist him, a million why she should scramble off the bed and put as much distance between them as possible. But before his lashes lowered, she'd seen something raw and aching in his eyes. Something that reflected the loneliness inside of *her*. A part of her had given up on intimacy long ago, resigning herself to a life where everyone thought her sweet and happy while inside she withered. She scared most men for reasons she didn't understand and thus couldn't change. Something they sensed in her, about her, that sent them on their way before they ever got close.

But Santo seemed immune to whatever it was that frightened the others. More than that, he seemed captivated by it.

He searched her face, giving her time to back out.

Common sense urged her to take it, but his touch had lit a fuse that hissed and sparked. It took forever for him to close the distance between their lips. Forever, while her heart thumped excitedly and her breath caught with anticipation.

Then his mouth touched hers. His kiss felt like fire in the middle of the darkest winter. Hot and welcoming, it burned in her blood and flared with her pulse. She couldn't get close enough, and it seemed that neither could he. The blankets had tangled around her hips, and they both tried to free her without breaking the kiss, fumbling. Clumsy. So desperate that each failed attempt added to the spice. The taste of him set off a chain of reactions she'd never known. It made her ravenous for more. She wrapped her arms around his neck, wanting to shed clothes and press her skin to his, but as she twisted closer, she tore at her still-healing wound and a cry burst from her lips.

Santo jumped back. "I hurt you. I'm sorry."

"I'm fine—"

Something moved just at the edge of her vision. Roxanne saw red . . . blue. . . . She turned quickly as a figure she recognized began to form.

Manny sat in the corner. Manny, who she'd seen shot, bleeding on the kitchen floor. He perched on the chair with his head down and shoulders hunched. Though he was in his early thirties, Manny dressed like a kid. He wore his favorite red Iron Man T-shirt and blue jeans rolled up at the cuffs because they were too long. Feeling her gaze, he glanced up and smiled sweetly.

A strangled noise burst from her lips as she pushed Santo away and slid off the bed. But by the time she reached the chair, Manny was gone.

"What's wrong?" Santo asked, coming to stand behind her. His hands went to her shoulders, moving gently over the muscle and bone.

"I thought I saw . . . Manny. The dishwasher who was shot." She let out a shaky laugh. "I thought he was here."

She looked over her shoulder, expecting to see disbelief and withdrawal in Santo's expression. Expecting him to take a step back and turn away. Instead, he shifted his gaze from the chair to her face, his expression thoughtful.

"Has it happened before?" he asked.

"What? Seeing Manny?"

"Seeing anyone that shouldn't be there."

She shook her head. "I'm not crazy. I don't see things."

But she just had and he'd seemed so real. Right there, in the corner.

She turned away from it, shaken. What did it mean, that the beloved young man had appeared that way? Was he dead? Was she seeing ghosts?

Why not? According to Santo, she'd seen demons, too.

An image flashed on the muted TV, pulling her attention. "They're showing Love's," she said in an urgent tone.

Santo reached for the remote to turn up the volume as the camera zoomed in on the street outside Love's. At least seven police cruisers were parked in front of it with an ambulance nearby, their flashing lights chasing back the dark. A fresh-faced Korean reporter standing in front of them recounted what Santo had told her before she'd fallen asleep. There'd been a robbery and a shooting. Bugs they'd now identified as locusts had unseasonably and inexplicably swarmed the street during the attack. Police suspected up to five victims, but no bodies had been found.

She knew where *her* body was, but where had they taken Reece and the others? She glanced uneasily at the chair in the corner where Manny had sat.

"They haven't mentioned you yet," Santo said broodingly.

But they would. No way would the media let a sensational opportunity to explore the Love twins pass by.

"What time is it?" Roxanne asked.

Santo glanced at the clock on the nightstand. "Three thirty."

The reporter continued, speaking to anyone awake enough to listen. "Love's is a privately owned restaurant and bar that opened in the late sixties and is run by the four Love siblings."

Roxanne braced herself. She knew what was coming. It *always* followed any mention of their name. As if on cue, the reporter began to recite the mysterious deaths and resurrections of Roxanne and Reece Love. Each came with its own canned footage. Pictures of gurneys wheeled from the shores of Canyon Lake. Then years later, an ambulance pulling away from the twisted wreckage of Reece's car. Fortunately their birth had not been filmed, or no doubt that would have been featured for the viewing audience's entertainment as well. Nothing like a couple of freaks to boost ratings, after all.

"You'd think they'd get tired of showing the same old footage," she muttered.

Beside her, Santo said, "Why do you let it bother you?"

"I don't," she answered too quickly, feeling her face redden. "It just gets old, being *unique*. How can I ever have a normal life if they keep showing that over and over and over?"

"And is that what you want? A normal life?"

More than anything in the world. To be just like everyone else. A wife, maybe. A mother, like the one she'd never known. Someone who worried about running out of peanut butter, not how she would face people and explain, yet again, that she didn't know why she lived when others irrevocably died.

"The idea of being ordinary has its appeal," she said with a dispassion she was far from feeling.

"You are many things, Roxanne. But ordinary will never be one of them."

"You don't know that. You don't know anything about me."

He smiled that sexy, *I know a lot more than you think* smile. The reporter was still going on about Roxanne's history, exposing the most personal elements of her existence to a faceless, cruel world. It would all start up again. The reporters camping out in front of her house, harassing her and her family. The zealots stalking them, cursing them . . .

"I just don't understand why they feel it's necessary to rehash the same old stories every single time—"

She stopped abruptly, but he heard what she didn't say. *Every single time I die.*

"It could be worse, Roxanne," he replied in that husky voice that danced over sensitive nerves. "Would you rather they were airing your funeral procession?"

The dry question startled a surprised laugh from her. "No. I guess not."

His lips twitched in the barest hint of a smile. It was there and gone so fast she thought she'd imagined it. His gaze moved over her face, and she felt the heated questions in it. A few minutes ago, she'd been ready to strip down to bare skin with him. What was she willing to do now?

She tucked a strand of hair behind her ear and looked away. She wasn't prepared to answer him.

He made a sound of disappointment and said, "I need to take a shower, then we'll get going. Let me know if they say anything else about what happened."

She nodded, watching him pull some clean clothes from his duffel and disappear into the bathroom. The water came on and all she could think of was Santo, stripped beneath the spray. Her imagination didn't have to work at painting a picture of muscles gleaming and flexing as he soaped up all of that bare skin.

The water shut off just as the newscaster's voice drew her attention once more.

"Just in. Fox News has uncovered exclusive footage following last night's robbery at a local Tempe bar."

The reporter who'd given such an earnest account of the incident earlier leveled a serious look from the studio before his face segued into a bird's-eye view of Mill Avenue. His voice became background to the footage that had been taken from the security camera positioned at the ATM next door. The lens was just wide enough to show the front of Love's.

Roxanne watched in horror as a brown swarm invaded, remembering how they'd sounded as they'd pelted the window. A few strays found their way onto the camera. Locusts. Seeing them sent a full-bodied shudder through her.

She was so repulsed that she almost missed what happened next. The front door of Love's burst open and

Santo charged out with Roxanne clutched in his arms. He was only in the frame for a matter of seconds, but he'd managed to look up, and the camera had captured a crystal-clear print of his face.

The reporter's voice overlaid the picture, and Roxanne listened as disbelief and dread built inside her.

". . . officials have named this man as a person of interest in the disappearance of Roxanne Love and the alleged shooting of Reece Love, Manny Gormin, Sal Espinoza, and Jim Little. All alleged victims have been missing since approximately eleven last night."

A picture of Santo appeared in the upper right corner of the screen. Young—perhaps midtwenties—he wore a pressed uniform and a proud, if stern, expression. "The man caught fleeing Love's has been identified as Santo Castillo, a Flagstaff police detective currently on suspension. Castillo was reprimanded three months ago under a hailstorm of controversy concerning alleged police brutality in the arrest of accused drug dealer Marshall Ralston."

Roxanne was aware that the bathroom door had opened. A moist breath of soap-scented steam drifted out. But she couldn't look away from the newscast.

"Castillo was cleared of all charges by an internal investigation that determined he did not use excessive force in the arrest. However, unofficial sources tell us that Castillo has been unstable since the murder of his wife two years ago in a retaliation shooting by a local gang, and his return to duty is pending a psychiatric evaluation."

A new image appeared, Santo again, only this time he wore a smile that revealed dimples she'd only glimpsed. His eyes glittered with laughter. A woman stood behind him, arms wrapped around his shoulders, cheek pressed to his. She had the same toffee skin and dark gaze that Santo did, but her features were softer, feminine, where his were starkly masculine. Roxanne could see love in every detail, from their laughter, to the way she leaned in, the way his big hand rested over hers where they lay clasped against his breastbone, the tenderness of a shared moment immortalized on film. Something weighted and yearning shifted inside Roxanne as she stared at the happy couple.

Santo made an angry sound as he stormed across the room, grabbed the remote, and clicked off the TV. She stared with shock at the sight of him, furious, wearing only a towel around his hips. His wet hair stood in tufts, and his eyes blazed as he hurled the remote across the room. It smacked into the wall with a bang that made Roxanne jump and sent batteries scattering into the corner. Anger radiated from him as he strode to the window and cracked the curtains to peer out.

Mouth open, she watched him. Drops of water clung to his broad shoulders and trickled down the long, supple slope of his spine. He turned, still glaring, and some numb, dazed part of her hiccupped at the view. A light sprinkle of hair covered his chest and traveled faintly between the ridged muscles of his abdomen before disappearing beneath the towel.

"It's time to go," he snapped, stalking back into the bathroom. He didn't close the door, and she heard the towel drop and the rustle of clothes. A minute later he was back, dressed in jeans, a T-shirt gripped in his hands.

"Is that true, what they said?" Roxanne asked.

Santo glared at her, and in the pitch depths of his eyes, she saw pain and fury, knotted so tight that one could hardly be discerned from the other.

"Which part? Beating the shit out of a drug dealer or getting my balls busted for it?"

"The part about your wife," she said softly.

For a moment, the question seemed to steal the oxygen from the room. He stood, shaking his head, lips parted in a silent plea for her to take it back. He'd wanted a fight. He'd wanted to lash out. She could see that, read it clearly.

But now his shoulders slumped. He tossed his T-shirt on the chair and ran a weary hand over his face. With a labored breath that seemed to pain him, he crossed to the bed where she sat. Sinking to the edge of the mattress, he fell back across the foot of it. If she stretched out her legs, she could touch his bare torso. He stared at the ceiling with haunted eyes.

Roxanne pulled her knees up and rested her chin on them, watching. Waiting.

At last he spoke in a deep, thick voice. "Yeah. It's true. She was eight months pregnant. She'd just come home from the grocery store. They gunned her down on the doorstep with her hands full of diapers and ice cream."

(8)

The spare statement held a serrated edge. It lacerated pieces of the human inside him and somehow grafted the raw remainder more tightly to the being he was becoming.

"Why?" Roxanne asked, her eyes rounded with concern. His pain—a pain he didn't even understand—had somehow become hers as well. Empathy, they called it, but like so many things, he'd never grasped what it entailed. He still didn't.

"Why would they shoot your pregnant wife?"

"It was a message to me. Revenge for an arrest I'd made."

The words came easily enough. They'd festered in Santo's heart like splinters in a pocket of pus, just waiting for the slightest pressure to eject them. It hurt to speak them, and yet it somehow brought relief. As if recounting this tragedy to the woman listening with her heart somehow lessened its impact.

Again, he didn't understand, but the human within him—that part of Santo that had wrapped around the reaper—understood the succor Roxanne offered. Understood and grasped at it like a dying man would his last breath of air, even as the part that *wasn't* human, that would *never* be human, fought it.

"What was her name?"

"Marisella," he said.

The name resonated inside him, calling up memories of dark, laughing eyes and warm, welcoming arms.

"Marisella," Roxanne repeated.

He nodded, wanting to be done with it. Roxanne knew what she needed to know, and they didn't have time for this. *He* didn't have the desire to rehash Santo's failures. "I was on the job when it happened. I should have been taking care of my family."

He turned his face away, unsettled. Confounded by the power of the emotion. How did humans deal with this hour after hour?

Roxanne reached out to touch his bare arm. Her hands were cold against his heat but the gentle brush of her fingertips soothed, healing the lesion that bled inside him. "You can't blame yourself for not knowing what was going to happen. For not thinking clearly.

Death—it doesn't just kill the one we lose. It kills a piece of us, too. The ones who live."

He stared at her in shock, her statement such a blatant contradiction to the truth that it left him speechless. No one knew death the way he—*a reaper*—did. He took life in a clean sweep. No stray pieces of their human loved ones got shuttled along. Yet, he could feel the gaping craters inside. Feel that somehow Roxanne was right. Those missing chunks in Santo Castillo had been stolen with his wife's life.

"Who have you lost that made you want to splatter your brains on the wall just so you didn't have to face yourself in the mirror?" he asked gruffly.

"My mother died when I was born. I know that doesn't compare, but I miss her—miss that I didn't get to know her. Then I lost my dad when I was a teenager."

"I'm sorry," he said, because it seemed to be the words humans spoke at times like this.

She lifted a shoulder. "I'm sorry about your wife."

A strange stinging irritated his eyes and blurred his vision. Tears, he thought, surprise chasing them back.

He stood, pulled on his shirt, and crossed stiffly to the window, then braced his hands against the window frame and rested his head against the glass. The morass of emotions had brought him to a place he needed to escape. He couldn't think clearly when so many things churned inside of him and he still needed to deal with Roxanne.

She wouldn't like what he had to say next. She'd feel betrayed when she fully realized their circumstances. He knew she hadn't put it all together yet. But she would. She would.

"We need to move," he said, not turning around. "It will only be a matter of time before they run my credit cards and track them here."

"They?" she asked, confused.

He gave her a cool glance over his shoulder, relieved to have tempered the roiling confessions, breaking free of the sticky tentacles of Santo's feelings. Roxanne watched him with those stormy eyes, wanting to understand and yet innately circumventing the obvious. She did that, when confronted with something she didn't want to handle.

She tucked a strand of hair behind her ear in a gesture he'd seen her make before. It had a defensive quality, the way she let her fingertips brush her cheek, as if checking to see that her disguise was in place. Inside him, he could hear the echo of her words.

How can I ever have a normal life?

And here he was to tell her to give up that dream because she'd never be *normal* by her standards. The longer he spent in her company, the more convinced he became of that.

"The police are looking for us, Roxanne," he clarified grudgingly. "We need to be gone before they find us."

"The police?" she repeated. "But I thought . . ."

Suddenly, everything the newscaster had said registered in her expression. She'd been sidetracked by the story of Santo's wife and obviously missed it at first. Now her jaw fell open as she thought about what had been said. She stared at him with hurt and shock that he could do nothing to change.

Mired in another emotion he didn't know how to parse, he waited for her wrath.

(9)

Roxanne couldn't believe it. Couldn't believe *him*. He'd lied. About who he was. About *what* he was. He'd said he'd been sent by the police to help her. He'd told her he'd spoken with fellow officers just a few hours ago. He'd promised that someone would be in touch with Ryan and Ruby. She'd taken some measure of comfort from knowing that, whether true or not, her brother and sister thought she was okay. But he hadn't done it. Any of it.

He wanted her to *run from the police*. He'd flashed his dimples and shown her his badge—*twice*—and used both to manipulate her.

And she'd *let* him.

And now he expected her to run with him as if none of that mattered.

"That reporter said you've been suspended," she said, pointing at the television, hearing it again in her head. It hadn't sunk in at first because she'd been so distraught about the story of his wife.

Santo said, "Would I still have my badge and my weapon if he knew what he was talking about?"

He reached in his bag and pulled out a holstered gun she hadn't seen before. At her enraged look, he clarified.

"They'd have taken them away if they'd suspended me."

"Then why is it on national news that they did?"

"Why do they say things about you that aren't true?"

"That's different."

"To you."

She stared from the gun to Santo again. "Did you have that last night? Why didn't you use it? You could have saved—"

"No. I didn't have it. I left it in the car."

"Why would you do that?"

"I planned to be in and out."

"You ordered a *drink*. You were there for almost an hour *leering* at me." His brows went up, saying in the simplest terms that she wouldn't know that if she hadn't been leering at him, too. Roxanne felt her cheeks warm. "You *were* watching me."

"Yeah. That I was."

He didn't say anything else, but his gaze moved

over her features, unapologetically letting her know that given the chance, he'd do more than look.

"I didn't know what your brother was up to," he told her. "I didn't think I'd need to be armed when I went in."

She gave him a sideways look. "But you said you were here to *protect* me from *demons*."

"I am."

"But if you didn't know about the demons, what did you think was going to happen to me?"

Santo went still and watchful. She felt him weighing options, gathering and discarding statements, deciding what to tell her. What *not* to tell her. She waited impatiently, her anger flaring, tired of him editing his lies. She wanted to force the truth from him, but she didn't know how, and she probably wouldn't believe it anyway.

"I was there because I knew you were supposed to die last night."

She gave an unladylike snort. "Is that how this is going to go? You're just going to keep lying to me?"

"I'm not lying, Roxanne."

"Is this fun for you? Kidnapping me and scaring the crap out of me by talking about demons?"

Santo raked his fingers through his hair in frustration. Roxanne watched, equally vexed.

"You saw what came through that kitchen door," he said. "You know they don't belong in this world. And you know I'm right. Your brother invited them in. If you want to pretend it was something other than that, knock yourself out. But we *both* saw Reece talk to him. We *both* heard the one with the mask call him by name."

She hated him for making her remember that. Hated the doubt that crowded in on her thoughts.

"I know demons don't fit in with your idea of normal, Roxanne. But even you can't lie about what we saw last night."

Roxanne glared at him. "You didn't just call me a liar, right? Because you've got me beat there, Detective. Why don't we talk about your wife some more? Was any of that the truth?"

His face paled, and now his dark eyes looked like pits. She shook her head and pinched the bridge of her nose, refusing to release the tears that pressed against her eyes. But he'd hurt her. She'd trusted him and he'd hurt her.

"I don't understand this, Santo. Any of it. I can't figure you out. What do you expect of me? Just tell me who you are."

His guarded look fueled her anger. He was sorting his words again, determining which version of his lies to tell her.

At last he said quietly, "You know who I am."

Fury built inside her and she had no desire to bring it down. She strode to the table, snatched his badge holder up, and threw it at him. It bounced off his chest.

Santo didn't even blink and she wanted to scream. She wanted to pummel his chest until he told her the truth. The *real* truth. The one that would make sense.

She shoved him. Hard. It barely moved him so she did it again, putting all her strength behind it. He staggered a step back and caught her up to him, pinning her against his body.

"Who *are* you?" she shouted at him.

"Ask better questions, Roxanne."

"No. You answer the one I want. You tell me."

She tried to squirm free and he tightened his grip, keeping her arms pinned at her sides. He was a big man with hard muscles and more than a bit of his own anger. She should have been afraid to have rattled his cage. Instead she wanted to do it again.

He put his mouth near her ear. "You know who I am."

His voice throbbed with something that spoke to her tumultuous emotions. She jerked her head away.

"I'm the one," he went on softly.

The one.

Through her anger, she heard it, felt it. And against her will, some part of her understood it.

When she stilled, he moved his lips to the other ear. "The one who won't let anyone hurt you. The one who's going to keep you safe when they come for you. And they will."

She leaned back so she could see his face. She'd be

a fool to believe anything he said. But she'd be an even bigger fool to ignore the warning even when it came from lying lips. She *had* seen the monsters—demons—come through the back door. She'd heard the masked man say Reece's name. And she'd known when he'd looked at her standing next to Santo that she'd become a blip on his radar he wouldn't ignore or forget.

Santo had tried to protect her then. He'd stood between her and danger. He'd tried to pull her out of the fray. And after she'd been shot, he'd gotten her away instead of leaving her for dead. Even if she couldn't believe what he said, she couldn't deny his actions. He would protect her if—*when*—they came again.

"They will come," he repeated in a tone as dark as midnight. "And if they catch you, they'll make you wish you *could* die."

His words echoed in a cavernous place inside her, too terrifying to take in all at once. Her lips felt numb as she whispered, "Why . . ."

Why did they want her?

Why did he care?

He cupped her face in his palms, his hands blissfully warm against her cold cheeks. They felt like an anchor in an unpredictable storm—a storm he himself had brought when he'd walked through her door. She didn't understand her own reactions when it came to Santo. A few seconds ago she wanted to hit him and now she . . .

"Trust me a little longer, *angelita*," he murmured.

"Don't call me that. And I haven't trusted you yet."

"Now who's the liar?"

She didn't dispute it. He was right. Again. She didn't know what she believed or what she wanted. The moment had turned without her knowledge, and her fury had faltered in the shifting winds. Mixed within her confusion, something stronger than rage smoldered red-hot. Something that sparked when his mouth touched her throat. She felt drugged by his nearness.

He felt it, too. His arms encircled her, his fingertips tracing up her spine to her nape, where they began a slow, lazy courtship with her knotted muscles. His hips rolled gently against hers as he kissed her neck, her chin, her ear. Her breasts felt tight and sensitive and she arched against his chest. She couldn't help it.

From the first instant she'd seen Santo Castillo, she'd been aware of him, of the subtle thrumming signal he seemed to emit just for her. She didn't know if this was a moment out of time or a moment that would seed the future. At that moment, it didn't seem to matter.

He refused to let her look away as he leaned closer, sweetening the tension of waiting for his lips to find hers. It made her ache to close the distance, to taste and touch . . . to feel all that his nearness promised. But she understood his message. Here was her chance to say no. Here was her chance to refuse him.

She believed him when he said they would come

for her. Perhaps in some deep subconscious well, she'd expected it. She believed he would help her. He would protect her. For all the unpredictable darkness he exuded, she felt safe with him.

And she wanted the kiss he held just out of reach. She wanted it very badly. She slid her fingers through his hair and met him halfway.

His mouth was hot and open and his tongue found hers in a seduction that made her knees wobble. In two steps he backed her to the wall, holding her hips to his and rocking the hard length of him against her belly. His body surrounded her as her hands explored his stomach and chest. She slid her fingers beneath his shirt so she could feel him without barriers. In an instant, he'd shucked it and yanked hers up and over her head, too. He gathered her to him, and she nearly swooned from the feel of all that skin and muscle up against her own soft curves.

Who was this man who could break her trust and then bend her to his will in the next moment?

He lifted his head and gave her a somber look.

"Quit thinking."

Then his hands cupped her breasts as his mouth moved over them with hot, lingering kisses she had no will to resist.

She quit thinking.

He pushed at the stretchy waist of her borrowed sweatpants and slid them over her hips before swiping his notebook and papers off the table and sitting her down on it. The action spoke of a desperate need that blew through her like a storm. The table's hard surface felt cold, but Santo was a raging furnace that kept her burning.

She braced herself and tried not to buck when his mouth moved to her nipple, but the feel of it consumed her. His scent had drawn her from the start. Now she lost herself in it, lost herself in *him*.

His hands roved on their own, from breasts to belly, down to the heat of her, the place where every nerve, every sense had gathered to wait for his touch.

"Fuck, Roxanne," he breathed against her skin when he discovered her wet and wanting.

His tongue was hot on her flesh. Tasting, savoring while his fingers made a rough and wonderful friction against the most sensitive part of her. The world narrowed down to the feel of his touch, the heat of his kiss. He pressed his nose to her throat, breathing her in, the burst of his breath hot, his nearness electric.

"What are you doing to me?" he muttered.

Roxanne should have been asking *him* the same question, but she couldn't quite form words when her body was drawn so tight.

His kiss demanded a response she had to give. His tongue was like velvet, his taste like an exotic, addicting wine. He took his time. Deep. Slow. So completely entrancing as he explored her mouth. She'd never been kissed like that before, as if nothing were more important than the way she tasted. The way she felt. She didn't think she'd be able to breathe if he stopped.

"I'm sorry," he said against her mouth. "I shouldn't have lied. But I swear I did it to keep you safe."

From somewhere in the distance, an eerie sound rose up and banked against the window, piercing the sexual haze that drove her. A cross between a bay and a shout, it howled like a northern wind, shredding the quiet and leaving behind a gritty foreboding. Immediately, Santo stiffened and eased back. His eyes narrowed as he listened.

It came again, that shrill and oily wail, racing across the miles, unlike anything Roxanne had ever heard. He caught her hands and stilled them as goose bumps broke out on her skin and a dance of shivers tangoed down her spine.

"What is that?" she asked.

Santo closed his eyes and his shoulders slumped. "You better get dressed."

He pulled away from her with obvious reluctance, taking her inside-out shirt from her fumbling hands, righting it, and pulling it over her head. His fingertips traced her breast before he jerked the soft fabric down to cover them. When he looked up, she saw the depth of his yearning and regret.

The howling came again, still distant but moving fast.

Santo went to the window and peered out. His back to her, he said, "Come look."

Frowning, Roxanne crossed to his side and peeked out of the small gap he'd made between the panels of the ugly drapes. He shifted so that she was in front of him, his body hot and hard where his chest pressed against her back as he leaned in. "Look there," he said in her ear, his arm reaching over her shoulder to direct her.

Three stories down, the parking lot stretched to a frontal road. A scattering of cars took up about half the spaces. The coffee shop that had provided their meal perched at the corner, and in the distance she could hear the roar of traffic from Highway 101. Bright lights still lit it up, and shadows loomed long and dark as she scanned the lot.

"What am I looking for?"

The words had barely left her lips when she saw it. A flash of white lurching between two cars. An instant later, she saw a second one. He paused in his dart across the lot and unfolded from his crouch to stand erect. He wore all black, from stocking cap to gloves, but his face gleamed like polished pewter, so white that the fat October moon sliding from the sky gilded it with a silver sheen.

Unbidden came the memories of the masked, icy-eyed man. His eyes had been the coldest, lightest blue she'd ever seen. Though she couldn't tell from this distance, she knew the man below would have the same lifeless glow in his. Did all demons have eyes like that?

And what about the creatures that had followed the demon last night? Their eyes had been white. No iris— just terrifying white orbs surrounding the black dot of their pupil.

It had been so terrible that even now she couldn't quite bring the memory into focus. They'd looked like something out of a mad scientist's wet dream. A conglomeration of human and beast that defied labels and descriptors.

The man in the parking lot turned slowly, as if feeling her watching. She couldn't see his eyes from the window, but she felt them tracking. Santo pulled her back before that disturbing gaze came to rest on her. He jerked the curtain closed.

"Who are they?" she asked.

"Is that really the question you want answered, Roxanne?" he replied as he moved through the room, grabbing the notebook and papers he'd knocked to the floor and shoving them into a bag.

"You mean *what* are they, don't you? Even with that smart, sane, *normal* mind of yours, you can't pretend they're human."

"Okay. What are they? More demons?"

"The ones you see now, they're scavenger demons. I call them scavengers."

"Scavengers," she repeated, grimacing.

"They are reviled even in the Beyond."

"And what about the others? There were others in the kitchen last night."

He paused and gave her a serious look. "I've been trying to figure that out since I first saw them."

"You don't know what they are?"

"I didn't. Not until just now. Not until I heard them."

Roxanne gave an uneasy glance at the window, thinking of the sound that had crawled into this room and ripped Santo from her arms.

"Are you going to tell me or make me guess?" she asked.

"Hellhounds. I think they're hellhounds."

She stood there like a moron, unable to even conjure a *no way* or *bullshit*.

Santo went on. "I didn't even think they existed until now. In five thousand years, not one has been seen in the Beyond."

"Beyond. You've said that before. What is it? Like . . . hell?"

"Heaven, hell, and everything in between."

What could be in between? she wondered but didn't ask. This was already too much to take in.

"And that's where they're all from? The scavenger demons? The hellhounds?"

He hesitated. "Yes."

"But?"

"Condemned creatures come from Abaddon. It is . . ." He seemed to search for the word. "It is a part of the Beyond, but it's more than that. It's both a place and a state of being. And it is controlled by the father of all hells."

Fabulous.

"Abaddon is the King of the Abyss." He looked away. "The Angel of Death. The Destroyer."

Wasn't that just what the party needed. "I've never even heard of him."

"I'd introduce you, *angelita,* but you wouldn't thank me for it."

She smiled grimly, her own disbelief adding a layer of surreal to the moment. She should be terrified, but without a recognizable framework for her fear, it felt strangely removed.

Santo went into the bathroom, gathered up his things, and dropped them in his duffel.

"But they're all considered demons, one way or another," Roxanne said.

He nodded, watching her take it in, seeming to wait for her to make a connection she couldn't see. She swallowed, hearing his voice. *Ask better questions.*

"Why are they here now?"

"That a girl," he said, zipping up his bag. He grabbed her hand and led her to the door. "Why do you think?"

She didn't want to think. She wanted to go back to the hours before the robbery. She wanted to listen to Reece and close Love's early and go home before anything bad happened. But she'd asked the question. Now she had to answer it.

"It has something to do with me and Reece, doesn't it?"

"Yes."

The blunt response made her flinch. And suddenly other questions took shape in her head. Questions she liked even less than that one. Questions she was afraid to have answered.

And they all began with *why. . . .*

"Why are you here to protect me, Santo? Why do you even know who I am? Why do you know so much about this *Beyond*?"

He stared at her, and she watched as he battled a conflict within. Filtering facts yet again, balancing truth against lies, scripting his response. He let out a deep breath that spoke of resignation. He looked down at his feet and shook his head. A small, broken laugh came from his lips, and she knew in that instant that he'd decided on the truth.

Roxanne steadied herself, but she couldn't have known what was coming.

"I know because *I'm* from the Beyond, *angelita*. That's why."

(10)

Reece Love hesitated outside the door with the words *Gary Knolls, Chancellor* spelled out across it in precise, hand-painted letters. He'd only known Gary for a couple of months, yet he'd begun to believe him a friend.

Gary had a wild side to him and a darkness that Reece understood all too well. The two of them played chicken with death and skirted the law like old-world gangsters. Two weeks ago, they'd taken their dirt bikes into the Superstition Mountains and ridden Graybel's Pass, trails no sane person would attempt. For good reason. The pass hugged the ragged edge of the mountainside so close that Reece had skidded off a drop that had come damn close to killing him. Again.

He hadn't told Roxanne about that. He hadn't told anyone.

He and Gary had had a good old laugh after he'd recovered, but really, Reece hadn't thought it was so funny. Dying was scary business, even for him, and he didn't like to fuck around so close to its edge. And honestly, hadn't some part of him wondered whether Gary had given him a little push just to see what would happen?

It hadn't mattered enough for him to say something, though. For the first time, Reece actually felt like someone *got* him. A friend in a world where he had few.

Now he didn't know what he felt. Seeing *Chancellor* attached to Gary's name sent a cold chill down Reece's spine, the first inkling that Gary was more—or *less*—than he'd led Reece to believe.

Chancellor. The officious title didn't bode well. Nor did it fit the rebellious fuck-you attitude Gary wore with the same negligence he did his clothes. Reece glanced over his shoulder, weighing the pros and cons of knocking or simply walking away. But he doubted the two *escorts* who'd brought him here would let him go. They said he wasn't a prisoner, but he sure didn't feel like a guest.

The door opened before Reece could make up his mind, and Gary stood on the other side. "Cold feet?" he asked with a smile.

Reece entered the room, pretending that he wasn't freaked out by this meeting. He still felt foggy when he thought of how he'd come to be here. Death had a way of clouding his memory and making him doubt what he recalled.

"Sit down, Reece," Gary said now.

The first time Reece had ever seen Gary, his brain had coughed up an unlikely comparison: Colin Farrell meets Brad Pitt. He had all the rough edges of a shattered whiskey bottle with the smooth charisma of a consummate player. He could coax a smile out of you an instant before he cut your throat. He seemed to operate under a very strict code of principles—the likes of which Reece still didn't understand.

They'd met during a pickup game of hoops, and at first Reece had thought him a kindred spirit. Gary had seemed dangerous, wild, troubled. But here, behind that door marked *Chancellor,* he seemed disturbingly mild and frighteningly controlled. The contrast of the two impressions made Reece feel like a tightrope walker, poised over a bottomless pit.

Gary crossed his arms and leaned against a battered desk, flexing his tattoos—Christ bleeding out on a cross. The Virgin Mary sobbing over her slain, bloody son. Jesus looking heavenward with an expression of sorrow and betrayal as scarlet drops oozed from the puncture marks made by his thorny crown. Not exactly badass, but against Gary's pasty white skin, the three holy tattoos gave an impression of menace.

Reece slouched into the chair on the other side of the

desk, feeling like an errant schoolboy in the principal's office—trying to look cool when his insides burned like they were on fire.

"A bit on the pissed side, are you?" Gary said. He had a distinctive voice, gravelly and overlaid by an unidentifiable accent. At times it sounded Irish, but at other times it took on a peculiar quality that gave it a harsh and atonal inflection.

"Pissed?" Reece asked, lifting his chin in challenge. "Why the fuck did you bring me here?"

Gary's eyes crinkled at the corners, too benevolent to be trusted. "Well you sure as hell couldn't have walked, could you, now?"

"Maybe because you put a bullet in my chest."

Gary threw back his head and laughed. For reasons Reece would never understand, Gary's laughter always made him want to join in. Even now. Now, when it scared him.

At last Gary's amusement died down and he wiped a tear from his eye. "If you could've seen your face when I pulled the trigger," he said, shaking his head. "You were all, *whatthefuck*?"

His voice rose an octave and he burst into a fresh bout of mirth. Reece sat very still, waiting. Afraid. It was a new emotion for him. Never dying had a way of making scary things seem like no big deal.

So why was he terrified out of his fucking mind right now?

At last, Gary gave a final chuckle and exhaled softly. In a mild, almost musical brogue, he said, "I wasn't trying to kill you, Reece. I was protecting you. Do you see that?"

"No. No, I don't fucking see that. I see a lunatic laughing his ass off over planting a round in my fucking heart. That's what I see."

Reece lurched to his feet. His wound had already begun to heal, but he was still sore, still felt as if a cast-iron skillet had passed through his chest instead of a bullet.

"You shot the *dishwasher,* Gary. Manny was harmless. Innocent."

Gary nodded sympathetically. "That was a tragedy," he agreed. "But I was only trying to save you, Reece."

"From a disabled dishwasher?"

"I didn't intend to shoot him, but he caught me by surprise. Don't worry, though. He's doing fine."

"He's alive?"

"Yes, yes. I'm no murderer. That would be a sin, wouldn't it? Your boy is upstairs in the infirmary."

"He's *here*?"

Gary smiled. "The other two as well. What are their names? Jim, Sal? I couldn't leave them behind, defenseless, any more than I could *you*."

"What about my sister?"

Gary gave him a look from the corner of his eye. "What about her?"

Reece's blood felt thick and cold. He chased this question around in his head, trying to peer through the veil of his unconscious self that night, trying to see what had happened after he'd been shot. But he got nothing—nothing that made sense anyway. Just before he'd slipped away, he'd thought he'd seen . . . *ogres*. Huge ones, hunched and hideous, coming through the door in single file. He knew he couldn't really have seen them, but the images stuck with him, as if burned into his retinas. And they rubbed against something deep in his subconscious—something dark and sequestered. He couldn't imagine what it might be, but it added an edge to the jittery angst in his gut.

"Did you hurt my sister?" he asked, his voice low, shaking. His lips stiff.

Gary shook his head, then spoke the word "No" so there'd be no misunderstanding.

Reece wanted to stand tall. To look imperturbable. But his knees gave a desperate wobble of relief and he sat again. He'd been convinced his stupidity had finally caused irreparable harm to his sister. Gary watched him with those pale eyes, noting his every move. Cataloguing Reece's weakness.

"I want out," Reece managed at last.

"Sure, sure and didn't I expect that?" Gary said. "But first let me explain."

Reece glared at him. *Explain?* He thought he could

explain the clusterfuck that had happened in the pub's kitchen?

"You were supposed to rob it, Gary. Nothing else. Get the money, get out."

"Aye," Gary said. "That I was."

Reece raised his brows and waited, his heart beating hard and fast. The feeling of standing at the brink of something both great and terrible swelled up in his chest, making it difficult to breathe. Goose bumps raised on his arms and a shiver wanted to dance down his spine. Gritting his teeth, Reece fought it.

"But you see," Gary went on after a pause that felt so much longer than the second that passed. "I wasn't after the money, was I?"

"What's that supposed to mean?"

"You've known me now for a month or two. Isn't that right?"

Reece nodded warily.

"In that time, have you ever known me to give a flying fuck about *money*?"

"You said you needed it," Reece insisted stubbornly.

"No, my boy. *You* needed it. *You* dug yourself an early grave with your bookie, didn't you now?" Gary leaned in, threatening. "Answer me. Did you really think I'd steal just to turn a buck?"

"Ten thousand bucks," Reece said.

"Oh, it was quite a bit more than that."

Surprised, Reece asked, "How much more?"

Gary gave him a cryptic shrug. "It doesn't matter. Not to me."

Reece wanted to press, but he kept quiet, flicking his gaze over the three bulging Christs inked on Gary's white skin. He'd seen Gary kick the shit out of a man who'd been fingered as a rapist, but not convicted. He'd seen him stuff a hundred-dollar bill into the collection bucket in front of St. Mary's. And he'd seen him smile when he'd pulled the trigger and shot Reece dead center. But no, he'd never seen him steal, and he'd never seemed short on cash, though Reece had no idea what he did for a living. Something connected to *Chancellor,* evidently.

"So where's the money?" Reece asked.

"Someplace safe."

"I want my cut."

"So your bookie doesn't decide to chop you into tiny pieces."

Yeah. Because of that.

Gary's smile was knowing. "I've taken care of your problem with that man and his associates."

"Taken care of it, how?"

"It doesn't matter."

When Reece opened his mouth to say, *It matters to me*, Gary stopped him.

"Why do you think I shot you, Reece?" he asked.

"Fuck if I know," Reece mumbled.

"Do you remember when we met? You asked me what I did and I told you I search."

But he hadn't said what he searched for.

Reece stared at him, unsmiling. "Is there a point to this?"

"You know I'm a religious man."

Reece's snort of breath was his only answer.

"Yes, I'm supposing that's obvious. But perhaps you don't fully grasp just how strong my faith is or what, exactly, I believe in."

Reece felt his breath catch as he watched Gary. There could only be one reason why Gary would bring up his faith. He was one of the psycho assholes who'd been stalking the Love family with their pointing fingers and their condemnations. As angry as Reece was, as confused and uncertain, the realization hurt all the same. He'd trusted this man. He'd called him a friend—and Reece didn't have many of those. Now he realized the full range of his own idiocy.

Reece pushed out of the chair again. Furious. Gary waved him down with a casual flick of his fingers.

"Hear me out. You might be interested in what I have to say. I told you the truth. I'm here to protect you, Reece."

"By shooting me? Fuck you, Gary."

"I knew you wouldn't die. You've survived worse, haven't you, Reece? But I had to get you out of there."

"Out of my family's restaurant because . . . why? It's a hotbed of terror?"

"There's someone coming for you, Reece," he said. "Someone a hell of a lot more dangerous than I am."

"What the fuck are you smoking?"

Gary gave him a tight smile, reached for a remote, and turned on a small television/VCR combo—the kind that used to be popular ten or fifteen years ago when people still recorded things on VHS. Reece watched with angry disinterest as a grainy newscast came on the screen. Numb, he watched it play out.

Roxanne. Gunshots. Gone, with a cop named Santo Castillo who wasn't a cop anymore. The guy who'd sat in the back and smelled of trouble.

Stunned, he looked at Gary as he clicked the remote and turned the recorded newscast off.

"Who is he?" Reece demanded.

"A more appropriate question would be, *What is he*?" Gary answered calmly, crossing his arms and flexing all his Jesuses at Reece. "He's not a man at all. He's a hunter and he's got your sister right now. Sit down, Reece. It's time to talk about monsters."

(11)

S anto realized the confession had been coming since
he'd looked into her startling eyes and filled his
senses with her elusive scent. He'd come to her world
to deceive and devour her, but after meeting her in the
flesh, all of his preconceived assumptions had been destroyed. His purpose had changed so drastically that he
didn't even understand it himself. All he knew was that
he didn't want to add fresh lies to the old. He'd turned
a corner when he'd kissed her, when he'd touched her.
But he'd turned it blindly. He didn't know what happened next.

　　Was that disappointment he saw on her face or
disbelief? Would one be better than the other? How
could he navigate from this perilous point back into her
arms? He zipped his duffel, so far out of his depth that

he didn't know what to say. He'd thought there would be more time before he had to explain. Time to dice the information and dole out only the bits he thought vital.

No, that wasn't true. He hadn't expected to explain at all. He was a reaper. He didn't give explanations. He came. He took. He left.

But now that he'd held her in his arms and sampled the feast that humans called life, everything had changed. *He'd* changed.

He didn't like it. He didn't want to *become* something new. Yet he sensed that he would do everything possible to have more of her. He'd been changing with each ticking second, and now the deceptive grip that Santo seemed to have on the reaper morphed into a full embrace and the floodgates that kept him separate eroded completely. His identity, already abraded by Santo's, roiled and twisted in the flotsam until even *he* couldn't determine where one ended and the other began. The line of demarcation between the two vanished in the torrent. In the beginning he'd had one single goal. Reap Roxanne Love. Now he only wanted to finish what they'd begun in this room.

"What are you thinking?" he asked, willing her to give him a sign of how to proceed. She kept her eyes averted and shook her head.

"I wish I'd called in sick last night," she muttered.

And never met him? Is that what she meant? He

swallowed, hating the hurt that coiled in his gut. At last she looked up. Her eyes looked huge and anxious in her drawn face.

"Are you really from this Beyond place, Santo?"

He nodded, wishing for the first time that his answer was different. Would she be repulsed by him now?

"And what does that mean, exactly? What does that make you? You're not a monster, like the others?"

It tore a hole through him that her voice lilted in question at the end. Was he a monster? Was he worse than a monster? He was death, the end of all things. The fire that incinerated them, the ash that blew away.

He chose his words like footsteps near quicksand. "More than demons live in the Beyond, *angelita*."

"Heaven, hell, and everything in between," she parroted his words, eyeing him cautiously.

Did she expect him to sprout fangs and claws?

"So if you're here to help me . . . If you were sent to protect me . . . Does that mean you're like an angel?"

He'd been braced for the worst, certain she'd see the grim reaper just beneath Santo's skin. But he should have known she'd find a more acceptable explanation. Hadn't she told him that faced with something they didn't understand, humans saw what they wanted to see? And she wanted an angel watching over her. Not death breathing down her neck.

An angel. She thought *he* was a fucking angel.

"Is that what you are?" she asked again and now a note of hope filled her voice. "An angel?"

At once appalled and relieved, he stared back and answered the only way he could. He lied. "Yes."

She gave a faint laugh. "An angel from Flagstaff."

It just got crazier by the second. The smile he forced felt wooden. "What is it with you and Flagstaff, Roxanne?"

"I don't know," she said with another small laugh. "I just never pictured it being a mecca of the supernatural."

He shrugged, seeing Santo's memories, his impressions of the wholesome mountainous city where he'd grown up. She had a point.

From outside, another chilling howl drifted across the miles. Was it coming closer or moving away? The desert warped the sound so he couldn't tell. But he could guess. Roxanne gave the curtained window a worried look.

"What do they want?" she asked.

"I don't know. They let you go last night. I don't think they knew who you are."

"And now they do?"

"It would seem so." He took a deep breath and pushed on. "I get that you don't want to face it, but the fact is, there are demons coming for you. Somehow, your brother is involved with them. Now so are you. You can't pretend they don't exist."

"You're not here just for me, though, are you?

You're here to hunt them. To send them back where they came from."

Again, she spoke with hope. Again, he gave her the answer she wanted.

"I have to destroy them to protect you," he said.

"You know how to do that?"

Her lack of faith offended him. "Yes."

"Is that why you're helping me find my brother?"

"Roxanne, creatures of the Beyond can't cross over into your world at will. They have to be invited."

"Were you?"

"A billion prayers are made every hour. Angels are always invited."

"I wasn't praying."

"Weren't you?"

The question made her eyes round and her lips soften. He knew he'd hit upon something secret, something she never shared. What prayer had she kept hidden just for herself? What plea had gone unanswered for so long that she'd forgotten she'd asked?

"So you're saying that for these demons to be on earth, they had to be invited in."

"In a manner of speaking. When your brother died, I felt a pressure in the air that I couldn't explain. I think it was a door opening in the Beyond." He paused. "A second later, the hellhounds came in."

She'd grown very pale but she kept her chin raised, her eyes steady on his face. "I don't understand."

"I'm not sure I understand it either. But we don't have time to talk this out now. They're coming."

He could feel their approach. They emitted a dark pulse of power that hummed like an electric line coursing with energy.

"I know someplace we'll be safe until we figure out what to do. But first we've got to lose *them*. They're watching the lot. They know what car we came in."

"They," she repeated softly. "Scavengers. Hellhounds. Demons."

There was no derision to her tone; no skepticism lingered at all. Intrigued, he nodded and said, "We need to get out of the room, circle to the back of the building, and find another set of wheels."

"Find? You mean steal?"

The innocent umbrage in the question cut through his tension and made him smile. "Yes."

She grimaced at her bloodstained shoes but quickly put them on. The bedside lamp did little to chase away the gloom, but he could still see the fear gleaming in her eyes.

He lifted his duffel with one hand and took her icy fingers in his other.

"Trust me, Roxanne," he said, his voice husky with all that entailed.

Doubt clouded her expression, but she nodded. He tugged her hand, urging her forward and toward the door. He paused before he opened it and looked down at her face.

She gazed back, eyes wide. Her long, gold-tipped lashes cast feather-light shadows on her cheeks. The color had drained from her face, giving her an ethereal look that made something inside him clench.

She thought him an angel.

What would have happened earlier if he hadn't heard that baying in the distance? If reality hadn't knocked on the moment and demanded attention? Would he be lost inside her, even now? Delving in the heat of her, taking what she offered? Basking in the exciting and forbidden? He'd wanted things he'd never even imagined.

He wanted them still.

He leaned closer and she swayed in response. He took the infinitesimal motion as an invitation and his lips found hers without blunder, without hesitation, a skill that must have come from the human who'd kissed a thousand times or more. But for the reaper, it was still new. The taste of her on his tongue. The surge of power that came from knowing he could make her go soft and hungry with his touch.

Her mouth was lush, her breath sweet. The feel of her lips couldn't be measured. In all the eternity of his existence, he'd never been jealous of humans. But that was before he knew the curve of this woman's body, the softness that felt like mink against his brawn. The breathy sounds she made when kissed just so, touched her, right there. The sensations turned him inside out and consumed him. He parted her lips like he'd been doing it his entire life and let his tongue slide against hers. A tremor went through him as the need to have her urged him to ignore the danger lurking outside and take her now. He wanted to pull her to his bed—yes, *his bed*—and lay with her, touch her, explore her. Make her call his name.

Outside, another long, eerie bay careened across the silence, mocking him. Warning him. Definitely closer now. Coming this way.

Reluctantly he pulled back, feeling raw and overwhelmed as her incredible eyes opened and focused on him with a dazed, yearning look that nearly incinerated him.

He forced himself to turn away.

"Stay with me," he said in a tone so desperate it pained him.

He waited for her softly spoken "I will" before he opened the door.

(12)

Roxanne's insides felt scrambled, her thoughts a jumbled mess. His kiss lingered on her lips, tripped up her senses, tangled her emotions. Her fear made her numb.

"Let's go," he breathed.

She could smell them before she even stepped over the threshold. A thin but noxious odor that stank of graves and sulfur and violence. It slammed into her with the power of a memory. The same rankness had been present last night, but she'd managed to forget—*deny*—it. Just as she'd managed to convince herself that what had come through the kitchen door at Love's couldn't be what she'd thought.

But now her eyes were open. There would be no more denial.

A silent walkway with a rusted metal railing ran outside each floor. To the left, she could see the stairwell they'd come up, to the right a pattern of doors and windows, all shut for the night. Large pillars ran at even intervals the whole way around. The walkway ended at a sharp corner.

Santo gave her hand a light squeeze before he slipped out, pulling her along as he quietly shut the door behind them and moved to the first pillar. They paused there, waiting for sounds of discovery, but all they heard was the roar of traffic in the distance and the loud tapping of a woodpecker in a nearby palm tree.

Her heart thudded in her chest as she tried to stay calm, but with her fear came the questions that preyed upon her composure. Santo followed the cracked concrete walkway from pillar to pillar as he headed toward the nearest stairs and the elevator that led to the parking lot. Roxanne followed, as silent as a shadow. Up ahead, she saw an alcove with an Exit sign. A mechanical hum announced the elevator rising. It *ding*ed on the floor below.

Santo paused, considering their options. She could tell he didn't like the idea of getting into the elevator, where they'd be trapped and vulnerable while the doors slid open and shut. But the stairs were well lit and exposed on all sides. They'd be targets the whole way down.

He leaned back and whispered in her ear. "When the elevator stops on this floor, we get in."

She didn't have a better plan, so she gave him another reluctant nod, trailing behind him as he crept through the predawn shadows and hit the down button.

She could feel the shuddering vibration as the elevator resumed its climb, but it didn't come close to matching the trembling inside her.

"What will they do if they catch us?" she asked.

He turned those dark eyes on her, unreadable in the gloom. An air of power and threat that was as much a part of him as the black hair and broad shoulders surrounded him. He looked so badass it was hard to picture him as the gentle, caring, *passionate* man he'd been earlier.

"You sure you want to know?" he asked in a low voice.

"Yes."

"They'll rip out your soul and feed on it."

Oh.

He brushed her cheek with his knuckles. "But they have to get through me, first. And that's not going to happen."

Another blood-chilling wail lifted from below, and the reassurance his words had given her vanished. She didn't know what they were up against. In a battle between scavenger demons, hellhounds, and an angel, who would win? Which one had the greater power?

"Do they always make that sound?" she asked. She'd never heard anything so frightening.

"Not when they're dead. I hope."

She didn't think she could be more scared, but terror of a new kind seeped into her bloodstream, an incurable disease that ran rampant through her system. Her heart was pounding so hard that it hurt. Her fingers and toes stung as adrenaline and cortisol flooded her system.

Dark humor moved through Santo's black eyes. "*Angelita,* quit thinking."

His words took her right back to those moments on the table, when all she'd known was his hands, his lips, his tongue.

The sound of dragging footsteps coming up the other stairway—the one behind them—echoed just as the strident bell of the elevator *bing*ed ahead. She didn't look back. She didn't need to. She could sense the creature on the stairs. Could it sense her, too? Did she carry a scent that demons could sniff out? Was the one on the stairs testing the air even now and asking, *Where are you?*

The elevator opened and a laughing man and woman emerged. Santo gave her hand a short, reassuring squeeze, then the two of them sidled in behind the exiting couple.

Inside she punched the number 1 over and over, as if it would make the doors respond faster. Stupid, but she couldn't seem to stop. Santo watched with hooded eyes until finally the doors closed and the elevator jerked as it began its creeping descent.

She stared at the numbers on the display overhead as they transitioned from 3 to 2 and finally to 1.

The elevator shuttered to a stop, then the doors groaned open onto a small alcove on the ground floor. She hadn't realized she'd been holding her breath until she saw the deserted walkway. It forked in three directions—left, right, and straight ahead. Signage told them what they'd find at the end of each path. The one that ran straight would take them to the lobby. The other two raveled around, intersecting with the tiny pool, ice machines or parking lots along the way.

Santo leaned close, his clean scent momentarily banishing the sulfurous air that seemed to be everywhere now.

"I saw a shuttle earlier," he said in her ear, his voice pitched low. "Makes airport runs. We aim for that."

"What if it's locked?" she whispered back.

He didn't answer her. What had she expected? If it was locked, they were screwed.

"Get ready," he said a moment before he pushed away from the wall and sprinted straight ahead, around the bend to the front of the motel, never loosening his grip on her hand. She kept up, though. Her adrenaline had spiked, and running—even for her life—was a relief.

She had a quick glimpse of a front desk with a big bowl of fresh fruit and the deserted air of the night shift before Santo pulled them both to a stop beside an old van with the motel's faded pink-and-blue logo on the side. He reached for the handle of the front passenger door, but a dent in the side had wedged it permanently shut and it wouldn't budge. The sliding panel glided back without resistance, though, and he pushed her in and climbed in after, closing the door as quietly as possible. Still, it sounded abnormally loud as it latched.

She reached over the driver's seat and hit the master lock button on the door. At once the thud of the locks engaging echoed down the van. Roxanne glanced nervously at the lobby again, but whoever was supposed to man the desk had abandoned his post. Nothing moved behind the wall of glass and automatic doors.

When she turned back, Santo had moved up and slid behind the wheel, where he was yanking out some wires and working with the kind of competence that came from experience. If she didn't know better, she'd guess he hot-wired motel shuttles every day.

Only an instant had passed, yet it seemed that time warbled between ticking seconds. Anxiously she scanned the parking lot for movement, for a flash of white skin rushing toward them, for a glimpse of something worse.

Her heart labored, so stressed she couldn't tell if it had sped up or slowed down. The eerie stillness stretched hard and tight over them, an imperceptible cellophane wrapper that trapped them. Panic made her short of breath; terror convinced her that she'd find the oxygen siphoned away from their dubious refuge if she tried to fill her lungs.

Santo worked silently, stripping the wires and twisting them into a new configuration with complete focus. His hands didn't shake and his eyes didn't shift from the task. He didn't even look anxious. She envied his calm, even if it was all on the surface.

She peered through the dirty windows, finding only darkness pressing back in silent, inert layers. Maybe the hellhounds had been headed somewhere else? Maybe they thought she and Santo were still in their room, unaware of their pending invasion. Maybe he'd get the engine to start and they'd drive away without ever being detected.

Or maybe the piece of crap van would just transform into Optimus Prime and save the day.

She double-checked the locks on each door and finally allowed herself a deep breath.

Sulfur filled her nose and mouth. It coated her tongue and clotted in her throat. She could almost see it now, colored green by her imagination, gritty as sand and thick as syrup. With the stench came the sound, so soft at first that she could only discern the timbre and tone. Menace and vibrato pursuing her in the night.

She twisted around so she could see out the back window, leaning right, then left to check the sides. The stillness felt dissonantly solid and cold.

"I hear something."

Head still under the dash, Santo didn't catch her frightened whisper, but the sound came again. Louder. Deeper. What was it? Not the blood-chilling bay, but a growl. The deep rumble raised the hairs on her arms and sent a cascade of ice down her spine.

"Santo," she whispered. "They're here."

His head came up from beneath the dash. "Where?"

Roxanne shook her head, maneuvering down the length of the van to check each window. "I can't see them. But I hear them. I smell them."

"Another second and I'll be done," he said sharply.

Roxanne nodded, though he couldn't see her, and began compulsively checking locks again. She caught herself muttering under her breath.

Hurry, hurry, hurry, hurry, hurry. . . .

The engine roared to life as she saw the first one. It wove through the cars like a dog on a scent, bolting toward the van at full speed. It came so fast that it made a blur of white and black. An optical illusion that filled her gut with sharp, pricking spikes. From the corner of her eye she glimpsed another one darting through the shadows and then more, converging on the van like fired arrows.

She'd never seen anything like them.

Huge and monstrous, the creatures had the same colorless skin as the scavenger demons Santo had pointed out from the window, but it was as if something had warped the wretched beasts into a shape that crossed human with animal.

They looked like rabid dogs with the size and mass of a full-grown man. Not the furry humanoid wolf-man of Hollywood—no, these nightmarish monsters challenged anything the imagination might conjure. They alternated randomly between running upright and charging on all fours. Misshapen skulls connected with blunt necks and distorted torsos. Legs too long, eyes too human, jaws like a great ape's—wide with vicious, sharp canines.

The first of them slammed into the hollow shell of the van with a *boom* that rocked the vehicle on its wheels. Three more came at the windows, smashing into them with barrel chests, thick-skulled heads, wicked claws, and bared teeth.

Roxanne gripped the dash, trying not to scream when the biggest of the creatures lunged at the window beside her with enough force to crack the glass.

"Hurry, Santo," she breathed, when she wanted to scream.

Santo popped the brake and hit the gas, and the big engine roared. Before he could jam the gear into drive and get them out of there, the delivery boy—what was his name? Chandi? Cheli?—rounded the corner at that moment and froze, a grease-stained paper sack in his hands. His eyes widened as his mouth dropped open with shock. He stared at the van. At Santo sitting behind the wheel. At Roxanne in the passenger seat. Disbelief pulled at his features.

"Stop," he shouted. Then he turned his back—
turned his back on the wild beasts attacking—and yelled
something at the deserted lobby. Roxanne couldn't
make out every word, but she thought the foolish young
man was reporting the theft of the van, not that there
was anyone to hear him.

"What's wrong with him?" she demanded, turning to Santo. "Why isn't he running?" *Why wasn't he
screaming in terror?*

The creature that had slammed into the window
took advantage of their momentary distraction, regained
its feet, and tried again, this time hitting glass already
weakened. The force of its weight shook the van, and a
baseball-sized hole splintered the center of the window.

The delivery boy jumped at the sound, and at last
fear filled his eyes. He looked around him, as if searching for the source. Roxanne couldn't keep the scream
inside this time as tiny shards of glass peppered her skin.

The beast had hands—*feet?*—with fingers that
looked like they'd been jammed into the mold of a paw.
The two parts didn't match—those long, prehensile
appendages attached to the rough pads of a massive
paw on one end and long, deadly claws on the other. It
swiped at her through the hole it had made, caught the
flesh of her shoulder and tore at it.

They'll rip out your soul and feed on it.

Santo jerked his gun from its holster and fired at
the creature, once, twice. The *bang, bang* in the compact

space made Roxanne's brain feel like it would spurt out of her ears, but the beast withdrew. As Santo hit the gas, though, the delivery boy—*Chidi, his name was Chidi*—dropped his paper sack and rushed forward, grabbing the passenger door handle.

"Let her go," he shouted angrily as he tried to wrench the door open. "Drop the gun."

The words were so unexpected, so ridiculous, that at first they made no sense. *Let her go? Drop the gun? Was he insane?*

"Run!" she screamed as two of the creatures pounced.

But Chidi seemed aware only of Roxanne and his misguided perception that Santo meant her harm. He didn't—apparently *couldn't*—see the real danger, or he would have run as fast and as far as he could.

The first beast sank its teeth deep in his arm, the second went for his leg. Chidi's shriek of pain and confusion mixed into the howls and snarls.

"No!" she shouted.

But there was nothing they could do to help him. Any attempt would most likely end with them all being ripped apart. She knew Santo had already come to that conclusion, just as she knew it was the *right* conclusion if they meant to survive.

But Roxanne couldn't just sit there and do nothing while the delivery boy who'd thought to help her was torn to pieces.

All this went through her mind in a blink as she reached for the door. Santo yanked her back.

"What the fuck are you doing?" he demanded.

"He was trying to help me. We can't leave him."

"He's as good as dead," Santo said. He gunned the engine and the van shot forward, just as another of the bloodthirsty beasts jumped over the hood and slammed into the windshield, turning it into a network of fragments.

They're learning. They'd seen the other one break through the glass, and now they knew where to attack.

The hysterical thought snapped her out of her paralysis as Santo swung the van at the pylons that marked the motel's drop-off area, careening into one and dislodging the animal but not slowing it down. He cranked the wheel in the other direction and she realized he meant to keep going, down the ramp and away.

The sound of tires squealing distracted the two animals that had the delivery boy pinned, and they both charged the van. With cunning that astounded her, one came at the window beside her and the other at the windshield. The first managed to get its thick skull through the hole to snap its jaws at her. The beast caught her between the seat and the door with no way to escape and sank its teeth into her arm, braced its limbs against the frame and jerked with incredible power.

The safety glass came free in one piece, shattered fragments held in place by film. It made a spiked collar around the creature's throat, piercing and drawing blood, but the beast didn't care. It had full access to Roxanne, and it wasn't letting go. She felt it dragging her through the window as she frantically twisted and fought to get free.

Pain sliced and burned from her shoulder to her toes as the creature tore at her flesh and heaved her to the ground. Santo threw the van into park and scrambled from behind the wheel through the window after them, landing on his feet with her sprawled between his spread legs. He unloaded five rapid shots into the monster until it released, snarling and snapping with rage. The bullets had slowed it, hurt it, but they hadn't stopped it.

From the hard asphalt beneath her, she watched as its muscles bunched. It flew at Santo, but he was ready. His aim didn't waver as he put a bullet between the creature's white devil-eyes, blowing its head into a gelatinous mass of matter and blood. Roxanne felt the splash of it, warm and gooey as the impact knocked the beast back and laid it out on the ground beside her. Its hind legs twitched, its unhinged jaw snapped, but it didn't get up.

Her shock mixed with her agony, but there was no time for suffering. Santo yanked her to her feet with one hand, still spraying bullets at the monsters that remained standing.

Chidi had managed to get his legs under him while the beasts had been busy with Roxanne and Santo. Roxanne couldn't believe he was still alive.

"Get the fuck out of here," Santo shouted, popping the cartridge from his weapon and inserting another in a quick, smooth action. Chidi stood stunned and frozen in place. His wild eyes darted everywhere, searching for the danger he couldn't see, couldn't hear, and couldn't fight. Santo lifted his gun again and fired at the ground near Chidi's feet. The delivery boy jumped back in surprise.

"Run or die," Santo snapped. "Your choice."

The remaining creatures faced Santo in a pack. Huge, ugly, fierce. Roxanne quaked at the long, sharp teeth and slathering maws, but Santo didn't even wince. The creatures stood in formation, the biggest at point, the other two fanning out behind him, leaving Chidi for later. Shoulders as broad as a man's. Legs warped and muscle-bound, terminating in those grotesque hand-paws. Claws scrabbled at the asphalt.

"Get in the van, Roxanne," Santo said quietly. "Get behind the wheel and start driving. Don't look back."

"I'm not leaving you," she croaked.

Santo cursed under his breath. "You're a stubborn pain in the ass. You know that?"

"Yeah, I get that sometimes. But I'm still not leaving you."

"Just get in and get ready."

That she could do. Carefully she backed away, feeling for the van behind her, convinced she'd find her fingers in a hot, wet mouth just waiting for a treat. She rasped her knuckles against the handle as Santo took a step back with her, keeping his gun on the creatures.

The biggest one in front stood on its hind legs and eyed Santo with a cold canine grin.

"Get away from him," she breathed as she fumbled for the handle without taking her eyes off the creature.

It sniffed the air in front of Santo and then warily did it again.

Get away, get away, get away. . . .

Watching with terrified fascination, Roxanne saw it recoil. The reaction came so fast that she almost missed it, and in the next second it returned to all fours and growled. But for that instant it had almost seemed . . . afraid.

Her fingers closed over the handle and she pulled. Nothing happened. She tried again, turning to see it, as if that might bring another outcome. It hit her then. She'd locked, double-locked, triple-checked all the doors. Cursing, she moved to the right, climbed the tire like a step to the hood, and heaved herself up and through the window. She clambered over the console and hit the master button, unlocking all the doors before dropping behind the wheel and gunning the engine to let Santo know she was ready.

"Chidi," Santo called to the boy as he took a step back toward the van. "Get inside the lobby."

At last Chidi seemed to comprehend that standing still would only get him killed. The four remaining creatures growled, fur standing on end down their ridged backs, hungry eyes shifting between the two targets.

Chidi stumbled to the glass wall that looked in on the motel's lobby entrance, leaving a smear of blood as he used it for support. An overweight clerk now stood just inside, staring out with big eyes and an open mouth. He held a cell phone in his hand, and his gaze moved back and forth from screen to parking lot.

He was recording.

Fury and disbelief warred inside of Roxanne. They were fighting for their lives and the moron was *filming them*?

Chidi paused on the mat that should have triggered the sliding doors to open, but nothing happened. Confused, he jumped on it again and again, still expecting the doors to part. But Roxanne understood in a second what Chidi had yet to comprehend. The clerk had locked the doors.

God in heaven, no.

She snapped her gaze back to Santo, who'd taken his eyes off the beasts to watch Chidi. The creatures advanced, moving like a hunting party, closing in on all three sides. Santo's back was almost to the van's sliding door, but he stopped, aimed, and fired, hitting one dead on between the eyes and killing it. He got another with a solid shot to the chest. That one went down with a howl, but an instant later, it regained its feet and came again.

For all the shots she'd heard fired so far, only the ones that Santo had put through the brain had done the job. The beasts were too fast, too sly for him to keep up. He and Roxanne couldn't count on help, and they couldn't defeat the creatures if bullets only slowed them. So what could they do?

She revved the engine, distracting the creatures as she yelled at Santo to get in. He fired a spray at the monsters before diving through the sliding door while she shifted the gear and floored it. He tucked his legs inside just as the door slammed shut, catching one of the beasts that had tried to follow at the neck. It snarled, still trying to bite even as Santo shoved his gun in its mouth and pulled the trigger.

Roxanne cranked the wheel, took the van around the horseshoe drive, out one side and back in on the other, adjusting to aim for the glass door. She hit it hard, and the door exploded with a *boom* and a hailstorm of glass. The desk clerk ran for the office with its solid door, but Chidi was right behind him and she had a moment to hope. She thought they'd make it. God, she prayed they'd make it.

They were one step short when the beasts pounced and brought the desk clerk down. She watched in horror as they began to chew and tear at him. Chidi had made it, though, and he had only to close the solid office door to be safe. Of course he didn't. He came out to help the man who'd ignored his cries of fear and pain.

Everything seemed to slow, and sounds became exaggerated and excruciatingly loud.

A siren, screaming in the distance as it came closer.

The creatures, snarling and slathering as they attacked.

Chidi's screams, the desk clerk's shrieks, Santo's shouts. The *bang, bang* of gunshots. Another creature squealed and went down. And then she heard the heart-stopping click of an empty cartridge. Santo reloaded with lightning speed, but even Roxanne could see that bullets wouldn't help them. There was no way either the desk clerk or Chidi would escape.

"Look away," Santo told her as he tugged on her uninjured arm, pulling her from the driver's seat so he could take her place. He reversed out of the lobby, tires squealing as he cranked the wheel, straightened out, and floored the gas pedal. Tears burned her face as she turned to watch the carnage they left behind. The hellhounds had all converged on the easy prey, but one of them—the big one that had scrutinized Santo with such shrewd eyes—left the party to watch them go.

It didn't give chase, though. Not this time. But the threat of it hung in the air like the stench of sulfur. Inescapable and foul.

"Roxanne," Santo said sharply, and she realized he'd been speaking to her. She had no idea what he'd said.

Santo took her hand and squeezed it. "Roxanne, look at me."

She turned dazed eyes his way, noting the splatter of blood and gore that covered him. Knowing she looked the same.

"How bad are you hurt?" he demanded.

She made a sound that bordered on hysteria, but when she spoke, her voice was eerily calm.

"I'll live," she said and then she turned away.

(13)

The room that Gary assigned to Reece was on the second floor at the top of the stairs. It was an average room in an average house, built at a time when families tended to be big, and wide front porches were mandatory.

And it was out in the middle of fucking nowhere. Seriously.

The view from the front porch was miles and miles of desert. Back porch, same thing. A cultivated lawn butted up to several acres of farmland and pasture, then sand, rock, and cactus for as far as the eye could see. It was like that out here. Oasis in the midst of desert.

Gary's slaves—for lack of a better word—all worked like busy little bees, tending to the property grounds and doing other odds and ends. The house wore a fresh coat of blue paint, with blinding white trim and rails. Around the porch, bright flowers grew in nurtured beds. The tended lawn with its winter rye sprouted dark green and lush. A virtual paradise in the bosom of the hostile desert.

After Reece's stranger-than-fuck meeting with Gary, he'd been given a tour of the compound—that's what they called it. A compound. In addition to the wannabe-plantation, there were four outbuildings and a greenhouse. One of the buildings held an array of shovels and hoes, rakes and picks, all shiny new. A big John Deere tractor kept company with something that might have been a seeder or just as easily a harvesting machine. Reece didn't know jack shit about farming, but he'd been told they grew most of their food here. Evidently, Gary wasn't a fan of preservatives.

Another building had been converted into a training center, with mats for hand-to-hand combat exercises in one corner. A portion of it had been walled off in a skinny chamber that ran the length of the building. Inside he'd found a shooting range complete with targets and safety gear. The third building held weapons—weapons like Reece had only seen in movies about Mexican drug lords. Stacks of automatic and semiautomatic rifles. Boxes of ammo piled to the ceiling. A launcher that looked lethal even unassembled.

"You guys think there's going to be a war?" he asked, only half joking.

"There already is," his ugly escort answered. The guy had the worst complexion Reece had ever seen. He looked like he'd never been in the sun, and his eyes were a milky brown, disconcertingly fishy. It took Reece a moment to figure out he wore colored contacts. The man carried the faint scent of rotten eggs.

"What's in the last building?" Reece asked, eyeing the thick chains and double padlocks on the door. This one had no windows and only one exit.

"None of your fucking business."

The tour couldn't have ended fast enough. Reece needed some downtime. A moment to process the insanity that Gary had served up with such finesse and a moment to come to terms with what it meant for him. When Reece returned to his room, he closed the door with relief. But only a few minutes passed before someone knocked. The door didn't have a lock, and Reece figured it would be pointless to ignore whoever was out there.

"Come in," he said.

He expected it to be Gary, coming to put the cherry on top of his crazy, but two women stood on the threshold. The first was St. Pauli Girl hot, with big blue eyes, long blond hair, and a scattering of freckles across her nose. She wore a tight T-shirt, no bra, and short shorts with flip-flops. She was creamy-fair like Gary and the ugly guy who'd given him the tour. She gave Reece a big smile and held up a tray.

"Hi. I'm Karen, that's April," she said with a drawl that spoke of the South.

She used her chin to point at the silent woman standing beside her, in case he couldn't figure it out. Where Karen was long, lean, and fair as a summer day, April was petite, compact, and dark as a winter night. Her rich color stood out like a red rose in a field of daisies. He realized she was the only person he'd seen with any color about her at all. Everyone here looked as pasty as cave dwellers in a subzero climate.

April had short hair only a few shades blacker than her skin, full, pouty lips drawn in a tight, disapproving line, and high cheekbones that made her look runway-model arresting, though she didn't have any makeup on that he could see. Not simply pretty, like Karen. Her suspicious expression alone told him there was little about her that could be termed *simple* at all. But she was beautiful in a complex and interesting way.

She avoided his eyes and ignored the introduction completely. Instead, she hunched in her oversized flannel shirt and baggy jeans, looking like she'd rather be anyplace in the world other than here.

He knew exactly how she felt and liked her for it, despite the frown.

As if she'd heard his thought, she glanced up with an assessing glint in her warm brown eyes.

"Gary sent us with some food," Karen said, increasing the wattage of her smile as she stepped into the room. "He thought you might be hungry. He wanted us to be sure you're settling in okay."

Hungry? Settling in? His stomach was in knots and he felt about as settled as a rabbit in a pen of pit bulls. Every time he thought of Roxanne and the fake cop who'd abducted her, he wanted to hit something, someone. What if the story Gary had told him was true? What if the world was being invaded by demons?

What if Reece could use that dark thirst inside him, the cravings that yearned to be released, to do some good? That's what Gary offered him. The chance to fight evil with evil.

As horrible as the idea of demons was, the offer had its appeal. He could hurt things that deserved it. He could unleash those longings on something that needed to die.

"Not hungry?" Karen asked, cocking her head to the side and scrunching up her nose. She was cute, he'd give her that. A little ray of sunshine in this strangely skewed place. By contrast, April hovered just inside the door like an angry thundercloud, clearly not happy to be part of the welcoming committee. Karen gave her a pointed look that didn't make sense until April quietly shut the door and leaned against it.

Eyeing them both, Reece said, "No, not hungry and hell-and-gone from settled. Just trying to take it all in."

Karen nodded with understanding and put the tray on his nightstand before making herself at home on the side of his bed. "I didn't believe it at first either," she told him. "But it's hard not to believe what you've seen with your own eyes."

Curious, Reece pulled the lone chair from the small desk and positioned it in front of the bed where she sat. He almost forgot his manners, but his dad's voice in his head reprimanded him at the last minute.

"April, would you like a chair?" he asked.

April looked surprised by the offer, but shook her head and continued to lean against the door and ignore him. With a shrug, Reece sat down and turned his attention back to Karen. "So you've seen . . . them?" he asked.

Gary had called them demons. *Demons.* But Reece couldn't bring himself to speak such an outrageous concept.

"I've seen them," Karen said. "They killed my family. April's, too."

Reece stared at her, nonplussed, waiting for the punch line. When she didn't recant, he swung his gaze to April, wishing she'd join them so he could see them both.

"Is that true?" he asked.

April stiffened and gave a terse nod.

"Don't mind her," Karen said. "She don't talk much anymore."

"Anymore?"

"Since her family got killed."

"You knew each other before?"

"Oh, sure. We lived right down the street from each other. My family moved north when I was in high school. We rode the bus together."

That surprised him, almost as much as any of the bewildering things he'd learned since arriving. He'd pictured the people here as strangers, united in a common cause. Her assertion that they'd been friends before the . . . well, *before* . . . tilted his perceptions.

"When did it happen?" he asked, trying to sound sympathetic but unable to keep the note of suspicion from his tone.

"Last month," Karen said calmly.

"Where?"

"Harvey, North Dakota. It's where we lived, me and her."

He shot April another glance. She didn't stand taller than five-four or five-five to begin with, but as Karen had been talking, she seemed to withdraw, making herself smaller. Even her fingers had curled into tight, little fists.

Reece said, "You're a long way from home."

Karen made a small humming sound, and he turned back to catch her eyeing April with displeasure. As soon as Karen felt Reece's gaze on her, she masked the look with another smile.

"Can you tell me about it?" Reece asked. "What happened to your family?"

"Sure. Like I said, the demons killed them. I wasn't home when they came. Probably why I'm still alive, you know? But I saw what they did. I saw what they left behind."

She folded her hands in her lap, staring at her linked fingers. "We never did find my sister. No one knows what was done to her. She's dead, though. Isn't another way it could be."

"I'm sorry," he said, meaning it. Praying to a God he'd never had much time for that he wouldn't be recounting a similar tale someday. If Gary had told the truth, though, his sister had been taken by a demon disguised as a cop.

Mentally, he rolled his eyes and slapped his forehead. It didn't come much crazier than that.

Karen gave a sad shrug, pulling his attention back. "I'm luckier than most. I'm alive. I'm here to fight another day and all that."

He leaned forward and touched her hands. Her fingers moved under his and gripped him tightly, startling him with their strength. As if realizing it, she let go and gave a small laugh.

"We're just so glad *you're* here, Reece."

Yeah, Gary had told him just how *glad* everyone was. They had expectations of him that boggled his mind.

"What about you, April?" he asked, pulling his hand back and turning his attention to the other woman. He caught her watching him and held her gaze before she could look away.

"She was home for the whole thing," Karen said. "Gary got there just after they killed her daddy. Everyone else was already dead. Her three sisters and her brother, Jeremy. He used to play football. Isn't that right, April? Jeremy played for UND, didn't he?"

April nodded, her gaze still prisoner to Reece's. Her eyes were big and so dark that he could see the light reflected in them. Her lashes made an outline around the whites, turning the brown into a rich and vividly expressive chocolate. She had the kind of eyes that spoke, though he had no idea what they said to him now.

She blinked and looked away.

"You saw them, April?" he repeated.

"I saw them. I saw what they did," she said, surprising him. He'd come to expect silent responses.

She had a low, musical voice that made him wonder if she sang. Trying to picture her face alive with music and joy, he crossed the room to stand in front of her. Blocking her from Karen's view with his body, he willed April to look at him again. He could feel her reluctance as she lifted her chin, focusing on a point just past his left ear.

"What did they look like?"

The question hung like a mist, obscuring things he didn't understand, blanketing the space between them.

"Big," she said after a moment. "Pale. So white they glowed. And their eyes . . ."

A shudder went through her body, and Reece found an answering shiver creeping down his spine. Flashes of memories he couldn't believe were real crowded in. Had he seen something like that the night of the robbery? He didn't know. He felt like he'd been pumped full of some type of hallucinogenic that clouded his thoughts and blurred the lines between reality and imagination to the point where he could no longer tell one from the other.

"What about you, Reece?" Karen asked, suddenly standing right behind him. He jumped and turned. "Have you seen them?"

"No." He stepped back, moving away from both women. "I've never seen anything even remotely close. I'll be honest, ladies. I don't know what happened to your families, but this whole idea of demons . . . well, it just doesn't sound believable or right. I guess I'll have to see it for myself before I can get on board with it. Sorry."

April started to shake her head, but Karen's quick glance stopped her. He wished he could figure out what was going on with these two.

"Don't be sorry," Karen said, running her hand up and down his arm. "And I sure hope you never have to see what we've seen. God, no. I hope you . . . I mean . . ."

Her pause felt weighted, and Reece braced himself.

"I mean, what about your sister?" she finished softly.

"What about her?"

"Gary says they have her. They took her."

From the corner of his eye, he saw April watching him again. "I'm not entirely convinced Gary isn't a lunatic."

Karen smiled at that, and the expression was so sweet and genuine that Reece let his guard down, just a bit.

"I didn't believe him at first either," she said. "Even after I saw the carnage they left behind, I managed to talk myself around to thinking that it'd just been bad guys, out on a rampage. You hear about them on the news all the time. But Gary showed me pictures."

"Pictures?"

"In the Bible." His blank look made her smile again. "Seriously. Ask him to show you. The Bible talks of Satan, and there's pictures in the one he has. They look just like . . ." She paused and swallowed. "I've seen them since, and when I think of them coming for my family . . . I'll do whatever I have to do to stop them, even if it means dying."

Her impassioned words resonated inside him. Whether bad guy or demon, he'd do whatever it took to save his sister, too. Death notwithstanding.

Without meaning to, he looked at April again. "You've seen these pictures?"

She shrugged.

Karen tugged at his arm, leading him back over to the bed. "I know it probably sounds like some religious mumbo jumbo if you haven't seen what you're up against, like we have. But it's God's truth, Reece."

She believed it. He could hear it in her voice. But that didn't make it true. She sat on the bed and tugged him down beside her, then inched over so she was practically in his lap.

"You should eat something," she said.

But he wasn't really listening to her. Instead he focused on the questions buzzing like a hornet's nest in his head. Finally, one slowed down enough for him to grab it. "Why?" he asked. "Why *your* family? Either of you. Why were they targeted?"

He could feel April's gaze drilling into him, but Karen spoke first. "Convenience. Harvey's a small town. Even if everyone in it got up in arms to fight back . . ." She shook her head. "They'd still win. We both lived out off Hunt Street." She laughed. "Wasn't much of a street, wasn't even paved. Our house was the last one. April lived two up. Everyone else who lived there's gone now."

"Jesus. I'm sorry."

"Jesus didn't have a thing to do with it," April blurted.

Watching her, Reece asked, "Why haven't I heard about this? Why wasn't it on the news?"

Karen said, "Gary and the others, they killed the demons who did it. Then they lit the whole thing on fire.

Burned it out all the way to the Coopers' house, but that place had been abandoned for years. Wasn't no one home to care. But even still . . . for every demon they kill, there's another taking its place. It's a losing battle."

"Yeah, that's what he said. There's too many of them."

"And more come every day. That's why Gary was so excited to get you. He wanted—"

She stopped with a stricken look on her face. In the sharp silence that followed, he glanced from Karen to April, trying to fill in the holes between what they said and what they meant. It almost felt planned, those blurted words. Bait that he couldn't resist.

With doubt edging his awareness, he said, "Gary wanted . . . what?"

Karen stood. "I shouldn't be talking about this."

"Why not?"

"Because she's got shit for brains," April said unexpectedly.

Karen didn't look offended in the least. "It's true. I'm not as smart as some people," she said.

"You seem smart enough to me," Reece responded.

Her smile could have powered a small village. But Reece couldn't shake the feeling that he was being played any more than he could say why he felt that way.

"I won't tell him you said anything," he went on, watching April from the corner of his eye. She shook her head and turned, grabbing the doorknob.

"Where you going?" Karen demanded.

April threw a speaking glance over her shoulder, yanked open the door, and let it thump loudly behind her. Reece had no idea what had set her off, but the tension in the room eased with her exit.

"You'll have to forgive April. She's been through a lot."

"Sounds like you both have."

"That's for sure."

Karen sat next to him again, just as close as before.

"Do you know what Gary wants from me?" Reece asked.

She looked down at her feet and said nothing.

"I swear I won't repeat it. Anything you say."

She took a deep breath. "You promise?"

"Yeah. I promise."

"Gary thinks you and your sister are chosen," she said, laying her hand over Reece's heart.

Pretty much what Gary had told him, but Reece had let it roll off. They thought he'd been chosen to fight evil because of his inability to stay dead. As explanations went, it was out there. But in all his twenty-five years, Reece had yet to hear a better reason for the fact that he kept coming back. That still didn't mean he believed the bullshit.

"He says you can't die because you're meant to save us."

Somehow he'd hoped Karen would tell a different

tale. Because Gary was off his fucking wheels. Reece couldn't save himself. Hadn't saved his sister.

He shook his head, looking into Karen's hopeful eyes. "I'm sorry, but that's crap. I *can* die. Chances are, I will again sometime soon. And maybe it will be the last time. Maybe I won't be lucky enough to have some surgeon on standby when they bring me in."

"He said you'd say that. That's why we aren't supposed to talk about it. I just get so excited when I think . . ."

He stared at her, waiting for her to finish that thought.

"He says with you and your sister on our side, we can't lose."

"Gary seems to be living in some fantasy land, Karen. I'm sorry. I'm sorry about what happened to your family. But I don't believe there are monsters—"

"Demons," she whispered.

"*Demons,*" he corrected. "I don't believe they're out walking around killing people. I think there's crime. I think there are people who are so fucked-up they act like monsters."

Sometimes he feared he might be one of them if he ever let himself go.

"But they're just humans with a lot of wires crossed the wrong way. That's all they are."

He paused, looking away. Feeling the acrid bite of disgrace in his throat. Talk about fucked-up wiring.

"I wish you were right. But you'll have to see them for yourself, I guess."

His skin got cold at that, but he didn't let his gaze stray from hers. "I guess I will."

She nodded, looking very young and more than a little bit scared. "You promise you won't mention this to Gary?"

"I promise."

She searched his face, as if seeking the lie in that. He gazed back, trying to appear reassuring.

"Thank you," she said and leaned forward to press a kiss to his cheek.

The action startled him, and for a moment he didn't move. She stayed where she was, leaning across the gap that separated them, her breasts pressed against his side. Then she wound her arms around his neck and wiggled closer, trying to push him back against the bed.

"Whoa," he said. "Karen, whoa."

He managed to grab her wrists just as she reached for his fly.

She looked up, gave him a siren's smile, and said, "What's wrong?"

He found his feet and moved to the other side of the room before she could lay another kiss on him. She was nice, beautiful, and sexy as hell. But nothing about this encounter sat right with him. He felt as if he'd been led into a dark alley—one he'd entered willingly only to call himself every kind of fool when he was jumped.

He heard her move as she crossed to his side. He held out a hand, keeping her at bay.

"What else did Gary tell you to do?" he asked. "Bring me food, settle me in, and . . . ?"

Karen faltered, the big blue eyes blinking at him.

"Did he tell you to make me feel at home? Did he tell you to show me a good time?"

She didn't answer. She didn't have to. He saw it there in her face, and for a moment he was disappointed. He realized he liked her, this fair, freckled woman with her big eyes that fear shadowed now.

"Don't worry. I'm not going to tell him what we talked about. I gave you my word. If he asks, tell him you did your best to . . . you know. Tell him I'm an asshole and it's going to take more than—" He stopped, unable to voice the scathing words that he wanted to throw in Gary's face. This girl was obviously a pawn. It wasn't her fault that Gary had manipulated her.

Reece moved to the door and held it open for her. "It'll be all right," he said as she walked out. She gave him a wounded look, one that held a gleam of trepidation. It was so stark, so unmistakable, that he almost stopped her. But common sense halted his instincts. She was playing him. Just like Gary had played him.

Before he turned back to his room, he caught a movement in the shadow at the top of the stairs. April stood watching him, the look on her face unreadable. But there was something desperate in those dark eyes.

Something that touched him, that beseeched him. Something he would be thinking about long into the night.

With a sigh he shut the door.

It was best he remembered that in this place, nothing—and no one—was what it seemed.

(14)

Santo wanted to put as many miles as possible between them and the horror they'd left behind, but morning traffic and the need to avoid major roadways kept the going slow. Roxanne had grown so quiet, huddled in her seat, that he feared the worst. She'd been mauled badly, but she'd recovered from a gunshot with more alacrity than she showed now.

She was hurt and her pain rode him like his own. It made him wish he *was* an angel. One that could make this horror go away for her.

You can, a treacherous voice whispered in his head. *Reap her and be gone.*

Why did the idea fill him with dread now instead of pleasure? Was it because he suspected that Roxanne was the only thing standing between an invasion of the human world and the most abhorrent of the Beyond? Or was it because he couldn't let her go, even when it meant taking her with him?

His lacerated hands tightened on the steering wheel and he glanced her way. What was she thinking? It consumed him now, that query. That need to know what went on in the depths of her mind. Were her thoughts consumed by him, as his were by her? Or was he merely another passenger on a journey that, for her, had begun long before he'd stepped into Santo's skin?

If he left without her . . . if he abandoned his goal and returned to the Beyond deprived of her soul . . . would *she* feel the loss? Would she mourn him as Santo mourned his dead wife? He almost laughed at the emotional traffic jam that thought created. He would not wish that pain on Roxanne, yet it would destroy him to know he'd been nothing more than a speed bump in her life.

"Roxanne," he said, reaching across the seat to settle his hand over hers. As soon as he touched her, he felt better. Still, her silence bothered him. He was beginning to know her enough to guess that behind it she'd be feeling guilt. Guilt, over the deaths of two strangers.

"You did everything you could. The beasts were out for blood. You know that. No scenario would have ended with the delivery boy and desk clerk alive."

"Really?" she said softly. "How about one where I wasn't there?"

"*I* brought you to the hotel. You didn't have a

choice. If you're going to play *what if,* you'll have to start with me."

"You were only there to protect me."

Shame kept him from responding. In this quagmire of emotion that trapped him, he'd found a well of guilt that was all his own. He'd lied to her from the start. Lied to her still.

She thought he was a fucking angel sent by God, no doubt, to save her.

What would she think when she learned the truth?

She stared out the window, lost in thoughts of her own.

"Talk to me," he said, frowning at the yearning he heard in his voice. "What's going on in your head?"

"You don't want to know."

Oh, but he did. Desperately.

He waited her out until she finally took a deep breath and began to speak in a halting, monotone voice.

"I was just remembering . . . After the last time . . . the last time I died . . . When I got out of the hospital, I saw this woman. Everywhere I went, she was there. In the grocery store, the mall. At work. I saw her at the library once, just sitting at a table, watching me."

He looked away from the road to ask, "How long ago was that?"

But he already knew. Four years, six weeks, three days.

"Four years give or take. I could tell you the date, but it's not important."

To her, maybe. "What did she want, this woman?"

Roxanne shrugged, the gesture tight, her expression so desolate he wanted to stop the van and pull her onto his lap.

Fates help him, he was lost.

"She was just this ordinary lady. A little overweight. A bit haggard. She looked like a mom, the one who always makes a cake for the school bake sale. She was everything I've ever dreamed about."

"You dream about making cakes?" he teased, but Roxanne didn't even smile.

She cleared her throat, avoiding his eyes. "It went on like that for weeks. Seeing her, but never speaking. I tried a couple of times, but she managed to disappear before I ever got close enough to ask her why she kept following me. Then one day I turned around and there she stood, right behind me. She looked at me like . . ." Roxanne shook her head. "She said, 'Why you? Why you and not my Suzanne?' After that, she just walked away. I never saw her again."

"Who was Suzanne?"

"Her daughter? Sister? Friend? Does it matter? She was someone who died when I didn't. The look in her eyes . . . I'll never forget it." Roxanne paused and stared at her fingers, knotted together in her lap.

"You can't blame yourself for things you can't control."

"Can't I? Think about it, Santo. Why me? Why *me*? That young man, Chidi? He didn't even know me, but when he thought I was in danger, he risked his life to help me. A stranger. Why not him? Why can't he get up and go on after what happened?"

Santo shook his head, wondering at the woman's capacity for self-reproach. She wouldn't hear a wrong word about her brother. She defended strangers and tried to save them from their fate, then held herself responsible when she failed. She seemed to put everyone and anyone above herself. But who watched out for Roxanne? Why was there no man in her life, ready to stand between her and danger? Why was she alone?

"I'm a coward and yet *I'm* the miracle. The human Energizer Bunny."

He didn't get the reference, but he understood it wasn't a good thing.

She took a deep breath and slowly let it out.

"Explain to me again about this door you felt open when Reece was shot," she said. "You think his death caused it, don't you? You think that's what opened it."

"Yes."

"What makes you so sure?"

Not the conversation he'd have chosen, but honestly, he was surprised it had taken her this long to ask. He'd assumed shock had kept her quiet, but he'd known she would have questions sooner or later. Roxanne always had questions.

"I'm not sure about anything, *angelita*. But I felt the barrier between the Beyond and your world go down the moment your brother died. I didn't put it together right away, though. Not even when the hellhounds came through. But I think his death made it possible for them to cross over."

"How is that even possible?"

"Death and resurrection, Roxanne. It's a cycle. A birth on earth brings a soul back to its human origins. A death returns it to the Beyond."

Her brows pulled together and her lips thinned.

"Do you remember anything about dying?" he asked in a low voice.

She shifted uncomfortably and said nothing for a moment. Then, softly, hesitantly, "The first time I was just a newborn. I don't remember anything from that. But the second time I was ten."

"Reece was with you then, too."

"Yeah. A family trip to Canyon Lake. We drowned, both of us. It took thirty-five minutes for them to find us. Another ten before they had a pulse. We were both gone for a long time." She tucked a strand of hair behind her ear, letting her fingers trail the line of her cheek.

Mask in place, he thought.

"I remember being someplace dark. I was alone. Scared. Then someone came."

"Who?" he asked, so intent he could hardly form the word.

She lifted a shoulder. Shook her head.

"I just remember feeling comforted until I opened my eyes again."

Comforted. He'd brought her comfort. She'd been so young, so scared. He'd been moved by her sobs, fascinated even then by the beauty of her soul, of how it changed the darkness, having her there.

"I woke up in the hospital and everyone called me a miracle. The news stations made a big deal of the twins that had come back from death twice. Strangers sent us stuffed animals and flowers. Cards that said things like *You are blessed.*"

She leaned back against the headrest. "It was almost fun, being famous. But after that . . . that's when Reece started to change."

"Change how?"

"He was always this sunny boy. Always smiling. But after the lake, he withdrew. Sometimes for days. Sometimes weeks. Then he'd come back and pretend nothing had happened. But I knew."

"What did you know?"

She swallowed. "For him the darkness held no comfort."

Something swelled inside him. He didn't even know what to call it. It felt too big to name, too important to label.

"Did you feel your brother, when you died and went to the darkness? Was he there, with you?"

She struggled for a moment, trying to articulate whatever it was she felt. "He's there. I sense him, but he's not with me." She shrugged. "I can't explain it."

"It's okay," he told her. "I just wondered."

Santo waited to see if she'd say more. When only silence stretched between them, he tried again.

"What about the third time?" he said, his voice so husky it sounded raw.

"I was with Reece again when it happened," she said in a low, unsteady voice. "He was on a rampage. Angry at life. He hated working at Love's. Still does. But we're all kind of trapped there. It's part of who we are. Maybe if the economy were better, we'd sell. But we can't even get out from under it right now. So Reece being an ass about pulling a few extra shifts . . . it wasn't cool. I'd suggested we go hiking in the Superstitions that morning, hoping to talk some sense into him. To tell him that when he bitches about working, it makes it miserable for all of us. But he was in a mood and I knew better than to bring it up. We were driving back when he just . . . exploded. It was like he couldn't help himself."

She paused, and Santo sensed a moment of revelation for her. He could almost see her putting things together that had never quite fit in her mind before. Her breath caught, and she stared sightlessly at the passing roadside.

"He was like that last night. I remember thinking that the last time he'd been strung so tight . . ." She trailed off, her expression dumbfounded.

"What happened after the hike?" he prompted.

"He drove our car right off the road and into a ravine. Right off. And it was a long way down. It seemed to take forever, you know? Falling. And the sounds . . . Metal twisting. Me, screaming. I couldn't stop. Later, I saw the wreckage they pulled us out of on the news. It's no wonder that the world went nuts and started calling us freaks. There shouldn't have been anything left to save."

"Did you go to the darkness again?" he asked. He couldn't have kept the question in if he'd wanted to.

She hesitated just a moment before saying softly, "Yes."

A small smile curled her lips. She looked down and she . . . blushed. That thing in his chest? It felt like it was going to burst.

"He was there again," she said to her fingers.

"He?"

"The one who waits for me."

"It's a man?"

She nodded.

"How do you know?"

"I just do. I remember him holding me and I felt so safe. So cared for. I wanted to stay there. I didn't want to be saved." She glanced at him and quickly away. "Do you think it was Jesus?" she asked.

It was his turn to be thunderstruck. "Jesus wouldn't have made you blush," he said before he could temper it.

Her face flamed at that and he knew, even when she didn't say it, that he'd made her feel more than *safe*.

"What about last night?" he asked, pushing his luck but unable to stop. "Was he waiting then?"

She shook her head and looked . . . sad. "Last night I was all alone."

He put his hand over hers again. "Not true," he said. "I was waiting for you to open your eyes. You were never alone."

He knew as soon as the words were spoken that he'd made a critical mistake. The soft light in her eyes grew sharp.

"Why?" she demanded. "What makes me so important that they'd send someone from the Beyond to keep me safe? If I were you, I'd be pissed to get such a shit assignment."

"I wanted to come. I wasn't sent, Roxanne. I volunteered."

He wanted her to ask *why* one more time. He even toyed with the idea that he might tell her, at least part of it. But that confession would truly be the end of it. And he couldn't bear to let it end.

"Oh," she said instead.

The one word caught in the air and hung like a bloated balloon, too fat to sail off, too full to sink. He caught her gaze and could almost sense the wheels and cogs of her mind turning, moving information from doubt to acceptance, earmarking that which she still questioned.

He thought she believed him, but he had the strangest feeling he'd hurt her. Damned if he could figure out how.

She stared at her clenched hands, her face like marble. The woman guarded what went on in her head like a warden.

"There's something else I need to tell you," he said. "Reece's death isn't the only factor we need to think about. His dying might have opened the door to the Beyond. But yours, Roxanne, closed it."

Her head snapped up and she stared at him.

"I don't know what it means," he said before she could ask. "I can't even swear the two are connected, but my guess is they are. I think that's why the hellhounds came for you tonight."

She shook her head. "I'm not following."

"The scavenger demon knew what would happen when he killed your brother. Shooting him wasn't a chance thing he did in the heat of the moment. I watched him. He meant to pull that trigger. I would say your brother is how the scavenger got here in the first place. But I don't think he knew about you."

He paused, wishing he didn't have to say it.

"Now he does."

She grew quiet again after that, and he was glad.

The conversation had left him troubled for more than one reason.

He'd been driving back roads, looking for a good place to dump the van and steal a less recognizable vehicle. Now he pulled into the parking lot of a busy Denny's restaurant and circled around to where the lot connected to a Days Inn hotel. He inched the van into a tight space behind a row of dumpsters and made his way through the dark to the sedan he'd spotted. Older model, peeling paint and cardboard over the back window made it easy pickings. Roxanne would probably protest that the poor slob who drove it couldn't afford to have his car stolen, but Santo didn't care. Humans found ways to cope with adversity. It was their nature.

While Roxanne waited in the van, he got the car going and pulled it around. She gave their new vehicle a sullen look but climbed into the passenger seat without protest. She winced, though, and made a stifled, pained noise that tore at something inside him.

He reached for the opened water bottle the car's owner had left in the cup holder and shrugged out of his T-shirt, turning it inside out and dampening it to wipe the blood that had dried on her face. She sat quiet and still as he worked, moving over her brow, her cheeks, her chin and throat. After he'd cleaned her arms—carefully avoiding the angry furrows from claws and the deep punctures left from teeth—he rummaged in the duffel he'd tossed on the backseat and found another T-shirt for her and one for him. He cleaned his own face and hands before donning it. A baseball cap lay abandoned behind the front seat and Santo fished it out and put it on. Silently, he took their bloodied shirts and tossed them in the trash.

Let the forensic team that pulled this investigation make what they would of that.

Before closing her door, Santo reached in and touched her cheek, cupping her face and turning it so she had to look at him. But once he held her gaze with his, he couldn't think of what to say. She looked so hurt, so broken. He didn't know how to respond to that.

Sensing that anything he said would be the wrong thing, he got behind the wheel without a word. As he drove away, he glanced at the dumpsters in his rearview. They made a perfect camouflage for the van. If he was lucky, no one would discover the van tonight and the owner of the car wouldn't notice it was gone until morning.

With the new wheels, he could breathe easier, and he headed for the one place he knew they wouldn't be turned away.

"Where are we going?" Roxanne asked.

"Someplace safe, *angelita*." At least for a while.

"Don't call me that," she muttered.

He smiled at the bristling command, taking it as a good sign. He didn't know what to do with the silent, morose woman beside him, but feisty Roxanne he could handle.

"I'm going to stop and get some bandages and antiseptic. After we get you patched up, you'll feel better."

"Something tried to eat me tonight. It's going to take more than a Band-Aid to make me feel better."

He shot her an amused glance.

"I want to call home," she said, wiping the humor from his face.

"That's not possible."

"Either you make it possible or I jump out of this car, Santo. Take your pick."

He hid his grin this time, knowing she'd be infuriated by it. She was deadly serious, he could see that, but having her fight back filled him with dizzying relief.

"And where will you go, *angelita*?" he taunted softly.

"To hell. I don't care. Ryan and Ruby have to be worried sick about me. That clerk, he filmed what happened, Santo. Filmed *us*. How long do you think it will take for the footage to be on the news?"

Santo shook his head. "You're mistaken."

"I saw him doing it with his cell phone. If they couldn't see those . . . things . . . the hellhounds, what do you think will be on that footage? You, shooting. Me, screaming. Chidi thought you were hurting me. Kidnapping me. The rest of the world will think the same thing."

She paused, peering at him expectantly, but he didn't know what to say. The opinions of the world mattered little to him. Keeping the female beside him alive, though, that had become a pressing concern.

"They suspected you of abducting me from Love's before. Now they'll have it confirmed. For all we know, they're accusing you of murder, too. There's going to be a manhunt. You of all people should know that."

"Any medical examiner who looks at those bodies will know that bullets didn't kill them," he countered.

The blood drained from Roxanne's face. Even in the dark interior of the car, he could see it.

"If there are any bodies to be found," she answered.

Excellent point. She didn't need to remind him of the people who'd been missing after the attack at Love's. He still hadn't worked out why, though. What were the demons doing with the bodies?

Roxanne said, "I want a phone, Santo. I want to call home."

Reluctantly, he nodded. "I'll see what I can do."

A half hour later, Santo entered a drugstore in a strip mall on the corner of *deserted* and *nowhere* with his head down, brim casting shadows over his face, and hands tucked in his pockets. He got in and out as quickly as possible, opened the door and tossed three bags onto Roxanne's lap, then reversed out of their parking spot.

"No troubles?" she asked as she rummaged in the sacks until she found the plastic-encased cell phone. She released a small sigh that told him she hadn't believed he'd follow through. Her lack of trust would have hurt him, but he felt like he'd finally gotten a handle on the human inside him, and he refused to let it.

"Thank you," she said, and something tightened smugly in his chest, mocking his idea of control.

"You can charge it at Louisa's."

Louisa was his dead wife's godmother. A sweet, recently widowed woman whom Santo Castillo, the human, had loved like a mother. Roxanne had given him a quizzical look when he'd told her he planned to take them there tonight, but she hadn't disputed the idea. An accepting Roxanne was novelty enough to take as a good sign.

Merging back onto I-10 headed north, he kept his speed at a steady sixty-eight, when he wanted to floor it and fly. It wouldn't do to get pulled over for a traffic violation and be forced into killing someone innocent in order to get away. Roxanne would never forgive him, and for reasons he chose not to examine, he cared about that.

After a while, she said, "You seem pretty sure that Louisa will let us in, Santo. If she's been watching the news, she might not."

"Louisa is like family," he told her. "She'll let us in."

"She's not, though. Related, I mean. Not even to your wife."

"No. But she and Jorge raised Marisella. When we got married, it was Jorge who walked her down the aisle. I never knew my own father. Jorge was that to me."

"Will the police be looking for you there?"

He shook his head. "There's no legal tie, as you say.

And I haven't seen or spoken to Louisa since we buried Jorge last year."

"Why not?"

He shrugged, but the gesture couldn't counteract the lump that suddenly formed in his throat. "Too much pain, for both of us."

"Will going there put her in danger?" Roxanne asked, ever concerned with innocents she hadn't even met. "Can the . . . demons track us there?"

Santo shot her an affronted look. "Do you think I'd put an old woman in danger?"

She thought about that before answering, which annoyed him to no end.

"No. I don't."

He didn't want to analyze the relief her simple answer gave him. It made his voice more brusque than he'd like when he said, "Why don't you try to sleep? We'll be there in about an hour."

He glanced at the clock on the dash. It was barely two in the afternoon, yet it felt like the day had lasted forever and it should be the wee hours, the witching hour, as humans called it. Roxanne said nothing more as she hunched against her door. She might have closed her eyes, but he doubted she'd sleep. Her soft heart wouldn't be able to let go enough for that, and she would fear the nightmares. He knew it without being told.

He pulled up to Louisa's house at three fifteen, and Louisa did, indeed, let them in.

Her brown, weathered face creased in a surprised smile when she opened the door, her features so familiar that they hit him like a punch in the gut, toppling all his arrogant disclaimers that he controlled the emotions inside. She pulled Santo into a bear hug, standing on tiptoes to embrace him, and her scent rolled him into memories so sweet and poignant that they drew blood.

Holding him tight, she whispered words in her native tongue, telling him how much she'd missed him, how she'd always known he'd come home. He answered in Spanish, and said that he was sorry. And he was. Sorry that Santo had ignored her when she'd needed him. Sorry that the man she embraced so warmly was only an imposter. Sorry that he'd come here, blithely taking advantage of a woman who would be heartbroken if she knew the truth.

Roxanne hovered in the tiny entryway, watching with her heart in those luminous eyes. She didn't need to understand the words to feel their meaning, and her empathy added another link to the complicated chains binding him.

At last Louisa pulled away, but she kept a frail hand on Santo's arm, like a mother with an errant little boy in a busy marketplace. "And who is this, *mijo*?" she asked, eyeing Roxanne with widened brown eyes. Louisa's gaze took in Roxanne's disheveled appearance, the oversized T-shirt, the baggy black sweatpants that fortunately hid the blood, and her sneakers, which didn't.

To her credit, Louisa hid the shock she must have been feeling, but when her gaze returned to his face, she looked uneasy.

He'd planned all along to lie to her, but now he surprised even himself. "Louisa," he said, "I'm in trouble."

"*Sí,*" Louisa answered, frowning. "I watch the news. They say you attacked two men at a hotel? You take them. And a woman. You shoot and kidnap all of them."

"It's not true," Roxanne said before he could find the words. "Santo saved me, and he tried to save those men, too."

Louisa looked like she wanted to believe it. She really did. But she said in a weary voice, "Someone films the whole thing."

"But it never shows Santo hurting those men, does it?"

"You, *niña,* were screaming." She covered her ears and shook her head. "And the blood. *Dios mío.* You were covered in blood."

Roxanne paled. "Santo and I were attacked, and he protected me. He was trying to give the men time to get to safety, but they misunderstood what was happening. It was dark. Very dark." The last came on a whisper.

Louisa looked uncertainly between them. "This is truth, Santo?"

He nodded, moved by Roxanne's quick defense.

Louisa let out a huge sigh. "I am happy to hear this.

I couldn't believe my Santo would hurt someone for no reason."

"He wouldn't," Roxanne said. "Have you heard . . . are the two men from the hotel still alive?"

"No one knows. They disappear. *Poof.*"

"Just like at the bar," Santo said.

"*Sí,*" Louisa said. "Is what they say on the news. Just like before. Gone."

Santo looked grim. "I'm sorry to show up like this, Louisa," he said, "but I didn't know where else to go."

These words seemed to cleave Louisa's heart in two. With teary eyes she embraced him once again, muttering furiously in Spanish that he'd done the right thing, coming to her. When she released him, she said, "Tell me. What you need? I give."

She would, too. Yesterday he would have been bewildered by it. Today, he was only grateful.

Louisa waited for an answer. With an uncertain smile, he asked, "Showers? Clothes? A place to sleep tonight?"

"Food?" she asked hopefully. "I make *carnitas.* I must have known you were coming, *mijo.* You go. Shower. I cook."

Before he could do as she ordered, she grabbed him up in another hug and gave him a big kiss on the cheek. "My angel," she said.

And the reaper inside him passed out cold.

Roxanne followed Louisa down the hall, aware of a brooding Santo right behind her. Their sweet hostess grabbed clean towels and pointed out the bathroom on one side and what appeared to be the lone spare room with its queen-sized bed on the other. Roxanne took a tentative step inside, trying not to look at the bed or think of sharing it with Santo.

While Louisa pulled him aside, Roxanne eyed the big cross hanging over the headboard, hearing Santo's voice in her head.

Jesus wouldn't make you blush.

No, she doubted he would. But evidently the man who waited in death for her did.

"She is your lady friend, *mijo*?" Roxanne heard Louisa whisper. "This is good. It's past time for you."

Roxanne's face grew hot. She peeped over her shoulder, waiting for Santo to contradict Louisa's assumption, and found herself looking straight into his eyes. He answered Louisa in Spanish, and whatever he said made the older woman beam.

"*Bueno!*" she murmured. "*Muy bueno.*"

The old woman left them alone in the bedroom together, promising to be right back. Roxanne and Santo avoided each other's eyes almost as diligently as they did the bed looming beside them. But Santo filled the room, crowding her. Taking more than his share of the air. Even dirty, banged up, and tired to the bone, he looked good.

With a determined sniff, she dug in the bags for the cell phone, fought the plastic casing until Santo took it and pried it open for her, then plugged it into a charger.

When she turned around again, Louisa stood in the doorway with a stack of clothes in her arms. "These were Jorge's," she told Santo. "They should fit." She pulled a gray and black jogging suit and shirt from the top and handed them to him before turning to Roxanne. "These are mine, when I was . . ." She trailed off, searching for the words. She squared her shoulders, sucked in her stomach, and thrust out her chest. "*Muy bonita, sí?*"

Despite everything, Roxanne smiled. "*Sí,*" she answered, taking the clothes. "*Gracias.*"

Louisa had brought her clingy pink velour warmups that had the words *Hot Mama* in glitter across the butt. Roxanne laughed when she saw them, and Louisa grinned broadly before hurrying off to the kitchen with a promise of a delicious dinner to come.

"You should let me look at those bites and scratches now," Santo said quietly.

He took her hand and pulled her into the bathroom, where the lighting was better. His palm felt warm and gentle against hers, his touch a low-frequency hum in her system. She sat on the closed toilet while he shut the door and pulled out the bandages and antiseptic.

"Which ones hurt the worst?" he asked as he lined up the supplies on the sink.

"All of them." And they did, even though they'd been healing at the usual rapid rate. Being hard to kill didn't mean she was immune to pain, though. She felt it just like the next guy, and right now not an inch of her didn't ache, burn, or throb.

Santo doused a gauze pad with disinfectant, cut his gaze to hers, and held it for a moment. Waiting. Embarrassed, breathless, and irritated with herself for the tension she felt, she turned away and pulled her shirt over her head, holding it in front of her breasts before she faced him again. He kept his eyes lowered as he began to clean her wounds, but she couldn't stop thinking about his dark head bent to her breasts, his hands against her skin, and his mouth . . .

She winced as the disinfectant seeped into a raw wound, and the erotic pictures in her head ceased.

"I'm sorry," Santo said with a worried glance.

"Don't be. I want them cleaned all the way down to the bone. I can't think of their breath, their saliva on my skin."

He took her at her word, tolerating her flinches and wet eyes as he cleaned each angry furrow. He worked his way down her shoulder and arms, and across the bones of her chest to the other side.

"You fought like a warrior today, Roxanne."

"I felt like a coward."

Startled, he looked up. "You hid it well."

She shouldn't have been so pleased by that, but she'd fast learned that where Santo was concerned, she had a hard time faking anything. She'd never told anyone the things she'd confided in him today. Not even her sister. But once she'd started, she hadn't been able to stop. And he'd listened. The kind of listening that left her feeling *heard* and better for it.

Santo finished cleaning and bandaging the bites where the hellhound had sunk in its teeth when it pulled her from the window. "You can put your shirt back on now," he said in a rough voice. "But let me look at your hands."

After finding tweezers in the medicine cabinet, he perched on the side of the tub next to her and began the painstaking task of removing the tiny shards of glass from her palms. She wanted to thank him for taking care of her. For putting himself between her and the hellhounds. For volunteering to be the one to help her out of this nightmare. But the words lodged behind her tongue and she couldn't set them free.

He paused and lifted that enigmatic gaze to her face, searching it for a moment before returning his attention to her hand.

"Why are you alone, *angelita*?" he asked in a deep voice.

She frowned at his bent head. "I'm not alone."

"You don't have a husband. Not even a boyfriend."

"You don't know that."

He gave her a questioning look. "I assumed."

Of course he did. And why not? She'd been ready to strip bare on a table in his hotel room just hours ago.

"You only wanted to call your brother and sister," he went on, a flicker of amusement in his expression when he noted her flaming face. "If there was someone else, you would want to talk to them, too."

She shrugged.

"But even before that I knew."

He reached up and brushed her cheek with the back of his hand. "You touch your face. All the time. When you think no one sees you."

"I touch my face?"

He nodded. "Like you're making sure your disguise hasn't slipped."

She didn't know why his words injured her, but

they did. She'd never considered the gesture that she made every day of her life. Never thought to attribute a meaning to the simple motion. But he'd hit a truth she hadn't realized, and it felt as if he'd attacked.

Her eyes stung, but she lifted her chin. "If you see me touching my face, it's because there's been blood on it. And I'm not *alone*. I'm single. By choice. There's a difference."

She could tell that he didn't believe a word she said. It was there in that half-amused, half-brooding look he gave her.

"A strange choice for a woman who dreams of baking cakes for the kids she doesn't have."

She called herself a fool for revealing so much to him, but she didn't say more. He would only find a way to use it against her. He finished with her palms, capped the antiseptic, and tossed the gauze in the trash by the sink. But he didn't get up and he didn't move away. Instead he put both of his hands on her thighs and rotated her with a gentle pressure until she sat facing him, knees trapped between his spread legs. He kept his hands where they were, wide and warm over her thighs as he imprisoned her gaze with his. She'd have to knock him back into the tub to stand, but to remain so close felt dangerous.

"Why?" he asked, features drawn. Intent.

Why what? she could quip and evade answering.

And she considered it, but to what end? He liked questions. She'd figured that one out early. He'd keep asking.

"I snore," she said dispassionately. "It drives them away."

He didn't even smile. "No, you don't. I've watched you sleep."

His fingers curled around behind her knees and he pulled her closer still. Off balance, her hands fluttered above his thighs, looking for a place to brace. He made the decision for her, guiding them down to his legs, letting them rest intimately close to his hips.

The position made her lean forward, on eye level with him. He cupped her face between his hands. "Why are you alone, Roxanne?"

She tried to push away, but it was like pushing against a stone wall. He held on to her. Gentle, but unyielding. Her lips parted and he shifted that focus and attention to the small gesture. He moved closer so that his nose lightly brushed against her cheek.

"I'm not alone," she said, tilting her head so he had better access, when she should have stood up and gotten the hell out of there. She felt like a traitor to herself, but Santo seemed to have some mysterious power over her body. It had been reacting to him with its own agenda since the moment they'd met.

His lips grazed her jaw. "Bullshit," he murmured against her skin. "You say you want to be like everyone else. *Normal*. But if that's what you really wanted, you'd be married. You'd have those cake-eating children already."

She managed to pull back, stung. Undeterred, his mouth moved to her throat, hot and wet and so enticing she wanted to melt into him. She twisted away, stumbling over his legs as she stood. Unbalanced, Santo caught himself on the faucet to keep from falling into the tub. She didn't stop until she reached the door.

"Who I marry and when I do it isn't your business," she said in a low, angry voice.

"*You* are my business, Roxanne. Haven't you figured that out yet?"

She wanted to turn around and glare at him. Show him that he hadn't hurt her. That he hadn't even pricked the surface of her feelings. But he had. He'd done more than prick it, and she knew she wouldn't be able to hide it from him.

"I don't care if that's what you think," she said, voice trembling with emotion. "Because you are not my business."

She turned the doorknob feeling justified and vindicated. His hands pressed against the door, blocking it from opening. Bracketing her as the warmth of his body burned down her back. She cursed the weakness that closed her eyes in surrender, even for just an instant.

"Is that what you do?" he asked, his lips by her ear, his breath a seductive lure meant to coax her into turning. "Push them away when they get too close? Tell them to fuck off?"

Damn him.

She spun around, but he didn't back away. He was there, filling her vision, overwhelming her senses. Muscled and broad, dark and dangerous. Gentle and protective. She didn't know how to deal with him. She fought the urge to touch him, but she *felt* him in every cell in her body.

"I didn't say fuck off."

"Only because you're too polite. Too worried about saying something you'll regret. Hurting someone's feelings."

Another killing blow that emptied her lungs. He was right again. Where was the point in denying it? In pretending he was wrong?

She was a polite, lonely woman who guarded every word and locked every door behind her. She said that she wanted to be normal, but inside she knew that wasn't possible. Normal women didn't die over and over again. Normal women didn't have to check their masks for fear someone would see too much inside them. Normal women didn't have six-and-a-half-foot guardian angels they wanted to touch more than they wanted to breathe.

She was the woman who tried to jump into a pack of ravenous creatures to save someone she'd never met but was too afraid to reach out to someone she wanted to know. Wanted to know very badly. Wasn't that the opposite of normal?

And why did she act this way? Because she feared she was more than just a freak who didn't die? In the darkest corner of her heart lived the fear that she was like the monsters who'd broken out of the Beyond. Unfit. Unnatural. Offensive.

She fixed her gaze on a point just below his chin and spoke to it. "Are you finished?"

"Why? Is it time to run away? Is that what you do, *angelita*?"

She turned and yanked open the door, forcing him to step back or get hit in the face. "Don't call me that. And while you're at it? Fuck off."

(16)

Reece waited on the back porch dressed like GI Joe, feeling like a dick. Beside him, Gary stood a head taller and looked like he'd been born to kick ass. He'd dressed in black from the cap to the boots, and acted like it was a Batsuit. Only his face remained uncovered, and his skin glowed, so pasty it appeared phosphorescent. He'd picked up a rash or a bad case of adult acne, and angry sores crowded around his hairline, making a mottled halo on his face. His eyes glittered eerily, like blue diamonds.

Reece had only ever seen the hours before dawn from the other side of midnight, when the rising sun meant the end of a good night. He'd never awakened early to watch it evict the stars and muscle down the moon like he did now.

Scattered in the yard stood a couple dozen of Gary's

minions, dressed in similar commando garb. Everyone held a weapon. Most had more than one, and the sweet scent of pending violence perfumed the air.

It made Reece's heart throb and sent a dark thrill through him. Blood would be shed this morning.

Yesterday had been filled with training. Shooting on the range. Lessons in tracking. Information about what to look for. Hard, cold facts that almost made him believe the unbelievable. Gary wasn't just fucking around. He thought demons were having their own little party on earth. He blamed them for the rise in crime, for the surge of brutality that seemed to be ever escalating. Every child who was molested, every woman who was raped. Even the goddamn war—all of it he attributed to the demons out there stirring the pot, cranking up the heat.

Reece didn't want to believe any of it, but Gary was convincing. He had a fucking army out here. Sworn to him. Fighting for him. Reece was one weak voice of sanity in a mass of conviction. And he didn't even know if he was right. All that Gary said, all that he pointed out—Reece could see it. How many times had he and Roxanne or Ryan or Ruby watched the news only to be stunned by what humans could do to one another? The cruelty and thoughtless brutality. It didn't make sense. Unless you bought into what Gary said.

And then it made perfect sense.

"Are you ready, then?" Gary asked him cheerfully.

Reece nodded, though he was learning to fear that tone.

"Right," Gary said. "You'll be hunting with Walter and Dave."

Hunting. Killing. His stomach made a queasy roll, but his brain worked overtime imagining every detail. . . . He swallowed hard, ashamed and angry all at once. But not even his disgust at his own fucked-up reactions could douse the excitement.

He nodded at Walter and Dave—privately nicknamed Casper and Shrek, though Dave wasn't really green. They'd been in charge of his training, and they'd worked him like an animal. He was so sore he could hardly lift his hands over his head. A lot of good that would do him if it came down to a fight.

"Where's Karen?" Gary demanded of no one in particular.

Reece heard the clatter of boots on the steps behind him, then Karen hurried over to stand beside the other two men. "I'm here."

"What about April?" Reece asked. Karen had been like a neighbor's kid he couldn't shake, but he hadn't seen April since yesterday. Whatever they battled this morning, he didn't want April in the middle of it, but he didn't want her facing something worse while all the cowboys were out fighting the Indians either.

"April?" Gary replied in that fucking lilt of his. "Like her, do you?"

Yeah, Yoda. He did. "Just wondered, man," he said coolly.

Gary's grin made Reece want to pop him one. *Fuck.* Having a conversation with Gary was like crossing an alligator-infested river. Just because it looked like a rock didn't mean it wouldn't bite your leg off.

"April!" Gary called out, surprising Reece. At the far edges of the gathered crowd, a slight form stiffened and stepped forward. "Fall in with Reece's team."

Reece tracked her as she moved closer, her skin nearly the same color as her clothes. She carried a rifle in her hands. No chance she'd be waiting back at the homestead. The whites of her eyes gleamed in the darkness.

At Gary's mention of "Reece's team," Casper and Shrek both stiffened like someone had shoved pokers up their asses. Morons. He would have told them that he didn't care whose team it was, but he didn't like either one enough to bother.

According to Gary, he'd be hunting demons before dawn even broke. And he had permission—no, *orders*—to kill them.

Since he'd been tumbled out of bed in the early hours by Casper and ordered to the training center, Reece had bounced between horror and hallelujah. He was buzzed, and he couldn't pretend otherwise.

Blood would be shed this morning.

"How are we supposed to find these demons?" He knew better than to ask Gary anything, but he couldn't hold it in.

"They'll find us," Gary said.

A straight answer. Who'd have thought it possible?

"Trust me in this, Reece. There'll be no mistaking what you're aiming at."

A few of the others voiced laughing agreement. They had the nervous energy of teenagers alone with the opposite sex for the first time. In fact, it felt a little like a party out here. Like kids waiting to go toilet paper a friend's house in the middle of the night. But beneath it, they were scared. Every one of them.

Something howled in the distance, and they all shifted uneasily. The sound came again, and a knot formed in Reece's gut.

"What is that?" he said.

"It's terrifying, isn't it?" Gary murmured. "A cry from the bowels of hell, that's what it makes me think of."

Yeah, that pretty much summed it up.

"And it belongs to?"

"Demons, Reece. What have I been telling you?"

He heard someone whisper, "They're coming back," and someone else hush them. Warily they turned their faces west, staring at the sound like it might appear in big notes on the horizon. It was stupid, but Reece couldn't look away either.

Casper appeared at his side and Reece jumped.

"Let's go."

The other man's voice sounded like a pressure gauge ready to pop. They all heard his fear and it spread like a spark through dried grass.

Reece adjusted the rifle on his shoulder and checked the wicked hunting knife in the sheath at his hip, praying he'd remember everything Shrek had drilled into him about using them. He'd practiced for hours until his arms felt like rubber. But the weapons still felt heavy and foreign in his grip. He was a city boy. He'd never even had a BB gun, though he'd wanted one in the worst way. He could still remember the clash with his dad over it and the crushing no at the end. His father had had too many concerns about Reece and Reece's *stability* to grant his son's wish, and they'd both known putting an eye out had been the least of them.

But they'd never talked of it. Never once. As he'd grown older, Reece had come to see that his dad had been right, though. Weapons implied violence. The last thing he needed was thoughts of *that* rooting any deeper in his mind.

April fell in behind him. He felt her there, alert and watching, and he wondered what she thought of all this. He wanted to drop back and speak with her, but Karen popped up at his side. "Don't be nervous," she whispered. "You'll do fine."

She looked scared shitless. Her face was the color of milk and her eyes and lips seemed almost superimposed. A clown face. Just what the night needed.

"You've done this before?" he asked.

She shook her head.

Odd that Gary would have assembled a team with

so many newcomers to accompany him. Reece couldn't see any good reasons for it. That left only the bad ones.

"What about you?" he called softly to Casper.

"I know what I'm doing," he said.

Which wasn't exactly an answer. Had he done this before or not?

"Don't worry," Shrek said, moving to take the lead. "We won't let the doggies eat you."

Karen made a soft, giggly sound that ignited Reece's jitters. April remained silent. The five of them trudged through the shadows and scrub, while the other four teams fanned out, canvassing the borders of Gary's compound.

The baying was all around them now. It felt like the desert grabbed each eerie note and slammed it home. Whatever had amassed in the cloying darkness, there were a lot of them and they were everywhere.

Casper went commando with the hand gestures to show where he wanted each of them positioned. Reece found himself crouched behind a boulder with April. She sat with her knees drawn up, her rifle resting on top of them and her arms holding it in place. Her chin dropped low to her chest as she stared into the hollow she'd made with her body.

"You know what's coming?" he breathed, scanning the horizon for a sign of movement.

"Hell," she answered.

Someone whistled, a loud, beckoning sound, and

the howling stopped for just an instant. Reece imagined heads cocked and ears pricked. The whistle came again, sharp and commanding. Calling in whatever waited out there in the dark.

He glanced at April, but before he could ask anything else, a low, rumbling growl came from somewhere to his left. He froze, all the hairs on his body standing on end. The fidgeting of Gary's soldiers suddenly ceased as they all strained to listen.

Christ, what was it?

Reece pressed his back tight against the boulder next to April, trying not to move. Trying not to breathe. He heard it again, a deep, menacing reverberation that seemed to come from just behind the boulder, and yet in front of it and all around it. The shadows gobbled the sound and spat it out in a million small, vibrating pieces. Beside him, April covered her mouth, trying to hold in her fear.

He reached over and took her free hand. She clutched his fingers desperately, her palm cold, clammy. A whisper brushed past his senses, his ears straining so hard that he couldn't tell if what he heard had come from his mind or the clearing in front of him. The air grew so still it seemed to thin until he could see the particles within, silver on gray, slate on black.

But then it shifted and became thick. Sulfurous. Suffocating. April began to breathe through her mouth, gripping his hand so tight it hurt. Why had Gary made her come this morning? She shouldn't have been here, reliving the slaughter of her family. Reece brought their hands to his lips and blew warm breath on them.

"It's okay," he whispered against her skin.

Somewhere across the clearing he heard a shout, a scream of pain, and more snarls and howls that made him tense. Hideous crunching sounds followed, then dark, wet slurping. April gagged and Reece put his arms around her, trying to keep her quiet. She huddled into him, gun abandoned as she tried to hide from what they couldn't see.

Another scream, this one closer, followed by three short, tortured shrieks and what sounded like a multitude of answering growls. A gun fired and another, but the bullets must have gone wild. No yelps of pain followed.

"Head shots," Shrek shouted with the angry impatience of someone forced to repeat himself over and over. "*Head shots.*"

The howls were everywhere now, echoing against the scrub and dirt, bouncing off the stars and velvet sky. He heard ripping, snapping, more tortured screams of agony, more gunfire. A man's voice—one he didn't recognize—begged for mercy and then begged for it to be over. A woman sobbed as those gruesome sounds went on and on. Soon the night was filled with them and the smell. Fuck, it smelled like death.

April pushed away from him and crawled to her knees, retching helplessly. Reece could do little more than rub her back and murmur soft hushing sounds as he scanned the hostile darkness, waiting for the hot breath that would precede snapping jaws.

He didn't know why they'd drilled him all those hours with the rifle. He couldn't see anything in the dark. But he could feel them, moving closer, stalking Gary's soldiers, picking them off one by one. Eating them alive.

The gunfire came fast and furious now, bullets winging in every direction but the right one, judging from the screams. He pulled April back behind the shelter of the boulder after one whizzed past his ear and lodged in the dirt. April cried big, silent tears. He could feel them against his chest. What had she expected to find here? Glory?

"*Shhhhh,*" he breathed as someone else went down in a torrent of bullets and screams. It sounded like a whole fucking herd of wild animals had ambushed them. But they'd all been set and waiting for them. Armed and dangerous. How had they been caught so unprepared?

The air shifted again, slapping him with a gust of blood and sulfur.

That's when he heard it. The soft *chuff* of an exhalation just behind him.

In his arms, April stiffened, her breath terminating in a gasp that barely emerged. His skin was hot and cold at once, drawn so tight it felt like it should split. He tried to swallow but couldn't force anything past his dry throat. He couldn't even breathe.

It came again. *Chuff, chuff.* This time he felt it, the moist warmth caressing his ear. April's hands fisted in his shirt, catching flesh in her grasp. The pinching pain focused him.

Slowly—*godsoslowly*—he reached for the knife at his hip as he turned his head and came nose to nose with something out of a nightmare.

The creature was huge. Standing on all fours, it was at least five feet from the tips of its pointy ears to the ground beneath its misshapen feet—*paws?*—hands. Whatever the fuck they were. A black and white pelt gave it better camouflage than he wore. Its skull was thick and heavy, with a protruding snout that sprouted long, curled canines. Thick as fingers, sharper than blades. Blood and gore covered its whole fucking head. The thing's nostrils flared as it took his scent.

Reece couldn't look away. The ice-cold gleam of its feral eyes had him trapped. Eyes so white they looked like halogens bearing down on him. Only the pinpoint of the pupil broke the bleached sheen.

Reece still held his gun, but there was no way to bring it up. The creature stood too close, watched him too intently. The knife, though. He might stand a chance with that. His fingers closed over the grip. The creature growled and Reece froze. It needed only to snap its enormous jaws around his throat so it could feast as its friends did all around them. He could feel April shaking beside him. She probably felt him, too.

The creature continued to stare, assessing. Beside it another appeared and another. The smell shoved him right past scared to ready to piss his pants.

They watched. But they didn't attack. Why didn't they attack?

Slowly, *fucking God, slowly,* he released April, carefully angling his body in front of her. Still they watched him with an almost doglike expression. Curious. As if they expected him to pull out a rubber ball and toss it. Except each one wore a coat of blood and guts. They were covered in it. Stinking of it. And they wanted more.

The one in the lead licked its chops and let its tongue loll out.

Watching. Watching. *Watching*.

What did they want? Why didn't they kill him?

Reece pulled his legs up, got his feet beneath him, and stood. "Easy, easy," he breathed.

The creature in front made a sharp, whining sound. Then it did the same: Stood. Like a twisted mutant in a really bad movie. It glared at him with those headlight eyes, red-tinted drool coming off its teeth. From his periphery, he saw the other two hunker down, haunches bunched, ready to go, ready to devour.

He flexed his fingers against the handle of his knife. All around him, the war went on. Demons like the ones in front of him chewed and tore and swallowed what was left, while men and women screamed in agony.

But he couldn't hear them anymore. He couldn't hear anything beyond the jarring thump of his heart and the hiss of breath as he tried to catch it. He could feel, though. His skin was so tight, so sensitive that it seemed he could see through every pore.

The creature in front of him made a deep, threatening sound that said, *I hear what you think, human.* It leaned forward, pressing its wet nose to Reece's throat and sniffing. *Once, twice.*

Then slowly it reared back again, hunching to bring its eyes level with Reece's. He stared into that white abyss, his insides rioting, his instincts screaming, and he thought, *Die.*

His hand moved of its own volition. He swung the blade into the creature's throat with the power of an ax, cutting through ligament and cartilage, burying it deep, then deeper still. Blood hit him in a hot gush that fired something inside him. He yanked the blade free and saw that only the spine kept the creature's head attached.

The demon fell as the second one lunged. He killed it the same way, then caught the third as it leapt over the corpses of the others and went for Reece's jugular. Less than a second had passed since the first cut.

Blood was everywhere. On his skin, his clothes, his hair. It colored his sight and fed the monster inside him. Long denied yet ever-present, it let out a howl of its own. He stepped into the clearing, whistling like he'd heard earlier. One by one, the handful of demons still standing lifted their heads and growled their warning.

A sharp *rap, rap, rap* came from behind him, and suddenly all the sounds that had muted rushed at him like a runaway train.

A spray of bullets caught one of the beasts from the left and its head exploded. Reece felt the splatter as he pivoted and cut another that charged him from behind. He missed the throat and sliced its leg. That pissed it off. It came at him full speed—moving so fast he couldn't see it.

Shots came from behind him and the demon dropped. Reece looked back to see Karen lowering her gun. They shared a quick, shell-shocked glance, then turned back to fighting. It seemed to last forever.

It seemed to end in an instant.

Reece stood, covered in blood, staring at the carnage surrounding him. Casper and Gary emerged from opposite sides, grim and gory as they called to the other survivors. Reece stared at them, trying to slow his heart rate. He felt as if his world had imploded.

He went to the boulder where April still cowered. He dropped to his knees beside her, wanting to touch her, to tell her that the monsters were dead and she had nothing left to fear. But he couldn't do that.

Because one monster had survived the battle. It lay awakened inside him, sated but not replete.

(17)

Roxanne perched on the bed in Louisa's spare room, listening to the phone ring at Love's. She could picture the office tucked away in the kitchen between metal shelves and the walk-in refrigerator. It was barely big enough for the bulky steel desk her dad had bought secondhand twenty years ago or the new safe Ryan had just installed last January. Lot of good it had done him. He'd be pissed about that.

She wasn't even sure if Love's had reopened for business, but she couldn't make up her mind on who to call first—Ryan or Ruby—so she decided to call the bar and leave it to fate who answered.

The phone rang again and a deep voice said, "Love's."

"You're open," she said to her brother.

"Roxanne? Jesus Christ, Roxanne, is that you?"

The worry in Ryan's tone made her eyes fill with tears. She blinked them back and leaned against the pillows.

"It's me. I'm sorry. I couldn't call before."

"Are you hurt?"

"A little banged up but nothing serious."

His pause told her he wasn't a fan of her answer, but he let it be. "Where are you?" he asked. She heard him moving before a door slammed, terminating the background din of banging pots and pans.

Santo had warned her it could be dangerous for her family to know where she was, so she kept it vague. "Someplace north. Someplace safe."

"When I get my hands on that fuck who took you—"

"Ryan, I know how it looked on the news. But you've got it wrong. Santo is helping me."

"So you haven't been kidnapped by a psychopath? Because that's exactly how it looked."

"No. There was something out there in the dark that the film didn't pick up."

"Something?"

She covered her eyes, knowing exactly how what she said would sound. Knowing the disbelief Ryan would feel hearing it. Only a few hours ago, she'd felt it herself.

"Demons," she murmured. "There were demons out there."

"As in entities from hell?" he asked calmly.

"As in the same entities from hell that helped rob the bar," she answered.

At last a reaction. The breath whooshed out of him. "So it wasn't Reece?"

"You thought it was Reece?"

"Yeah."

She considered telling him he hadn't been too far off the mark, but she couldn't. Not until she'd spoken to her twin herself.

"Okay," Ryan said. "Back up. Start from the beginning."

As quickly—as *sanely*—as possible, she told him about the stain, the bugs, the robbery and shootings. The hellhounds and how Santo had gotten her away.

"Those things that attacked us . . . you can't even imagine them. One of them tried to turn me into a squeak toy."

"Wait—did they look like wolves? Because one of the witnesses said something about wolves—"

"Only if they were mated to gorillas. They were huge and pretty much bulletproof, so I'm going to say *no* to the wolf theory."

"This Santo guy called them hellhounds? How does he know what they are?"

Her brother would never buy the truth if she told him that Santo was an angel sent to protect her. He might accept that Roxanne thought it was true. But swallow that fish whole? Not a chance.

When she didn't answer, he said, "Rox, did it occur to you that he might know what they are because *he's one of them*?"

"He's not. You're just going to have to take my word for it."

"But you know he's not a cop anymore, right? You can't take what he says at face value."

"They were hellhounds, Ryan. I was up close and personal with them."

"Christ." A heavy pause followed and Roxanne forced herself to stay quiet and let him work through his thoughts. Ryan could smell a lie. When she was a teen and he her guardian, that had really sucked, but she had faith that it would help him believe her now. After a moment he said, "The police are looking for you both, you know that?"

"I figured. No word from Reece?" she asked.

"Nada. We didn't even know if you were alive. I thought . . ." His voice broke. He cleared his throat and tried again. "I thought . . ."

"I'm sorry, Ryan."

"You know you can trust me, Roxanne," he said in a somber voice.

"I know."

"Whatever trouble you're in . . . whatever it is you think I can't handle, you're wrong. I'm your brother. I see more than you think I do."

"Like?"

"Did you die? Did it happen again?"

The question made tears sting her eyes. "Yes."

"Was *he* there?"

"Who?" she asked, stilling.

Ryan puffed out a breath. "Him. The one in the dark."

"How do you know about him?" she asked.

"You told me. After you . . . after you drowned in the lake. You were still in the hospital and you woke up and told me not to worry so much because you had a friend who took care of you when you went to the dark."

"I don't remember telling you that."

"You were kind of out of it at the time. You told Ruby about him after the car accident. You said you cried when you left him."

Roxanne's face felt like it was on fire and something ached in her chest at a memory she couldn't bring into focus. But she remembered the feeling of being safe, of being connected, of being where she was supposed to be.

She cleared her throat. "Ruby never mentioned it."

"Neither one of us wanted to bring up dying. Hell, I still don't."

She understood. It had been a taboo in their family for as long as she could remember. It hurt her, when she was young, that no one would talk about it, but how could she blame them? She wasn't the one who had to sit beside the bed and wonder what would happen next.

"Did Reece talk?" she asked. "After the lake or the accident?"

Ryan's silence stretched for a long moment. "No," he said at last. "Reece came back screaming."

"What?"

"Every time. They had to sedate him."

"The doctors always said that we couldn't trust our memories," Roxanne said. "They told us we'd had hallucinations."

"I know," Ryan said.

Yet his tone told her that he believed the hallucination theory about as much as she did.

"Why don't I know any of this, Ryan?"

"Like I said, who wanted to bring it up? We didn't know what to make of it and Dad said it would upset you to be reminded. I figured he was right."

"Santo thinks the demons are here to use Reece," she said. "When he dies, he becomes the freedom train from someplace called Abaddon."

"Abingdon? Maryland?"

"Ab-a-ddon. Hell."

"Yeah, yeah. I got it the first time. I'm just a little freaked out right now."

So was she. But at the same time, it felt good to be talking about all the things they'd avoided her entire life.

Ryan cleared his throat again. "So. What does Santo think *you* can do?"

She should have expected the question. It had taken him only seconds to form it. Had her brother always known something dark and twisted waited in the twins' future?

"He thinks I counteract what Reece does. He thinks I stop them."

"Do you?"

"I don't know."

And she didn't. Even now. All she had to go on was Santo's interpretation of what had happened.

In the background she heard Ryan's chair squeak. The sound was so familiar, it filled her with a longing to be there. To see him.

"Roxanne?" he said after a moment. "Be careful. Don't get in so deep."

"What's that supposed to mean?"

"Think about it. You *cried* when you left it the last time."

"You think I'm going to die and not want to come back?"

"Maybe. Maybe that's what dying is. For all of us. You just have more experience with it."

As she let that little gem settle inside her, she heard Ryan rap his knuckles hard on the desk. She could picture him, shaking his head, staring out the big window into the kitchen.

"Fuck. What do I know? We had a guy in here the other night bending spoons without touching them. Spoons. Bending them with his brain. I was amazed."

She almost smiled at his blatant subject change, but too much of what he'd said was bouncing around inside her, making her question everything she knew about herself.

"When are you coming home?" Ryan asked.

"I don't know."

"When *will* you know?"

"I don't know."

"I don't like that answer."

"It's all I got."

"I don't like that one either."

"I'm safe, Ryan. I'm with Santo by choice. That's all I can tell you."

"How do you know you can trust this guy?"

"You saw the footage on the news. Did you see where I was during it all?"

"Inside the van until Castillo shot out the window and you hauled ass onto the pavement."

"That's not how it happened. But just tell me this: Where was Santo?"

"Outside trying to shoot the delivery guy."

"Outside, guarding me from something that wanted to *eat* me."

"You need to come home."

"Why? So they can eat you, too? Santo thinks he can stop them. If I can help him, that's what I'm going to do."

"What the fuck, Roxanne? You're not some super-hero. Whatever has kept you alive before may not be around forever. You get that, right?"

Yeah. She got it. "You and Ruby need to be careful. Trust your gut, Ryan. If you see something that doesn't seem right . . . chances are it's not."

"I hate this conversation."

"I know. I just wanted to tell you I'm safe. Don't believe what you see on the news. Santo is a good man. I owe him my life."

A sound behind her made Roxanne glance over her shoulder, her senses already telling her Santo had come in. It seemed wherever he went, her radar followed, picking up the way he moved, the way molecules parted for him. The way her heart beat double-time when he was near.

He stood in the doorway wearing a clean white T-shirt and the soft sweatpants Louisa had given him. The shirt stretched tight over the taut muscles of his arms and chest, emphasizing just how *big* he was. How sculpted and hard. His black hair held a damp sheen. His black eyes held heat.

"I have to go now, Ryan."

Santo stepped in and closed the door behind him. He'd shaved, and his cheeks looked smooth and lean, his face imperfectly scarred and all the more interesting for it.

"I'll call again when I can," she said into the phone.

Ryan wasn't happy to let her go. She could hear it in his voice. But he said, "Be safe."

"I will. Give Ruby a hug for me. Tell her I love her. You, too, Ryan. I . . ."

"Just get your ass home alive."

Still caught in Santo's gaze, she said good-bye and set the phone on the nightstand beside her. The air felt thin, dissipated by the man who moved like a jungle cat through it, bare feet padding against the wooden planks. She waited for him to speak, wanting him to break the tension that had grown so thick since their argument, but he said nothing.

"Why are you staring at me?" she finally asked.

"Just wondering when I went from *fuck off* to a *good man*."

"You didn't. I only said it so Ryan wouldn't worry about me so much."

He gave her a veiled look. "Are you doing better now?" he asked.

"Better than what?"

"Better than you were before you called your brother," he said, brows raised.

He moved to the side of the bed and sat down. She scooted to the other edge and stood, intending to put the room between them. He leaned over, caught her wrist, and towed her back before she made it.

Mouth dry, she sat quietly beside him, chin down, avoiding the probing stare she felt on her face.

"Why can't I ever tell what you're thinking?" he murmured.

She didn't know why, but she was glad for it. She felt transparent where Santo was concerned and he riled too many emotions for her to share her thoughts with him.

"I'm sorry I told you to fuck off," she said softly. "I didn't mean it."

His fingers skimmed up her arm, pulling her a little closer. "I was out of line. I shouldn't have pried."

He leaned back against the pillows and tugged her down next to him. She resisted for about half a second before laying her head on his shoulder. He smelled of soap and cotton and Santo. She pressed her nose against him and breathed him in.

"What did your brother have to say?"

"That you're probably a demon, too, and I shouldn't trust you."

He nodded, as if he'd expected it. "You didn't have trouble convincing him that you'd seen demons?"

"He knows I wouldn't lie about something like that."

"But?"

"He's got this crazy idea that I wanted to stay dead the last time I died. That I might want to go there again."

Santo tucked his chin against his chest so he could look down at her. "What gave him that idea?"

She shook her head. "It doesn't matter."

Of course Santo didn't let her get away with that.

"Are you afraid it's true?" he asked quietly.

She laughed. "I'm afraid of everything, Santo. Haven't you figured that out yet?"

"Let's think about this. You heard a gun and charged into the kitchen to help your brother. You tried to jump out of the van to save that kid, the delivery guy you didn't even know, when hellhounds attacked. You'd have died trying but that didn't stop you."

"Maybe I knew you'd pull me back."

"Maybe you should give yourself some credit. You've got some stones, lady. Big ones."

She didn't know if he said it to make her feel better or if he really believed it. Either way, it worked. She settled her hand on his belly and the muscles tightened beneath her palm. He answered by wrapping his arms around her and holding her tight.

"Is being in this house hard on you?" she asked. "The memories?"

"No. I thought it would be." She felt his shrug. "For so long I've been carrying her memory like a weight. But now . . . it's hard to explain."

"She's moved from your head back into your heart where she belongs."

He exhaled heavily. "Yeah."

Roxanne propped her head on her hand so she could see his face. He had a strong profile, marked by the black brow, long nose, and firm chin. She remembered how flustered he'd made her when he'd entered the bar and looked at her with those midnight eyes. Had some part of her recognized even then that he would change her world?

"Are there other angels like you, Santo?"

He hesitated. "What do you mean?"

"You know. Living here among us? Angels who have lives. Who know how we feel when we lose someone we love."

He lowered his lashes. "I don't know. Probably."

"You don't see each other?"

"You mean at church or something? No."

"But how does it work? Your being here? And don't even think about filtering."

He raised his brows. "Filtering?"

"Don't pretend you haven't been doing it since you met me. I deserve the truth. All of it."

She held his gaze until he nodded.

"Have you always known what you are?" she asked.

"Yes."

"Did your wife know?"

He shook his head.

"That's a pretty big thing not to share with her. Why didn't you tell her?"

He shifted uneasily. Roxanne watched him, trying to crack the *Santo Code*. Because there was definitely a hidden message being sent, if only she could decipher it. His words said one thing, but his body told a different tale. She could almost see the tension in him. The fight he waged before revealing each fact.

He wasn't sifting and it didn't *feel* like a lie. But deep water ran beneath his answers.

"At first, because it's not something I told anyone," he said at last. "Later, because too much time had passed."

"What about when you got married? When she got pregnant?" Roxanne tried again.

"No."

It seemed impossible that he would have kept it from the woman he claimed to love, but his response left no room for doubt. What did that say about him?

He gazed into her eyes and she saw something there that made her feel like his next words would be monumental, filled with more subtext that she'd have to be sharp to understand.

"I guess I was afraid if I told her what I really am, she'd leave me."

"Why?" Roxanne breathed.

"I'm not human." He swallowed hard. "She might have found that . . . abhorrent."

He was serious. The look on his face was too naked, too raw for anything less.

"She wouldn't have," Roxanne said softly.

"What makes you so sure?"

"Trust me on this one, Santo. You're pretty much the opposite of abhorrent."

He blushed, looking so open and vulnerable that in that moment, Roxanne teetered over an edge she hadn't realized she'd been skirting and fell a little bit in love.

"Were you sent to watch over your wife like you were me?" she asked.

He shook his head and she felt him choosing his words again. When he spoke, they were flat and dispassionate.

"Humans aren't necessarily important to the Beyond. Not individuals, anyway."

It took a moment for that one to register and another for the lingering emotions he'd stirred to ease enough for her to understand.

"What *is* important to the Beyond?"

"Rules. The natural order of things."

"Things like demons running around in Tempe?" she said derisively.

"For one."

"What about you, Santo? Are humans important to you?"

"I've lived here. I have a different perspective."

"A *human* one?"

He looked almost shy as he nodded.

"I'm glad to hear it," she said with a smile. At last, he met her eyes, but something still shadowed his. She smoothed the worry from his brow with her fingertips.

"What happens after we find my brother?"

"We destroy the demons and send them back to Abaddon."

"How do we do that? Because in case you didn't notice, bullets only slowed them down."

Santo looked away. "I'm still working on it."

Roxanne stared at him with shock. He didn't know how to destroy them? They'd sent him to protect her and hadn't explained how to kill the bad guys? That circled in her mind, inciting other questions, making her doubt his motives even as her heart urged her to trust what she knew. She'd only just told Ryan that Santo had protected her without thinking of his own well-being too many times for her to start doubting him now.

"You're losing faith in me already, aren't you?" he asked.

"No. I mean . . ." She shook her head. "No. I'm not. But I am wondering . . . if humans aren't important, why am I? Why are you helping me?"

"Because you're important to me," he said, rolling on his side to face her. For a long moment, he simply stared, his gaze so intent she felt as if he was memorizing her features. Emotions echoed in that look. Emotions she felt reverberating deep inside her. He touched her cheek with gentle fingers.

"You're important to me."

The words were a balm to her battered soul. She

let them sink in and begin to heal wounds she hadn't known she'd been nursing.

"I don't mean to push you away," she said in a low voice. "If that's what you think I'm doing. It's not on purpose."

"That's good news. Because I wasn't going to let you."

He rotated smoothly, tucking her body beneath his and bracing above her. Without waiting for permission this time, he pressed his mouth to hers and kissed her softly. His tongue made a lazy sweep of her lips before parting them. Roxanne let her questions fade at the same time she let herself be swept away.

He tasted of toothpaste and heat, a drugging combination that made her want to lose herself in him and never surface. His weight pressed her back into the softness of the mattress, the hard shape of him filling an emptiness that had grown huge and hot since he'd touched her for the first time.

He didn't kiss like an angel. He kissed like sin itself.

His eyes were closed, his lashes fanned against his cheeks. He shifted his hips against hers and her legs fell open, letting him slide between. If he asked her to make cake-eating babies with him right now, she'd say yes without hesitation.

Her breasts felt heavy, sensitive to his touch, her nipples pebble hard. With his lips, he explored her throat, the hollows around her collarbone, the shell of her ear. But always he returned to her mouth and the melting kisses that she couldn't get enough of.

He'd said he was the one and she felt the truth of that with every cell in her body.

"Louisa's just in the kitchen," Roxanne breathed when his hands slipped beneath the waist of her stretchy pants.

Santo dropped his head and sighed. "Do you want me to stop?" he asked with a solemn look.

"I want you to lock the door."

He rolled off her and onto his feet in a single, graceful move. She heard the click of the lock and then he was back, stripping as he came. Long of limb, heavy with muscle, he was lean at the hips and belly, bulging in the places he should be. He lifted her shirt over her head and skimmed her pants down her legs, following each layer with kisses that turned her bones soft and her senses alive. His breathing was choppy, and his heartbeat raced beneath her hands.

He rested his forehead against hers and stared into her eyes. "I had to feel you," he said, his fingers moving from her bare thigh to her waist to her breast in a warm, possessive caress.

"Me, too."

Santo captured her mouth and kissed her again, seeming to lose himself in the heat. He shifted between her legs, his fingers hot and skilled as they circled the sensitive center of her. Roxanne forgot where she was as a groan of pleasure passed her lips. He watched her face as she arched into him.

"I didn't know," he said.

It certainly felt as if he knew everything, but she couldn't find the words to say it. "What didn't you know?" she managed.

"That you'd be so beautiful."

He replaced his fingers with his mouth and she forgot everything but how he made her feel. He found the very heart of her and devoted himself to setting her blood on fire.

She dragged her fingers through his hair and pulled him up, needing to feel him inside her with a passion she barely understood. Was it because of what he was that his touch was so electric? Or was it because of how she felt about him? From hello, he'd been chipping away at her defenses. Pushing her. *Seeing* her like no one had ever done before. He made her feel safe in the jaws of danger, alive in the sights of death. He made Ryan's fear that she'd choose darkness over *this* seem ridiculous.

Santo braced his weight, his gaze unfocused and his muscles bunched as she lifted her knees and locked her ankles behind him. He entered her in one long stroke that seated him to the hilt and made her head fall back into the softness of the pillows. He filled her, pulsing and hot, so hard that he stretched her swollen flesh and compelled her hips to move against his.

He buried his face in her shoulder and bit down so gently. "I didn't know," he said again, the words muffled against her skin.

He began to move in a slow, steady rhythm, driving his length deep inside her and pulling out just so. Just where she wanted him.

Her orgasm built fast and tore through her body, bowing it and clenching it tight around him. She covered her mouth with her pillow to muffle her cry. Santo muttered something in her ear that was both crude and exciting and he began to rock faster, pumping in and out, and before she knew it a second climax raged through her like a storm. Santo held her face, kissed her deeply, and came with low sound that revved her up all over again.

Her breath was shallow. So was his. He held her body so close that their lungs filled in tandem, each breath taking the space vacated by the other.

"You matter to *me*," he breathed and the words filled her as completely as he did.

The knock on the door startled them both. Roxanne's eyes went wide, and Santo gave a silent laugh and mouthed, "Great timing," at her before calling out, "Yes, Louisa?"

"Dinner is ready. You are hungry, *sí*?"

(18)

R oxanne could feel herself blushing as she followed Santo into the kitchen. She still couldn't catch her breath, thinking about the feel of him. How hot his body was as it entered hers. How desperately she wished she could stop time and stay there for just a little while longer. She couldn't help it.

Making love with Santo had rocked her whole world. She couldn't believe that Louisa wouldn't see how profoundly it had changed her and know exactly who and what was the cause.

For his part, Santo appeared as cool as could be. Until he looked her way. Then it was all heat.

Louisa had prepared a veritable feast for dinner. Tender spiced pork and hot salsa with the tang of cilantro and the bite of jalapeño. Beans so creamy they melted in her mouth and fat slices of Mexican *queso* as white and smooth as milk. Louisa warmed fresh tortillas and delivered them hot to the table, refusing to allow either Roxanne or Santo to do more than fill their plates and eat. Roxanne found herself shoveling it in like she'd never been fed before and only stopped when she realized that Santo was watching her. His grin made her heart do funny things.

"So," Louisa said once they'd both pushed back from the table. "What will you do now?"

"Roxanne's brother is missing," Santo said. "We think that whoever is after Roxanne has her brother, too. If we can find him, maybe we'll find everyone else who was taken as well."

And then what? They didn't know how to fight these demons. They didn't even know what the demons wanted.

"You think they are alive?" Louisa asked, surprised. "On the news they say everyone's dead."

"We won't know until we find them," Santo said, giving Roxanne's hand a reassuring squeeze under the table.

"You are lucky to have Santo helping you, *mija*," Louisa told her. "He has a good heart. He's a strong man." She gripped his bulging bicep, as if to prove it.

"Yes, I know," Roxanne murmured, looking everywhere but at Santo and his manliness.

"When Marisella died," Louisa said, "I thought I lose him, too. He don't come here. He just . . . *go*."

Santo shifted uncomfortably, and a dull flush stained his face.

"He feels it's his fault, *sí?* He thinks we blame him." She looked at Santo and shook her head. "Death comes when it chooses. It took my Jorge last year. It doesn't care that he wasn't ready."

"I'm sorry," Roxanne said.

"Jorge, he worry about Santo. He say to me, 'Santo will take this hard.'"

"He should've worried more about himself," Santo said gruffly. "Or about you."

"He knew I'd be fine. I understand how God works. When my time comes, I will go happily to meet my maker. I hope so anyway," she qualified with a laugh. "Although I have sinned."

Santo gave her an indulgent look. "No, you haven't, Louisa."

"We all sin. You sin, Santo, by blaming yourself for everything. It is not up to you who lives and dies. That is His job."

The words seemed to startle him, and for a moment Santo looked like he couldn't decide whether to laugh or argue. It was an odd reaction that brought to mind her first impressions of Santo. She remembered thinking his way of phrasing things was *off.* Had that really been just last night? It seemed like days had passed since she'd met him.

"I'm glad he has found you, Roxanne. I like how he

watches you. His eyes, they sparkle. Life. This is what is life."

Santo stood and carried his dish to the sink, but Louisa waved him away. "You two have much to talk about. I see. And this . . ." She indicated the mess. "This will take me no time to put away."

He stared at the older woman for a moment, and Roxanne felt the depth of his emotions. The tangled quandary he seemed to be mired in all too often. He looked lost, as if he had no idea how to respond to this woman he obviously cared for.

At last, he gave her a gentle hug. "I don't deserve you," he said.

"Ah, there you go again, thinking it is you who makes such decisions. Take your lady to bed, Santo. She looks tired."

Santo didn't need to be told twice. With a look of promise, he took a step toward Roxanne and her body immediately responded to the silent invitation she read in his eyes. She didn't know what future—if any—waited for the two of them. Odds were good that she'd end up with her heart broken. But she didn't care. Stupid or not, she was into him. She'd stay on the ride as long as it lasted.

A sound coming from outside the kitchen window stopped Santo before he reached her. Roxanne heard it, too, but wasn't sure what it was. His sudden stillness was her only warning that it was something to fear.

Santo crossed the kitchen and turned off the lights. Warily, he pulled the lacy curtain from the edge of the window and peered out. Moving as quietly as she could, Roxanne joined him there.

A fat moon gloated in the sky, diminishing everything below with harsh light. Bushes and trees seemed overlaid on a canvas of pitch. The night had no depth, and the eerie absence somehow magnified the absolute silence. Roxanne scanned the shivering quiet, feeling the chill that coiled around the trees and bushes, hushing the chittering leaves and restless limbs. Behind her, Santo held himself rigid, his tension feeding her own.

A sudden gust crackled the barren branches and agitated the leaves. A flutter caught the corner of her eye, then something darker than the night parted the shadows as it soared toward the window. Immediately she thought of the locusts and stumbled back into Santo.

An enormous bird—*a raven?*—alighted on the sill, black wings spread wide and beak open in a greedy smile. Easily the size of an eagle, it gripped its perch with clawed feet and stared at them with watchful, ebony eyes.

Behind her Santo sucked a breath between his teeth. He pulled Roxanne away and faced the room with worried eyes. Santo, who'd fought snarling, rabid *hellhounds* without flinching.

The bird rapped its beak against the glass, waited, head cocked, and did it again.

Knock, knock.

The sound, almost polite for all its insistence, lit a wick of superstition she hadn't realized she possessed. Louisa crossed herself and turned her back on the window, as if not seeing would make it go away.

A sound—bizarre and yet familiar in a way she didn't understand—*flapped* in the cryptlike silence. Roxanne found herself shaking her head as she tried to place it. Like a low sonic pulse, she *felt* it in her gut. When the recognition came, it stole the air from the room.

Wings. Hundreds of them. That's what made that sound.

Her imagination blotted out the swollen moon and covered it in birds, flocking like a plague. Santo turned his eyes upward as the scratch of clawed feet skittered across the tile roof.

Then his gaze shifted and met Roxanne's.

"This is going to be bad," he said softly.

Reece stood beneath the shower spray until his skin hurt. He'd scrubbed the blood and gore away once, twice, a dozen times, but still he felt it. Warm and sticky. A blanket of shame; a cape of pleasure. He'd *liked* the killing, the violence, the dirty mess of it. No amount of soap and water could wash that away.

When he finally gave up, shut off the water, dried and dressed, he felt no better. His reflection was different. His eyes looked hungry now. Desperate and dangerous.

He stepped out of the small bathroom to find Gary leaning against the wall in the hallway, waiting for him. "Feeling better?" he asked cheerfully.

"No."

Gary pushed away from the wall. "But you see what

we're up against, aye? No denying the face of your enemy anymore, is there?"

"No."

Yet a part of him did deny it. A part of him felt that despite what he'd seen, despite the blood he couldn't seem to wash off, despite the fear and the thrill, he'd been . . . duped. The facts had been laid out in black and white, indisputable, but ultimately false. As if everything had been prearranged so that Reece would be forced to draw a logical conclusion that made no fucking sense at all.

And that bothered him nearly as much as the secret joy he'd felt in killing.

Gary watched him, trying to track his thought process to its end. The corners of his mouth tightened when Reece said nothing else.

"What we fought this morning, Reece," he murmured. "It has your sister. Do you understand that?"

So Gary kept telling him. "The man who took Roxanne looked nothing like those things out there."

"You're right," Gary replied encouragingly. "The *man* who has your sister is no man at all, though. He's an imposter, isn't he? He pretends to be human so sweet little Roxanne will trust him. But she doesn't know what *we* know. He commands those beasts, Reece. Are you hearing me? They are *his* to control."

Reece couldn't imagine anything controlling the creatures that had attacked them, and the idea that someone might hold that kind of power terrified him. The thought that that same someone had his sister . . .

"What does he want with Roxanne? I still don't get it."

Gary nodded with understanding. "I couldn't explain it to you before. Not until I made you a believer. He wants your sister because he's a demon. It's as simple as that."

Simple? Reece shook his head. There was nothing simple in that.

"Hear me out. I know it's a bitter reality, demons on earth," Gary went on. "Every time I'm forced to confront it, a piece of me still doesn't believe. But the bigger pieces, they want to fight. They want justice."

Justice. Gary liked that word. He'd used it earlier when he'd laid out his theory about Santo Castillo, the cop who had taken Roxanne. The cop who was really a demon, if you took your crazy with whipped cream and a cherry on top.

"Let me tell you a story," Gary went on.

"Why don't you just tell me the truth?" Reece demanded, sick of Gary and his stories.

"'Tis one and the same this time, Reece. One and the same."

He paused, waiting until Reece gave a tired nod for him to continue.

"This story is about a man who never dies—or rather, a man who can't seem to *stop* dying."

Reece stiffened, skin chilling between heartbeats. And Gary knew it, the bastard. His sad little smile held a glint of satisfaction he didn't hide.

Gary went on. "Every time this man releases his last breath, he opens a door between our world and the other side."

"The other side of what?"

"The Beyond, Reece. Heaven, hell—Hades, Elysium. Call it what you want. But in the end it's the same. That door lets darkness seep in. And lurking in all those shadows, just waiting for a chance to scuttle through that opening, are demons."

Reece swallowed hard, wanting to tell Gary to shut the fuck up, but Gary moved closer, stepping into Reece's personal space, drilling him with a gaze that seemed to see everything he wanted to keep secret.

"These demons hide in plain sight. They slip beneath the skin and pretend to be human. They become the six o'clock news, only what we hear about is the man who rapes an eighty-year-old woman and burns her alive."

Gary took another step, and Reece fought the urge to retreat.

"Or the one who snatches a little boy from the playground and sodomizes him before dismemberment. Or the—"

"I get it," Reece said, pushing Gary back and stepping away.

Gary eyed him speculatively. "I hope you do, Reece.

Because even though that door between our worlds may be shut right now, the demon who kidnapped your sister knows how to open it again."

Reece felt like a puppet, yet he was powerless to stop the question that emerged. "By killing me?"

"Aye. By killing you."

There was more. Reece could feel it, hovering there between them.

"Is he using Roxanne for bait?"

Gary shook his head. "No. She has a purpose of her own."

Reece's stomach made a greasy roll. Lost, he shook his head. "What purpose?"

"How many times have you died, Reece?"

He shrugged, as if he'd lost count. "Four times. Almost five, because of you."

The other man smiled and Reece's doubts about whether Gary had deliberately run him off Graybel's Pass and into that gully evaporated. He still remembered the pain when he'd hit rock bottom, the agony as he'd fought for his life.

"I'm sorry about that," Gary said with no hint of apology in his tone. "I had to test my theory before I could be sure."

"So you tried to kill me?"

"Yes. But you didn't die, did you? I still can't believe it."

Reece looked at Gary coldly.

"Get to the point, Gary."

"How many times have you and your sister died together?" he asked.

"All of them," Reece said grudgingly.

"So you don't know if it feels different, if you died all alone?"

"Look, Gary. Either you stop talking in fucking riddles or I'm gone. You got that? I'm sick to hell of you and—"

"You don't even understand what you are, do you?"

"I'm pissed off, that's what I am."

"You open the door, Reece. But Roxanne . . . she closes it."

Reece shook his head.

"She is the light to your dark. Hasn't it always been that way?"

Reece's mouth felt like it had been filled with chalk. But the truth rolled over him like the tide.

Gary said, "Do not underestimate how much this demon wants that door to stay open. He wants to fill this world with his army. But to do that, he must destroy your sister and make *you* his slave."

Dread became an anchor Reece couldn't release. It kept him from drifting away even as it pulled him down, down under that rolling truth and into the nightmare Gary illuminated.

"You understand," Gary said gently. "You can see yourself caged, waking, dying, waking, dy—"

Reece raised a hand for him to stop. Surprisingly, Gary did. Reece wanted to escape the other man, escape this conversation. He turned and walked to his room without another word, but Gary followed.

"I'll think about what you said," Reece told him. He stood in front of his closed door without opening it in case Gary wouldn't take the hint and thought he was invited in. "But I need some shut-eye right now."

Gary's pause felt staged, but he didn't press. Thank the fucking Lord.

"Sure, and don't I understand that? Sleep on it. But think about this, Reece. We need you on our side. And you need *us* on yours."

(20)

Reece opened his door and stepped into the darkness of his room, apprehension crowding in with the shadows. Christ, could he believe what Gary had told him? How could he not after what he'd seen this morning?

He stripped down to his briefs and climbed into his bed without turning on a light. He'd seen too much this morning, and if something waited for him here, well then, hell. Let it have him. He couldn't take any more. His exhaustion felt like a friend, and he welcomed it in and begged it to make itself at home.

He'd just started dozing when he heard the click of his door. Instantly awake, he watched it swing inward and shut again. A willowy form parted the curtain of gloom as it moved to his bed. His heart stuttered for a moment before he realized who it was.

April.

She wore an oversized T-shirt that ended at her knees and nothing else. Against the drab color, her skin looked darker than the shadows. Silently, she pulled back the covers and slid in beside him, her flesh warm and silken against him. He inched over, making room for her.

Neither one of them spoke as he pulled her against his chest and held her. It didn't seem necessary, questions or explanations. Just the opposite. For the first time since he'd opened his eyes in this place, Reece felt the tight knot in his chest ease.

"I'm sorry," he said.

"For what?"

He shrugged, not exactly sure what he'd apologized for. Only certain that he owed her one.

"I'm sorry for your pain."

A taut quiet trailed his husky response. Thick and accusing, though he couldn't say if it came from within himself or from April.

"My pain," she whispered. "I deserve my pain."

"No."

She shifted, her bare legs moving against his as she pressed closer. Softly rounded and innately feminine, she felt good against him. Real in a world that had become so cockeyed he no longer recognized it.

"Why are you here, April?" he asked, but his arms tightened on their own, making sure she understood that he didn't mind. Not at all.

"I heard what Gary told you," she answered softly.

Reece stiffened, but she only wrapped herself around him more completely.

"So you know I'm the reason the world is all fucked-up."

She laughed, a low sound that warmed the sharp chunk of ice that had settled around his heart. "Yeah. It's all you."

He leaned back, peering at her through the dark. "Why aren't you scared of me, then?"

She turned her face into his chest, breath warm against his skin. He felt her inhale, taking in his scent even as he caught himself with his nose against her hair, doing the same. She was quiet for so long that he wondered if she'd refused to answer. Maybe she'd fallen asleep. God knew she had to have been as weary as he.

"When they came . . ." she began in a broken voice. She cleared it and tried again. "They came in the morning when we were all getting ready for the day. A normal day. Mom worked, so we didn't do a big breakfast. I remember scarfing down a piece of toast as I got my books together. I'd just started college. My little brother was annoying me. He hid my calculus book and then tattled when I smacked him. My older brother was yelling at me to hurry. He used to drive us both to school.

Daddy had just shouted at us all when the first one busted through the door." She let out a puff of air. "Isn't it funny what you remember?"

Reece pressed his lips to her temple. "Yeah," he said. Because as she talked, a background movie played in his head. One of Gary charging through the kitchen door, gun already drawn. An old song by .38 Special had been blaring on the radio. "Caught Up in You." Manny loved that song. But then Gary shot Manny for no reason. No goddamned reason at all.

"They killed carefully," she said. "Like surgeons."

"What do you mean?"

She looked up then, her chocolate eyes glimmering in the dark. Her lashes dammed the tears she seemed determine to deny. From the October moonlight edging the curtains, he saw so many things. Anger. Terror. Defiance. Remorse.

And he understood every last one of them.

"They didn't just kill my family. They did it carefully. So it wouldn't show. They took them, Reece."

He wanted to be incredulous. He wanted to ask naïve questions. *Took them how? Like hostages? But you said they'd killed them . . .*

Instead, he said, "The demons took their bodies?"

Her sigh held so many emotions that he couldn't begin to sort them. "I saw one break my mother's neck. I *heard* it snap, Reece. I watched the life go out. Like a snuffed candle. She looked like a rag doll when she hit the floor. Her eyes were open the entire time, and I saw it all. The fear, the pain . . . the death."

A few hot tears broke ranks and slid down her cheek. He felt them against his chest.

"A minute later, she stood up again and those eyes weren't hers anymore. I'll never forget the horror on my daddy's face when he saw it. When he realized . . ." She swallowed hard. "He fought them. He tried to protect us kids, but they kept coming. There were too many."

"What did they look like? The things we fought this morning?"

She shook her head. "Some were already . . . they'd already taken bodies. But the others . . . they were just shadows, shades of nothing that hissed across the floor, over the ceiling. They were everywhere, just looking for a way in."

She pressed nearer, as if she couldn't get close enough. What she'd seen could never be unseen. What she'd survived would never be forgotten.

"They possessed my family, Reece. All but the little ones—they just killed my baby brother and sister. Right now, those demons are walking around pretending to be my mother and father, pretending to be my older brother. Committing crimes—doing *unspeakable* things—dressed as my family."

Her words blew through him like a sour wind, churning up dust devils of superstition and fear. Demons, possessing humans. Turning average, everyday citizens into monsters. Gary had said it, but April made him *see* it.

They'd done this to her family. And now she'd dedicated her life to seeing them banished.

He moved at last, tucking her into the curve of his body and holding her tight. She gripped his shoulders as she finally released the rest of her tears, sobbing against his chest while he rubbed her back, murmured words of comfort in her ear, smoothed her hair away from her face.

His mind felt numb, his thoughts sluggish. His sense of self, of reality, battled with this vista she painted so skillfully. He felt like he'd missed something key in her story, but the images he'd retained were too vivid to allow him to focus elsewhere.

Gary's tales of demons joined April's narrative looping in his head.

Demons.

Possession.

Monsters roaming the land, dressed like Mom and Dad. *Families* who would commit *unspeakable* crimes.

And at the crux was Reece. The reason it happened. The way in.

April's weeping eased and the harsh, painful sobs subsided until she was silent in his arms. She sniffled and turned those wet, brown eyes up to look at him.

"I'm sorr—"

He kissed her before she could utter those words.

Because she had nothing, *nothing,* to be sorry about. Reece should be on his knees, begging her forgiveness.

She froze at the first contact, before her arms went up and around his neck and she pulled him closer still, kissing him back with fire and passion that seared away all thoughts, leaving blessed redemption in its wake.

She pressed herself to him eagerly, her response so unaffected that it touched deep inside him. She wasn't acting. She wasn't role-playing. She didn't kiss him because she'd been told to, as Karen had. She'd come because she'd needed the solace they could give each other.

Reece had been with a lot of women. But he'd never understood the difference between fucking and making love. Until now with this woman he barely knew.

Afterwards, she lay curled in his arms as the sun crested the roof and moved to the other side, leaving them in cool shadows. Her breathing evened out as she began to drift off, and the sheer trust of that—of her willingness to sleep with him, to depend on him to keep her safe—filled him to overflowing.

In that moment, he swore that he would protect her, no matter the cost. But as he began to drift off, the question that had circled in his brain as April had told her tale, that niggling doubt that had moved so fast it had evaded his attempts to see it, finally slowed and came into focus.

"April," he whispered.

"Yes?" she answered, her voice soft but alert.

She hadn't been asleep, and some sixth sense told him she'd been waiting for him to ask that missing question.

Reece swallowed hard, wishing it back even as he spoke.

"How did you get away, when they came? How did you escape?"

Her pause held the weight of a mountain, towering, unstable and immense.

"I didn't, Reece," she answered in a tone filled with anguish. She tilted her face up so he could look into her eyes, so he could see the truth he doubted he'd heard.

"I didn't get away from them. They caught me."

(21)

In the moments since Santo had seen the first raven, more had joined. Hundreds of them, by the sound of it. Their wings created a thundering symphony. They cawed and shrieked and flew wildly outside the house. The melee melded with the shadows and stretched the harsh noises into chaos. A tangled, torturous tension gripped them all.

Nothing good came from black birds. Ever. Only a fool would dismiss the threat of their presence.

Louisa shut her eyes and bowed her head over folded hands. Moving her lips soundlessly, she began to pray.

"Santo?" Roxanne said, touching his arm with icy fingers. She spoke in a hushed voice, but he heard the tremor, felt her fear. "Where are they coming from? Why are they here?"

"They're Abaddon's messengers," he answered simply.

The sound of Abaddon's name excited the birds. They screeched and battered the house and windows with fury.

He turned back to the window, unsure what their next move should be. They needed to find a way to escape, one that didn't involve exposing themselves to sharp beaks and razorlike talons. That many carrion eaters could strip the meat from their bones in a matter of minutes. He stared at the closed curtain, picturing the swarming mass of black bodies that flocked outside. What did they want? *Why* had Abaddon sent them?

Reaper, a crackling, inhuman voice spoke in his head. *Open the windows, reaper. Let us in.*

The urge to obey sank beneath his skin and took hold like a hooked lure. He reached for the edge of the curtain.

"What are you doing?" Roxanne asked.

Santo jerked his hand back as dread raced with his blood. The voice had *compelled* him. *Him.*

Reaper, let us in. . . .

He would bet the cat-sized raven that had tapped its beak on the window still perched there. Waiting.

He didn't have to look to know that the birds had filled the boughs up high, bent the twigs down low. Sinister winged predators that perched and pecked, cawed and jockeyed for roosts as they watched the house. They tapped their beaks against the doors and windows, and suddenly one of them slammed into the glass with a thud that sounded inexplicably loud. Louisa's head came up, and she gasped as a dish clattered in the cupboard from the impact.

Roxanne moved closer to Santo and his arms circled her automatically. Another bird hit the glass. And another. They began to screech, long, bloodcurdling shrieks that struck fear so deep he felt it travel through Roxanne's body to his own.

"Into the hall. Away from the windows," he said, taking Louisa's arm in one hand and Roxanne's in the other.

The woman is ours, reaper. Give her to us . . .

"They're talking," Roxanne whispered. "I can hear them."

She turned in place, looking at the ceiling with wide eyes. "They're telling me to come outside."

Something gripped Santo's chest hard and held tight. "Don't listen to them."

"They say they'll kill you if I don't."

"They tried that already. Hellhounds. Still here."

"But—"

He took her face in his hands. "Don't listen to them. And whatever you do, if they get in, if we get out . . . just don't look them in the eye."

"Why?" she breathed.

"Because when you see them, they see you."

The simple explanation drained the color from her face.

Louisa shuddered and wrapped her arms around herself, rocking side to side, muttering a prayer in her native tongue. The soft incantation silenced the birds, but just for a moment.

"I want you both to stay here—away from the windows and doors. I'm going to check the rest of the house."

He moved down the hall toward the two bedrooms, peering cautiously around the corner before he entered the first. The window in Louisa's room was shut tight, the curtains drawn. A big mirror hung over her dresser. He yanked the blanket off the bed and draped it over the reflective glass, keeping his eyes averted as he did.

"Why did you do that?"

Startled, he turned to find Roxanne hovering in the doorway with Louisa right behind her. Why had he expected any different?

"Mirrors can be used," he said, already brushing past them. He closed Louisa's door and quickly moved to the spare room, unable to stop his quick glance at the mussed bed. The memory of lying there with Roxanne mingled with his fear and anger, binding him as only thoughts of her could.

"Used by the birds . . . ?" Roxanne asked.

Reaper, give us the woman and we won't tell where you are.

Alarms jangled inside him, but he fought them down. He'd never had reason to fear punishment before. To fear anything. But by stepping into Santo Castillo's body, he'd committed a crime that would not be forgiven or forgotten. In his arrogance, he'd never imagined he'd be caught.

They don't know about you. Yet.

And why would they? In the Beyond, he didn't even have a name. But if they discovered him masquerading as a human, impersonating an *angel,* he'd learn about hell firsthand.

Reaper, you're out of time. . . .

Outside the birds had multiplied with astounding speed until the sound of their screeching, their talons on the roof and walls, their beaks pecking as they searched for a way in, had grown so loud that it seemed to come from everywhere.

He pulled back the curtains and checked the lock. The big raven sat just on the other side, watching him with those eerily human eyes. Though the window remained shut, a dark, unpleasant scent seeped into the room.

What future is there for you here, reaper? What do you care for the human?

He yanked the curtains closed and turned to find Roxanne right behind him. Louisa hovered in the hallway, her hands clutching the crucifix around her neck. Wondering what good it would do him, he took his holstered gun from the drawer where he'd stashed it before his shower and put it on.

"Louisa, do you still have Jorge's truck?" he asked,

suddenly remembering the old F150 that Jorge had driven.

Louisa nodded. "In the garage."

Relief swelled inside him. The door from the house to the garage was off the laundry room. They wouldn't have to risk going outside to reach it. Once they locked themselves in the truck, they could open the big garage door and escape. The birds would give chase, but at least on the road, they'd have a chance.

"Where are the keys?"

"On the hook, by the phone. Same as always."

He pointed down the hall. "Get to the garage. I'll be right behind you."

Louisa did as he asked, hurrying toward the laundry room, still mumbling her prayers. Naturally, Roxanne didn't.

She slipped her hand in his and followed him into the kitchen, muttering, "Just get the keys," when he opened his mouth to argue.

Outside the birds cawed and beat their wings against the house while that pervasive odor scurried down the hall. The biggest raven still whispered in his ear, but he blocked it out, focusing on the uneven cadence of Roxanne's breath and the rampant beat of his own heart.

Her hand in his gave him strength. It didn't make a damn bit of sense, but when he found the keys, he thought, *I'm going to get us out of here.*

And he believed it for exactly three seconds.

(22)

Everything happened at once, but Roxanne saw each minute event with impossible clarity.

The sound of the bird hitting the window reverberated and the curtains billowed just as a small hole appeared in the glass and cracks snapped from the shattered center. No longer buffered by a barrier, the shrill and raucous cries of the ravens hit like a ravaging storm.

Santo grabbed her arm as one of the smaller ravens wedged its body in the jagged opening, emerging with a *plop,* bloodied, right leg nearly severed by the sharp edges of glass. Santo pulled her through the archway as the bird hopped pitifully on the counter, its soulless eyes fixed on her. She couldn't look away. A second raven followed, then the glut of black bodies shattered the fractured window and exploded into the house.

Roxanne screamed as Santo shielded her with his body. Standing on the other side of the house, Louisa stared out from the open laundry room with wild eyes.

"Go!" she and Santo shouted at the same time as they tried to follow.

Louisa jumped and spun, dashing into the garage. Santo and Roxanne hurried after her, but the birds swarmed the house like giant wasps. They formed a writhing black barricade between Roxanne and Santo and their means of escape. The ravens swooped at her hair, grabbing it with their ugly clawed feet. Letting their talons graze her scalp and skin. Drawing blood and retreating in a vicious game she didn't know how to play.

Santo fought back, but there were too many. The birds surrounded them, a net of oily feathers and moldering stench that drew tighter and tighter, trapping them. Roxanne gagged, waving her arms wildly, terrified beyond rational thought. More birds swooped in, all sharp beaks and scythelike feet. She screamed again and then couldn't stop screaming as they surged in the small space.

In her panic, she stumbled over her feet and plunged through the mass of fluttering, jostling, *aggressive* bodies, hitting the floor chin first. She tasted blood on her tongue, but beneath the flock, she found a pocket of uncontaminated air and sucked it in. Still sprawled flat on her belly, she turned her head and saw Santo's shoes an arm's length away. She reached for him just as he fell to one knee. The birds flapped around his face, snapping their beaks at his mouth and nose, smothering him with their loathsome black bodies.

"Santo!" she screamed, but her throat burned and her voice emerged powerless.

Santo's left hand and his other knee hit the ground, then he lurched hard to the right and toppled.

"*Santo!*"

Roxanne lunged toward him, madly beating back the birds that congregated at his face. But for every one of them she swiped away, two others took its place, their bodies so close to his nose and mouth that he had no hope of drawing a clean breath. The ravens pecked and scratched at her, refusing to give up their spoils. They took hunks of flesh and left bloody gouges as she relentlessly struggled to get them away from Santo. In desperation, she used her body to protect his inert form, taking the brunt of the attack.

We see you, the ravens screeched in her head. *We've found you.*

She rocked back and forth, tucking herself into a ball, pulling Santo's head in her lap and curling her torso over him. She couldn't tell if he was breathing. She couldn't tell if she was either.

We found you, we found you, we found you. . . .

Found. By Abaddon. The personification of Death. The part of hell that every human lived in terror of, even when they didn't know it by name. And she didn't even know what he wanted her for.

But she felt like she'd been running from him her whole life—well, maybe not *him,* but some instinct had made her afraid. Urged her to strive to be *normal. Ordinary.* But here she was, in extraordinary crosshairs all the same.

Why was she still running? Why was she allowing this King of the Abyss, this Abaddon, to hurt the people she cared about? She could protect them better by just giving up.

That's right, the voice cooed. *It's time to give up.*

For a moment, she found her grip on Santo loosening, and she almost stood.

She shook her head, disoriented. What was she thinking? She couldn't quit. Evil surrounded her. Whatever gift it wanted to steal from her, it would use it against her. Against her loved ones.

He wants to help you. He wants to bring you home.

Home? Home, to a place worse than *hell*? She scoffed at the idea even as something insidious seeped inside her and painted another picture. One of warm welcome. One of belonging, at last.

Yes, yes. Come home where you belong.

She lifted her head and stared at the birds. The nearest ones skittered back. *See? We're no threat.*

No, of course they weren't. They were messengers, nothing more. And they would help her. She could see that now. Abaddon had sent them to show her the way. He didn't want to hurt her.

He was who waited for her in death. How had she not known that? *He* was the one who held her, who . . .

Her arms loosened their tight hold on Santo, and a strange numbness overtook her.

Yes, the ravens whispered. *Yes, yes yes. . . .*

She put a hand on Santo's chest for balance as she tried to stand. The birds retreated another inch or two, giving her space. Encouraging her to come . . . come. . . .

She could feel Santo's heart pounding beneath her palm. Labored, erratic. The beat of it almost penetrated the calm that enveloped her.

What was she doing? They'd gotten in her head. Santo had warned her not to look at them. She couldn't listen to them. She couldn't trust in winged messengers sent by Death.

She realized she was standing. She didn't remember when she'd gotten her legs beneath her.

It's you we want. Not him. Not him.

Of course, she thought. Santo would be okay. Abaddon wouldn't hurt him if she went with his ravens. Abaddon had little use for humans.

Yes, yes yes. . . .

But Santo wasn't human . . . he was an angel. An angel who'd come to protect her.

She blinked her eyes, looking down at the man who'd fought so hard to save her. What was she doing?

How could she even think of leaving him? The ravens had infested her thoughts, her vision, the air she struggled to pull in.

She took a step away from him.

Good.

The numbness filled her more completely even as a horrified voice inside began to scream for her to wake up, *wake up*, *WAKE UP*. The ravens clicked their beaks, receding another inch and then another. All except the big one with its glittering eyes. It gave her a sympathetic look and hopped forward.

"You can't win this one, kiddo," the raven said in a voice that sounded like her father's. The tone, the inflection. The bird tilted its head, looking so human that it started a quake of terror amidst the upheaval already going on inside her.

"You know I'm right, Roxanne," her father spoke from the black beak. He sounded so gentle and reasonable, so impossibly alive. "When have I ever steered you wrong?"

"Never, Daddy," she answered.

"Wouldn't it be nice to give up?" he said. "Forget this crazy game of hide-and-seek? You're never going to win it, and people are going to get hurt if you try. Your brothers. Your sister. Why would you put them in danger?"

Every nuance of her father's voice was just as she'd

remembered, and even though the soulless eyes looking at her didn't belong to the man she'd loved, the words rang true and the scolding brought tears to her eyes. "I'm sorry."

"Do the right thing, Roxanne."

Beguiled. That was the word for it. Somewhere deep within her mind, she knew it. But she couldn't break the spell. The raven puffed its feathers, then let them settle again. It smiled at her, black beak parting to flash the pale pink cast of its throat. It lifted its wings high and wide, ridged by long fingers of black feathers. Arms that welcomed her.

"Come home, sweetheart," her dad said. "We'll forget about all this nonsense. You'll be forgiven."

Forgiveness. It sounded like salve that would ease her isolation, her loneliness. But what was she being forgiven for? She struggled to reason it out. Had she done something?

Yes, Roxanne, you have sinned.

The raven smiled justly.

She took a step over Santo's body, while inside her terror squeezed at her heart. How had she sinned? What did it mean? Why did this feel so wrong? She needed to fight it. Fight this hold. Fight *them.*

Sweat broke out on her brow and careened down her spine. She was trembling with the conflicting forces within her. The compulsion to obey, to listen to her father battered against the insanity of doing just that. Her father was dead. If she listened to this imposter, she and Santo would be dead, too.

She took another step, her movements jerky, muscles aching as the waging war took down her motor skills.

STOP, ROXANNE. STOP.

Another step, the ravens dancing back to give her room—all but the one who spoke with her father's voice. The other birds settled in perches on the curtains, the lamps, the furniture, leaving her and Santo an island of carpet while they seethed like a black tide against a seawall.

A held breath hissed through her teeth, and the big raven hopped back in surprise, eyeing her with wary suspicion.

From a great distance, she seemed to see herself, poised on the edge of a dangerous unknown. Petrified. Tangled in commands she didn't want to obey.

She took another step and the birds kept up their merry escort, shifting along the curtain rods and furniture to keep pace. The big one took flight, hovering at eye level.

Tears burned her eyes, but rage kept them from escaping. Another step.

"Time to come home, Roxanne," her dad said.

She pulled in a burning breath, anger blazing in her gut as she forced herself to look away. Santo lay unconscious on the floor, the rise and fall of his chest shallow.

"Santo, help me," she whispered, even as she moved to the door. Knowing that no matter how she tried to fight it, she wouldn't be able to stop herself from obeying. She'd been summoned, and who was *she* to decline the summons of Abaddon?

Ask better questions, Roxanne.

"Santo," she tried again.

He didn't answer.

Peace—though she knew it was a lie—waited for her in the velvety shadows around the big raven. That she could both know it wasn't real and still crave it stoked the rage in her.

The ravens had grown quiet, expectant. How much time had passed since she'd risen and taken that first step? Seconds? Days? She felt like a radio tuned between stations, filled with disruptive static and intermittent surges of song. These ravens would compel her to her death and she'd go. Afraid.

As she'd been her whole life. She couldn't stop any of this. She didn't even know why they wanted her.

She made it to the door, and she knew that if she stepped out, she'd be lost.

She unlocked it.

Her tears overran her resistance, clouding her vision. She could hardly see past them or hear for the frantic screams that echoed in her head.

She turned the knob and opened the door.

A sound came from behind her, a great gust of

breath and movement, and then Santo grabbed her, knocking her off her feet as he tackled her.

It felt like something ruptured inside her—not bones or organs. A fissure splitting with a violent explosion. Her rage turned sharp-toothed mouths up as her fear plummeted down, down to be devoured.

Roxanne lay pinned on her stomach, her feet still inside the house, her body sprawled on the front porch, Santo's heavy weight across her legs. The birds exploded from the open door. The force of their exit made a sound that hurt her ears. They blotted out the mustard glow of the harvest moon.

The last twenty-four hours played in her mind. All she'd learned. All she still didn't know. Santo's voice inserted itself, explaining, teaching, challenging. He'd be so disappointed in her. He'd come to rescue an utter failure.

Roxanne shut her eyes, shutting down. Only the white-hot glimmer of her rage existed now. It burned so bright that it blinded.

Get away, she thought. *Get away from me.*

The ravens had crowded closer, and suddenly they fluttered and took a step back. Not much, but enough that she could breathe. She sucked in a breath and rubbed the knot in her chest, the place that seemed to swell within her. In her head, she heard Santo whisper, "*Shut the door, Roxanne. Come back to me.*"

She looked into the sea of black feathers and lethal claws hovering above her.

But she couldn't even *find* the mysterious door. How could she possibly shut it? How would she even know it if she'd done it?

Shut it. Shut it. Shut it.

"How?" she asked in a broken voice. "How?"

The answer formed like a rolling snowball, gathering speed and mass as it hurtled to its destination, and she realized that finally, at last, she'd asked the right question.

She shut her eyes and listened as the ravens began to scream.

(23)

Reece sat on the wide front porch he'd admired just yesterday and watched sunset turn the sky into a pink and gold menagerie of hooved clouds and horned doom. It would be Halloween soon.

His day was inside out. His night had come at dawn, his morning with dusk. He was wide awake at a time when he should have been winding down.

His coffee had grown cold and the jacket he wore provided little protection against the desert chill, but Reece didn't move. Since he'd staggered from his bed and down the stairs to this chair on the porch, he'd been numb.

In his head, he heard April's words over and over and over.

I didn't get away. They caught me.

And each time he heard it, he faced the realization anew. April hadn't been orphaned in Harvey, North Dakota, the day the demons had come and killed her family.

She'd been born. She was one of them now. A demon.

Gary hadn't ridden in and saved the day when the demons had attacked April's and Karen's families. He hadn't saved the survivors and brought him to sanctuary. No. Because Gary, the man Reece had once thought of as a friend, was the Big Bad of this crazy reality. He hadn't led the knights in shining armor to the rescue; he'd led an army of demons to attack.

The rest of the story Karen had told him was true. The demons had confiscated the dead bodies and now wore them like new suits. What she'd omitted was the fact that she was one of them. She and April both.

One of many, as it turned out. The compound was nothing more than a nest of demons disguised as humans. And here he sat within their terrible embrace, a human trying to pretend he didn't have his own monster to hide. It should have been a match made in heaven. He should have felt like he'd finally come home to a place he belonged. But Reece felt only horror.

He heard a noise behind him, but he didn't turn. He knew the sound of April's footsteps. Already he knew her scent. Silently, she took his coffee cup and replaced it with a fresh one. Then she curled up on the swing to his right, pulling the blanket she'd brought tight around her.

"There's more you should know," she said softly.

He thought there would be.

With a sigh, he looked at her. Still the beautiful young woman who'd intrigued him with her dark eyes and silence. Still as sweet and fresh and as all-American as the sunrise over the pines. Except she was none of those things. She wasn't even human.

"There's something that happens to us," she said.

Us. Demons. Reece swallowed the pain that came with the thought. Not an hour ago, he'd made love to a demon. He'd felt cleansed by her kisses. Healed by her touch.

"We didn't know it when we followed Gary out of Abaddon."

Abaddon. Hell on steroids if he'd grasped the concept.

"Know what?" he asked, when something inside him begged him to keep quiet.

But there was no turning back from this—no pretending it was something he'd misunderstood. He needed to learn everything he could about these *people* he'd come to be allied with. But he had to be very careful. If Gary even suspected that Reece knew the truth . . .

"Wait," he said, holding up his hand. "Go get dressed. Let's take a walk."

A few minutes later they headed out, skirting the inside gates of the compound until they reached the open pasture where the horses grazed with a scattering of sheep, goats, and cows. Here, the desert crept right up to the fence, taunting the nurtured pasture with its dusty, dry promises.

"Start from the beginning," Reece said. "Why are you here?"

She took a deep breath, and those dark chocolate eyes that had enthralled him from the first moment he'd seen her grew misty.

"We were considered scavengers before. That's why we were imprisoned in Abaddon."

"Things that prey on the dead?"

She nodded. "Before that, we were reapers. Reapers have a higher calling. They reap the soul and see it carried to its proper place in the afterlife."

"They kill people."

"No. Not at all." She looked down, and he could see a dull flush beneath her dark skin. "At least they aren't supposed to. But scavengers are reapers who can't get enough of death. They crave it. The fear that humans feel when death is upon them. The pain. The sorrow. The need for it becomes what you would call an addiction."

He knew she meant *humans* when she said *you*. But Reece felt like she spoke directly to him, confiding something she thought he'd understand. And he did.

"You're one of them? One of these scavengers who likes death too much?"

Her remorse touched something deep inside him, moving and jarring all at the same time.

"Yes," she said. "I was."

He noted her use of past tense but kept silent.

"If reapers are caught abusing their power, inciting terror, they're condemned to never reap again. It's like caging a lion and starving it to death."

He hated the picture she painted. Hated that this soft-spoken woman, who'd touched him in a way no other had before, had experienced it.

Reece couldn't look at her. "Go on."

"Reapers were created for one purpose, Reece. When that purpose is stripped away, what's left is . . . ugly."

"As opposed to the beauty of death?"

"It can be beautiful," she said in a wistful voice. "Death is as much a part of life as birth."

He thought of this morning. The violence. The blood. The death. There'd been nothing beautiful in that. But then again, there'd been nothing human in it either. And yet, he couldn't pretend that he hadn't felt the glory of it. The power. The electric *charge* of killing.

"Why didn't you want to join in the killing this morning, then? Wasn't that like a free buffet?"

She swallowed and looked away. "No, because the victims weren't human. But there's another reason."

He waited, knowing he wouldn't like the reason she gave but conversely glad it existed.

"I'm having a hell of a time wrapping my head

around any of this, April." He paused. "I guess April isn't even your name."

"It's the only name I've ever had," she answered. "Picture where I come from like a hive. Endless hives. Each hive has a ruler. Those are the names you know here on earth."

"What about the rest of you?"

"We aren't important enough for names. God, in His wisdom, chose not to make us individuals. Not to give us emotions that could confuse or derange us."

"Yeah. How's that working for you?"

She bowed her head and he felt like a dick for saying it.

"We were intended as creatures of service and nothing more."

"What about now?" he asked. At her blank look, he grudgingly explained. Because he wanted the answer. Wanted it with a desperation he wished he could deny.

"Do you have those things now? Feelings?"

Her smile held overwhelming sadness. "I do. I feel everything." She looked him in the eye, all artifice stripped. The anger that had simmered around her before, banished. "I don't have words to describe what it meant to come to you this morning."

A tightness had gathered around his heart; now it eased. "I thought it might have been an act. Something Gary put you up to."

"No. He thought Karen would be your sin of choice. I don't think it occurred to him that you'd want me."

Another flush colored her face. He brushed his knuckles over her cheeks, wanting to kiss her. In spite of everything she'd told him, he still wanted to kiss her.

"You're different from everyone else here," he said.

"There's a reason for that, too."

"Good."

She went on, determined to tell this tale. "I don't know when Gary first found the way in, but it's only been recently that he's figured out how to stay . . . how to take over the dead. How to inhabit a body after he'd killed the human inside it."

Reece watched her intently, but she avoided his eyes.

"It's tricky, taking the dead," she said in a hoarse voice. "It requires killing them without reaping. It has to be done quickly and cleanly because a death is a beacon to the Beyond. Gary figured out how to kill a person and possess their body in the same fell swoop. He abandons the soul because if he sent it on its way, they would know."

"They?"

"In the Beyond, life and death are catalogued on a strict schedule. If souls suddenly appeared before their time, it would cause problems. A soul without a death would be noticed."

He'd had to ask.

"Gary never told us how it would be, though. We followed him, not knowing the risks."

"But you knew you'd be killing innocent people and leaving their souls to be damned?"

"Not damned," she said. "Just lost."

"That makes it so much better."

"No," she whispered. "It makes it so much worse."

Her sorrow was too real, too aching to ignore. He didn't think she was pretending, even though a voice inside him warned him to be wary. There was so much he didn't know about her, about what she was, how far she'd go or how desperate she could be. She might be lying, manipulating. She might be the best actress in the world. Or, God help them all, she might be telling the truth.

"Gary sent us to April's home, to Harvey, to take everyone between the ages of twelve and fifty. The rest were killed and covered with the fire. Those who were lucky enough not to be home when it happened thought their loved ones had been burned to death."

It was too horrible to contemplate, but Reece forced himself to ask, "There are that many of you?"

She shook her head. "Most don't survive. They expire in the first few minutes. It's a dangerous thing."

Especially for the humans.

"What happened to April's parents and her big brother?"

"Clyde was with the hunting party this morning. Ellen works in the kitchen. James didn't make it."

Shock wended its way through him like an electric current. "Why tell me? Doesn't this go against Gary's grand plan?"

She nodded. "He'd destroy me if he knew."

"Then why?"

She faced him then, her eyes so filled with anguish that he felt her pain in his chest. But he still didn't know if he could trust it.

"You asked why I was afraid this morning. Why I didn't want to kill." She looked around, as if hoping to find her next words among the waving grasses and tumbled stones that littered the pasture. "Have you noticed that people around here seem to have skin problems?" she asked at last.

The random question startled him. "Yeah."

"The bodies we take, they fight us. Even dead, they fight us. They reject us. Bit by bit, they begin to degenerate. They deteriorate until they become our worst nightmare."

He thought of the rash on Gary's face. He'd noted variations of it on the others, but he hadn't equated it to anything like this.

"The rash is a symptom of what's going on inside. The weaker the scavenger, the faster the change. They start out looking human, but before long, the first signs begin to show. They lose all pigmentation. Their hair, skin, and eyes turn white, as if the human world is eating them away. Finally, they regress into something ravenous. Mindless creatures that live only to appease their hunger for souls."

He stared, uncomprehending for a moment, until the reality of her words took shape. In his mind, he broke down the creatures he'd fought this morning, remembering how freaked out he'd been by their paws, which looked so much like hands. The creatures had been huge—too big for a dog or wolf. Human-sized, but so grizzled and deformed that he hadn't made the connection.

"Once it begins, there's no stopping the deterioration. It eats away at them, *changes* them until they become creatures of death. Something not seen or heard of for thousands upon thousands of years. Even we thought they were myth. Evil without thought, without purpose. Hellhounds." She took a deep breath. "Gary is the only one who can control them. He keeps them locked up in a pit below one of the outbuildings. They're dangerous to the rest of us."

"Wait a minute," Reece said. "Those things, those hellhounds we fought this morning . . ."

"They were once like me. Like Karen or Walter, any of us."

"Why were they out there? Why did everyone know they were coming? Why—" He paused, answering his own question. "It was a show, wasn't it? All for me."

April nodded. "Gary had to convince you that our enemy was real. That we're on the same side."

"So he sacrificed his own?"

"You say that like you expected something different. They answer to Gary and Gary answers to Abaddon. The hounds were supposed to kill the police officer who's protecting your sister so Walter could bring her home. Here, to the compound. But they failed and they almost killed *her* while they were at it. Gary was furious. He moved to Plan B—use them and destroy them as an example to the rest of us of what happens to those who fail."

Too many thoughts crowded in his head. Rage over Gary sending those things after his sister. Hurt over the betrayal that seemed to go on and on. Horror over what it all meant and . . .

Suddenly Reece realized he'd missed an important turn in her story. He stopped and looked at her. "So what? You're saying that the rash, the deterioration . . . that happens to *all* of you?"

"Eventually. Inevitably."

He stared at her. She'd confessed to being a demon, and he believed her. It didn't matter that what she'd said was incredible. He *believed* her. He should hate her right now. He should want to kill her, this demon. But he couldn't hate her more than he hated himself. He was every bit as much a monster as she and Gary's other soldiers were. Just because he was human didn't make it less true. He understood what she meant about addictions. About craving the hot, sweet fear that came with death. He'd been fighting it his entire life.

April said, "Gary has been trying to find a way to keep our bodies from failing. He's doing experiments. He made me take this body—take April—before she drew her last breath. She was still alive when I stepped in, Reece. We both felt it when Gary ripped out her soul."

The pain in her voice washed over him, making him see it in every single detail.

"I feel her," she whispered. "She's a part of me now, or maybe I'm a part of her. I can't tell anymore."

She began to weep. Reece watched helplessly until finally, he gave in and pulled her into his arms.

"Did it work?" he asked, pressing his mouth to the silk of her temple. "Are you safe? Can you stay like you are?"

With me?

Fucked-up on so many levels, but there it was.

"No," she said, her face damp with tears. "I can't. Unless you have a really strong leash."

Neither of them laughed.

"It's happening slower than it has with the others, but I can feel it, the changes. I'll be able to see them soon."

"I'm sorry," he said. "I don't want that for you."

She seemed surprised, almost hurt by that. "You should. What I am, it's wrong. *Wrong.* I can feel her inside me. And I'm so sorry for what we did. I just want to die, but she won't let me."

"Why won't she let you?"

"She wants revenge, Reece. So do I."

He pulled back so he could look into her face. Wet, spiky lashes framed her big brown eyes.

"I can't let Gary destroy this world. Not now that I know it. I need you to help me stop him. I need you to tap into that part of you that you hate."

"What's that supposed to mean?" he asked, but he knew. *He knew.*

She smiled sadly, knowingly. "You don't have to lie to me, Reece. I see what you are."

"And what is that?"

"Someone who wants to be good."

(24)

Santo felt like he'd been hit by a train. Twice.

He shifted, coming awake all at once to unmerciful sunshine and a million aches and pains. He lay sprawled on the backseat of Jorge's old Ford pickup truck. His clothes were in tatters and his skin burned where the birds had clawed it. A few of them had gotten hunks of his flesh, and the bites throbbed. But as far as he could tell, he was still alive.

Irony. It followed him everywhere.

He couldn't tell where they were, but the truck moved at a good clip and scenery sped past the window. Gingerly, he sat up and looked around. Phoenix. They'd come south from the mountains back to the city. Roxanne sat behind the wheel and caught his movement in the rearview. She nearly jumped out of her skin. He waited for her to catch her breath before speaking.

"I guess we got away?"

"For now," she said with a weak smile.

She looked different, though he couldn't say exactly how or why. But something in her face, in the way she held herself . . . the angle of her chin . . . the squared shoulders . . . the tight grip on the wheel . . . All of it? None of it? He didn't know, only that in some indefinable way, she'd been altered.

She turned her gaze back to the road when he would have liked to search her eyes.

"What happened?" he asked softly.

"I'm not really sure," Roxanne answered.

"I meant, what happened to *you*?"

She didn't glance in the mirror. Didn't give him a hint at her thoughts. "About five hundred ravens tried to line their nests with my hair and skin, but other than that, not too much."

He waited for her to say more. The soft line of her mouth tightened, and tension radiated through her entire body. She didn't fill the gaping quiet.

Awkwardly, he maneuvered over the back of the seat and into the front. It hurt like hell, but now he could see Roxanne's face. The ravens had done a number on her. Scratches marred the porcelain perfection of her skin, and jagged holes gaped in her clothes. Blood had seeped through in several places. He pulled down the visor and looked in the mirror. As he suspected, they were a matched set.

He still wore his holster, but the weapon was gone.

"Do you have my gun?" he asked.

She gave him a surprised look, seeing the empty sheath. "No, of course not. It must have fallen out when Louisa and I were getting you into the truck."

Outstanding. Now he was confused *and* unarmed. Roxanne looked so worried that he touched her shoulder to get her attention again.

"No big deal," he lied. "Like you said, bullets only slowed them down."

She nodded, unconvinced, and grew quiet. He still didn't know what had happened and it appeared that he'd have to pry the information out of her. But carefully. That much was clear.

"Okay. Let's talk about the ravens," he tried again. "How did we get away from them?"

She shrugged, a grim, defensive movement.

"What about Louisa?"

"She hid in the garage. When the birds were gone, she came back. I couldn't figure out how to get the car started, so she told me to take the truck. Evidently, hot-wiring isn't in my skill set."

He nodded, still watching her, still trying to analyze the nuances of her reactions and that strange sense of *transformation* that he couldn't quite pinpoint.

He wanted to demand an explanation. Abaddon's

ravens didn't just *go away*. But Roxanne reminded him of a trapped animal that might be dangerous if her cage was rattled. He wanted her to talk to him, not come out snarling and bolt.

"How are you holding up?" he asked, backing off when she obviously expected a full assault.

She shot him a surprised, grateful glance and said, "I'd give my eyeteeth for a glass of water and a bathroom. Not necessarily in that order."

He checked the gas gauge. It hovered at a quarter tank, and Roxanne looked like she was running on empty. Gently, he reached out and covered her hand on the steering wheel.

"What's going on, *angelita*? Talk to me."

She nodded, then shook her head. "I just thought . . . for a while I wasn't sure if you were going to wake up."

In her voice he heard the ring of fear and, overriding it, responsibility. As if *she* could have somehow stopped Abaddon's ravens. He brushed his knuckles against her cheek and she bit her lip, exiting Highway 60 at Mill Avenue and taking a right.

"Where are we going?"

"Reece's condo."

He couldn't stop the shocked glance he shot her. "What about the reporters? The news? Won't they be there?"

She looked at the clock on the dash. "About fifteen

minutes ago, my sister made an anonymous call to the Channel Twelve tip line. She told them that Reece and I were spotted at a convenience store near Payson."

"Where I bought your phone," he said, impressed.

She nodded. "That should keep them busy, especially when they see you on their security camera. I told Louisa to wait two hours before calling in the abandoned car in front of her house. By now, anyone who's interested should be headed north."

"Pretty smart."

"Not really. But it might work. Reece lives in a gated complex anyway. The reporters aren't allowed past the street. If we can get there without being spotted, I know the codes to get in."

Santo let out a deep breath. It was a risky plan, but he could see she'd thought it through. They'd be hiding in plain sight, someplace that had been checked and dismissed already. They just might get away with it.

"Do you want me to drive for a while?"

She shook her head. "We'll be there soon."

Watery daylight spewed over the streets and sidewalks. Clouds offered thin cover as Roxanne took a back road that led to a side entrance of a sprawling condominium complex.

"They have security cameras here," she said, pulling the hood of her jacket up. "You should get down."

He did as she asked, wedging himself below the

dash as she punched a number in a keypad and waited. After a few seconds, she began driving again. "Okay, we're clear of the cameras."

Santo sat up and looked around as she turned down a twisting drive. The silence in the truck had become a presence, seated squarely between them as she navigated around the buildings of the complex. Desert landscaping crawled over rock gardens, and bright green paloverde trees offered low-maintenance shade to the walkways. A small pool positioned near the rental office and clubhouse glittered, surface as flat as glass, chairs at precise attention around the perimeter. All of it vacant and looking too serene to be real. It buzzed his already stretched nerves.

Santo had never been patient, and reapers did not require forbearance. Not surprisingly, the hybrid man he'd become didn't care for waiting either. But he forced himself to swallow his questions until they were safely inside. Then he would get his answers.

Roxanne stopped the truck in front of a single-car garage, put it in park, then moved to another keypad. A moment later, the big door groaned as it moved up, and she pulled in and closed it behind them.

The door from the garage to the house opened into a compact, immaculate kitchen with a breakfast counter and two bar stools. A strange transitional space—too small for a table and chairs, too big to be a walkway— joined the kitchen to the small living room, where a chocolate brown couch and a coffee table faced the all-important flat-screen TV. He caught a glimpse of two bedrooms down a short hall. No pictures hung on the walls, no knickknacks on any surfaces.

Roxanne dropped the truck keys on the counter and went straight to the bathroom. A few minutes later, she was back and still avoiding his eyes. She pulled two water bottles from the refrigerator and tossed him one. They both drank thirstily.

"Is your house like this?" he asked.

Frowning, she looked around. "What do you mean?"

"My hotel room had more personality."

Her gaze lingered on the clean surfaces and the blank slate of walls. "No, Ruby and I share my parents' old house. It's got more personality than working features. Hot in the summer, cold in the winter. We keep saying we're going to get rid of all the old stuff my dad left and move, but . . . we never do."

"Why not?"

She lifted one shoulder. "My mom died when I was born, but I like having her things around. It makes me feel like I know her, just a little."

She looked so lost and sad that he had to force himself to stay put. He'd finally got her talking. He didn't want to do anything that might bring back that heavy silence.

"Just you and Ruby live there?"

"Ryan moved out when I was eighteen and never came back. Reece went the same year." She took a deep, shaky breath. "Dad left us all some money. Reece bought this condo with his, but I don't think he likes it here. He spends a lot of nights on our couch. Or Ryan's."

"What did you buy with the money he left you?" Santo asked.

"Nothing." She turned to the refrigerator and rummaged for a minute. "Are you hungry?"

He wasn't surprised that she was hungry again. Roxanne was like a little wolf cub. But he sensed that what motivated her now had more to do with avoidance than appetite. He came up behind her, putting an arm around her waist and pulling her back so he could close the refrigerator door. For a moment the soft heat of her relaxed into him and he wanted nothing more than to swing her in his arms and carry her to one of those nondescript bedrooms.

Reluctantly, he eased back and guided her to the couch. With equal reluctance, she let him. When they were seated, he turned to her.

"What happened at Louisa's, Roxanne? What happened with the birds?"

"I told you, I don't know. It's the truth," she insisted when she saw the doubt on his face. "I think I blacked out."

"And when you came to, they were gone?"

"More or less."

He let his silence ask the next question. With a frown, she shifted, scooting away from him.

"I was trying to fight them off. I could see that they were smothering you. You fell and they just . . . they were everywhere. The stench and their sound. I came unhinged. I got so *angry*. I couldn't see past it. I think I screamed and I just kept on screaming. I remember curling around you, trying to protect you. Then the house lit up, like a spotlight got turned on somewhere. It blinded me . . . then Louisa was shaking my arm and the birds were gone."

"Where did the light come from?"

"I don't know."

"Louisa didn't see anything?"

"She said she saw the light, too. That it was so bright it came through the cracks in the doorjamb. It scared her, so she didn't come out until it was gone."

He looked away, stumped. What light? And why had it chased the ravens away? It didn't add up.

"I remember the birds breaking through the kitchen window," Santo said slowly. "I remember making it as far as the living room."

He scowled. He could still feel the ravens crowding around his face. They'd suffocated him in feathers and evil.

"Did they speak to you?" Roxanne asked in that toneless voice that revealed nothing. But her eyes . . . they spoke volumes. The fear hadn't vanished, but anger had shoved its way in and overpowered it. Sharp and biting, it snapped like lightning in the stormy colors swirling there.

"Yes," he answered. He couldn't tell if she felt relieved or terrified by that. He shifted on the cushions so he was closer to her and took her hand. "What did they say to you, Roxanne?"

"They said they'd found me."

"Abaddon found you?" he asked in a low voice.

"They said I should go to him. They called to me."

The last came in a low, shamed voice. He understood it. Their power sucked away the will to resist and left their victims feeling violated. He knew. He'd felt it himself.

Yet somehow she had resisted. Somehow, she'd escaped. And she'd managed to save him *and* Louisa. She couldn't know how incredible that was.

"The ravens kept telling me to come home," she said. "That I belonged with Abaddon. And for some reason, I believed them."

"You will never belong with Abaddon. Not as long as I have breath in my body. You belong here."

With me. It shouldn't have been so difficult to keep from saying it. But he felt as if a hole had been carved out of his chest and now all the emotions he'd disdained from the start had settled there, waiting for the moment when they would consume him.

"I kept hearing your voice in my head, Santo. You tried to stop me, and I could feel you holding on, protecting me. They were trying to kill you, but you kept protecting *me*."

She gave him a tremulous smile he didn't deserve. He'd succumbed to their power. He'd been the weaker of the two of them, and that shamed him. He might have lied when he'd said he had come to protect her, but he'd never meant to fail her in this way. Abaddon had almost snatched her away from him.

She said, "*Ask better questions.* I kept hearing you say it in my head. The ravens tried to tell me that it was Abaddon who waited for me when I died, and I knew they were lying. I knew that something so vile couldn't make me feel . . ."

She stopped and her cheeks pinked. But then she went on, passionately disputing the lies Abaddon had told her.

"I knew it wasn't Abaddon who waited for me when I died. And that made me think . . . if it's not Abaddon . . . then what does my *death* have to do with any of it? If you're right and I can really close this door that lets in all these horrors . . . then why do I have to die to do it?"

He felt himself go very still. "And what was your answer?"

She shook her head. "I couldn't answer. But you said you felt it close when I took my last breath. My *last* breath. Those were your words."

He nodded, thinking of those moments, the timing of each bizarre event. She was right.

"I don't know if the ravens could hear my thoughts or if they just sensed it in me, but they inched back. And . . ." She shook her head, her gaze far off, her brows pulled. "I felt it."

"Felt what, Roxanne?"

"What Louisa saw. The brightness. The light. I felt it right here."

She clenched a fist and pressed it to her chest before turning those beautiful eyes on him.

The heart he no longer scorned came to a painful, stuttering halt.

"I could feel *you* with me. Guiding me. And I thought, I have an angel to help me. I can do this."

And then his heart broke. He looked away, destroyed by the adoration in her eyes. Damned by the lies that had put it there.

She moved closer to him and took his face between her palms. "If not for you, I would have gone with them, Santo."

Her words tore into flesh and bone. Helplessly, he touched his forehead to hers. "No, you wouldn't have," he said. "You would have fought and you would have won. It was all you, Roxanne. It was all you."

He looked into her eyes and let his thumbs brush her cheeks. He didn't deserve her, this woman he'd come for. But he couldn't let her go. Her eyelids fluttered shut, but her lips softened in invitation.

"I know what you're doing," she said.

That might have been funny if he hadn't been so confused himself. He didn't have a fucking clue. He only knew he needed her. Roxanne. He needed the truth in her touch. The honesty in her kisses. Needed them though he knew she'd find none of that in his.

Her hands came up, tentative, seeking. They found his chest and settled softly there, fingers spread over his heart. Their gazes locked as he tried to find words, but he couldn't begin to decipher the complex and frothing mix of his emotions. His goal had been so clear when he'd stepped into Santo's skin. Find Roxanne Love and reap her mortal soul.

Now he wanted only to stay in this minute, freeze this small moment in time, and hold her. Forever.

But even he could see the fallacy of his plan. Roxanne was more special than she knew. More than he had imagined. If she'd figured out how to force Abaddon's ravens from her mind, from her world, then it was only a matter of time before she figured out how to do it on a bigger scale.

Soon she'd be asking herself how she could do the same thing to the demons who'd invaded her life. She'd be working on a way to send them all back to the Beyond, where they belonged.

All of them.

That meant his time was running out. She would learn the truth, then. She would know his lies.

Because along with the rest of the scourge she evicted, one reaper who had no right to her world would be exiled, too. One she considered her angel.

And there wasn't a damn thing he could do about it but help her.

(25)

Roxanne watched with confusion as Santo turned away. One minute he'd been warm and comforting, holding her like she was more important than breath. In the next, he'd lifted the duffel she'd remembered to grab from the car and started down the hall.

"Where are you going?" she asked, standing.

"I need to clean up. I can't think straight when I feel like I'm covered in feathers and blood."

She nodded, puzzled and a little hurt by his sudden departure. She'd been thinking along the lines of washing all of that away together. She stared after him, steeling herself not to beg him to come back. Before he stepped into the bathroom, he stopped, fingertips to the wall, head down.

Say something.

He glanced over his shoulder, his uncertainty a whisper she couldn't quite hear and definitely didn't understand. Then he closed the door behind him.

Not the reaction she'd expected. Not the one she wanted. But she'd seen the change in his eyes when she'd called him her angel. She just couldn't figure out what it meant.

Frustrated, she leaned against the wall and let her head thump back.

"Fabulous."

With a sigh, she moved to the spare room where she and Ruby both kept a few extra outfits, just as Reece had clothes at their place. Arms full, she headed to the bathroom in the master suite.

She washed and changed into some soft leggings and a battered ASU sweatshirt that had belonged to an old boyfriend who'd come and gone so quickly he'd left articles of clothing behind. The sweatshirt was worn soft, and it hung to her knees. Not exactly seduction material, but she didn't have a lot to work with here. She told herself that her decision to go braless had to do with comfort, but her breasts were heavy and tight, her nipples hard as she pulled on a T-shirt beneath the sweatshirt.

Her breasts were laughing at her.

She brushed her teeth. Her hair. Put it in a ponytail. Took it down again.

She was stalling. Since Santo had walked into the bar two nights ago, they'd been shot at, gnawed on, and attacked by devils with feathers. They'd been on the run and all alone. And somewhere in there he'd become important. To her. Not just because he kept saving her life but also because he made her see. Everything. He made her question. And sometimes he even made her answer.

She'd been given *four lives.* Sooner or later, her luck would run out. What if it happened tomorrow? What if it happened tonight? She wasn't afraid anymore. She knew that she wouldn't be alone, even in death. But right now she was very much alive, and she wanted to be with Santo. Be with him, no holding back. No regrets.

He'd been trying to get her there from the first, and she'd resisted. Why, then, had he walked away from her now that they finally had a moment of peace? A chance to be together.

Well, if he wanted her to ask better questions, he'd better brace himself for that one. If it meant marching right into the bathroom and demanding an explanation, she'd do it. Determined, she turned around.

Santo was leaning against the door frame, watching her. His gaze glittered darkly as it moved over her face and down, lingering on her breasts, her belly, her legs. How long had he been standing there? Had she been whispering to herself as she'd recited that little pep talk? Did he know what she was thinking this time? Her blush felt like a hot wave.

He'd replaced his tattered sweats with faded blue jeans that rode low on his hips. Scratches and bites covered his bare chest, and a thin strip of elastic from his briefs showed above the waistband, white against his burnished skin. His feet were bare.

She cleared her throat. "I was just coming out."

He stepped aside to let her pass, but not so much that her arm didn't brush his chest. Or had that been her fault? He made her want to touch. She could feel him at her back, following close enough to send a shiver through her.

In the living room, she sat on the far end of the couch, knees drawn up under her sweatshirt, chin resting on top. For all her determination, she was suddenly shy.

He dropped down beside her, and she tried not to stare. But it was hard. The shadow of a beard darkened his jaw, as black as his hair and brows. It contrasted with his skin and made his features stand out. The arrogant nose, the lover's lips. And the eyes with those long, lush lashes . . . She carefully avoided them.

Roxanne couldn't think of anything to say, and Santo seemed to be having the same problem. He leaned back, staring at the ceiling with a pensive look. His right hand rested low on his flat belly, fingertips just inside the waistband of his jeans. She didn't know just how long she'd been watching them with a fixed fascination, but when she glanced up, she saw that she had his attention. His eyes had become heavy-lidded and the air between them became thick with awareness.

"I've spent the last two days wishing I could read your mind," he murmured.

"It's a scary place in there," she said with a weak smile. "Be glad you can't. Besides, I gave you my life story in the car. That's all there is."

"No dark hidden secrets?"

"All my lives are an open book."

"Not to me."

She smiled, but she felt too self-conscious for small talk. Too vested for flirting. She wanted him. She wanted him to want *her*.

"What happened earlier?" she asked before she could convince herself not to. "You turned all broody again."

His brows went up at *broody*. She wondered how he perceived himself. Did he know how darkly dangerous he seemed to her?

"Nothing happened. I just needed some downtime."

"You mean away from me? Because it seemed like it was something I said that came out wrong."

He shook his head. "No. Not that."

"Then what? Are you worried that I'm going to expect something when all of this is over? I know I called you my angel, but I didn't mean it to sound so possessive. . . . I mean, you don't have to . . ."

"Roxanne."

"I just don't want you to think I have expectations."

"Roxanne? Could you look at me?"

That was the last thing she wanted to do. Because when she looked at him, she wanted to touch him. And if she touched him, she'd never want to stop. The whole speech she'd just bumbled through had been a lie. She had expectations. She had big ones.

He moved, leaning across the couch to touch her cheek and raise her chin. Halfheartedly, she let him.

"It wasn't anything you said. You just made me think."

"About?"

He let out a deep breath. "About what happens later. When I have to go back."

She frowned, feeling like his words had emerged mixed up and she'd have to order them before they'd make sense.

"Go back?"

He nodded soberly. "I won't be able to stay here when it's all over."

She couldn't have heard that right. "Define *here*."

"On earth."

"But you live here. You have a life here. You were *married* here."

He caught his bottom lip and nodded, but some out-of-control signal was flashing in her head, taking her back to the spare bedroom in Louisa's house and the conversation they'd had about his wife.

He'd never told Marisella what he was. Something

about the omission—something *more* than just his secrecy—bothered her about that. But she hadn't been able to pinpoint why.

Now a horrible suspicion began to grow inside her. A fear that she couldn't control. There was something hidden in this picture that she couldn't see.

"Roxanne," Santo said. "There was always a bigger plan for me. I came here for *you*."

"To protect me."

"And I stay until I'm sure you're safe. But then I go back. I'm not of your world, Roxanne. You know that."

"Bullshit." She reached over and pinched him. Hard. When he winced and looked at her in surprise, she said, "You feel like you're of this world to me."

He didn't rise to her anger. Instead he watched her with grave eyes that saw the hurt echoing through her.

"Why didn't you tell me?" she asked in a voice that wasn't steady. "Why did you let me believe I could keep you?"

Later she might regret how pathetic that sounded. How much of her heart it revealed. But right now all she could think was that somehow as they'd been running for their lives, she'd been falling in love. He'd stolen her heart and now he meant to leave with it.

"I wanted to tell you, but I couldn't. I was afraid you'd shut me out and all I wanted was for you to let me in."

There was too much honesty in his voice. It wrapped around her and squeezed until she thought she was going to cry. She bit down hard on her lip and fought it.

He took her hand, and she allowed herself to look at him, bracing for what she'd see in his eyes. "Roxanne, I don't want to go. If it was my choice, I'd stay here."

"Define here," she demanded in a tone that turned it into a plea.

"With you. Always with you."

The declaration drew her forward. Santo met her halfway. She kissed him with all of the hurt and pent-up longing inside her. Kissed him like it was the last chance for a taste of heaven. Santo made a deep sound that chased away her doubts and filled her with a twisted sense of hope.

He wanted to stay. If the two of them could survive demons, hellhounds, ravens from Abaddon . . . why couldn't they change their future? Why couldn't she hold her angel here?

He tunneled his fingers through her hair and held her face in his hands as he kissed her back slowly, deeply, his touch a reflection of all she felt. No man had ever kissed her like that. Touched her like that.

And if he left her, no man ever would again.

But he was here now, and he made her feel . . . exquisite. Rare. Precious. Something so special it had to be savored. While his tongue stroked hers, he pulled her onto his lap, her knees straddling his thighs. His hands were on her body, their heat cleansing, healing. Filled with promise.

He tugged her hips closer until all that separated her hot center from the hard length of him was a soft pair of blue jeans and stretchy leggings. When his hands slipped under her shirt and found only skin, he made that sound again, and her whole body bowed in response.

He carried her to the bedroom without breaking the kiss, and Roxanne thought he could have had her on the hallway floor as long as he kept his mouth on hers. He found the bed in the spare room without stumbling and followed her down until she felt the softness of a mattress beneath her, the seducing weight of his body above. The quiet groan of surrender he made in his throat turned her boneless. His fingers gripped the hem of her sweatshirt and stripped it off, leaving the T-shirt underneath. She needed that gone, too. She wanted to scream, *Hurry!* and beg for him to slow down. He did neither. Instead he continued his leisurely assault, taking his time kissing her, exploring her mouth, tasting the curve of her throat, the soft swell of her breast.

He tongued her through the thin cotton of her T-shirt, making her nipples hard and her breasts ache. It had seemed they would never have these moments together when they'd run from the horrors that chased them. And now it seemed that none of that could have been real. Only this. Now. With him.

She arched against him, reveling in the weight of his body, muscled and hard from sternum to calf. Her legs wrapped around his and a wave of desire went through her like electricity.

When her bare chest was finally against his, they both stilled. He had his weight on his forearms, his hands in her hair, and he stared down at her with a look so complex it stole her breath away. Their lovemaking had been explosive at Louisa's, a rush of passion and feeling that had left her dazed. Now she took the time to note the tremble in his arms, the hitch in his breath, the hooded look in his smoldering eyes. He seemed overwhelmed by the responsiveness of her body beneath his, overawed by how it felt to make love to her. And for just a moment, he looked lost.

"What is it, Santo?"

He kissed her instead of answering, and in the seduction of his lips, she forgot why she'd asked. She moved restlessly against him, and at last he stripped off the rest of her clothes steadily, determinedly, mouth still plundering wherever it roamed.

"How could you think I would choose to leave you?" he said against her shoulder.

She couldn't think at all, except about how to get closer to him, have more of him. Make it impossible for him to ever leave her.

She reached for the button fly of his jeans and he leaned back to help her. She yanked at the top button and the others opened in rapid fire. He hissed in a breath and laughed, the sound deep in his chest, vibrating against her bare skin, so masculine, so intimate that it left her scalded.

The feel of Santo naked beside her on the bed nearly sent her over the edge. *This* was what she'd heard of, what they portrayed in movies and books. She'd grasped the meaning of it without ever understanding how it *felt*. How breath couldn't come fast enough and, at the same time, could be forgotten completely. How even her fingertips tingled when she felt the velvet warmth of his tongue against her flesh.

She took him in her mouth and he made that sound again, the one that her body responded to like a signal.

He hissed in a breath as she pulled him deeper, letting her teeth graze ever so gently and her tongue swirl over the rounded head and down the hard shaft. He pumped against her, a small, reflexive movement that spoke of his need and her power to satisfy it.

Then he was pulling her up, turning her beneath him, and burying himself in the cradle of her body.

His kisses were long and lush, filled with desire that had been pulled and sweetened by the pressures of time. Chemistry that had sparked and fired from the conflict of their dance.

He began to thrust in a deep, steady rhythm that stroked every nerve, every inch of her, bringing the fiery feelings to flame and searing one thought in her mind.

She would not let him go. The Beyond would have to make do with one less angel, because this one was hers.

She held the thought tight and let it join with her passion, let it build with her pleasure. It became a vow she swore she'd see through to the end.

Breath ragged, heartbeat thunderous, she glanced down the length of their bodies, his as brown as desert sands, hers as pale as moonlight. The contrast was as beautiful as the feelings swelling inside her.

He rocked his body inside hers and his fingers joined the sweet assault, pushing her ever closer to that point of no return. She cried out when she came and he answered with a shout of his own, her name on lips that found hers once more. And all the while, Santo held her tight, riding through it with her until, exhausted, they collapsed together in a silence that felt as perfect as the moment.

With one last kiss, Santo tucked her into the curve of his body and pulled the covers over them both. The warmth of him sank down to her bones, and Roxanne held tight to the feeling, promising herself that they would have this together for the rest of their lives. With a deep sigh, she relaxed against Santo and let her eyes close. They fell asleep in seconds.

(26)

Santo woke up beside Roxanne, bare and warm and instantly alert. The clock on the nightstand read four fifteen, and the greedy shadows told him it was night, not afternoon.

Without moving, he searched the silence with his senses, finding nothing to explain the feeling that had awakened him. The only sound was Roxanne's soft, even breathing next to him.

Quietly, he eased from the bed, pulled on his pants, and reached for his weapon, remembering it was gone. Feeling naked without it, he left the room. Nothing stepped from the dim corners or growled from the hall. Nothing fluttered at the windows or spoke in his head. But the feeling stayed, a song playing too softly to be heard. The quiet held its breath.

Darkness shouldn't have bothered him. He was one with darkness. He had come from darkness. But this one held more than shadows.

The lights had been blazing in the living room and kitchen when he'd carried Roxanne to bed. Now a dank, pitch-black seeped from the edges of the room.

He drew even with the kitchen and paused. The front door was closed and locked but the sliding glass door that led out to a small balcony stood open. A cold wind gusted through it and banked against the walls. He smelled demons in it.

A big fat raven sat on the railing, wings tucked and eyes glassy. Locusts covered the balcony's floor. They hopped and scuttled. The bird watched.

It was the same cat-sized raven that had attacked at Louisa's but it didn't look so cocky anymore. Its feathers had a thin, diseased look; its eyes had a milky sheen. Roxanne hadn't banished that one to Abaddon, but she'd certainly managed to hurt it.

A deep growl came from behind him and slowly, he turned, braced for hot breath and sharp teeth. A hellhound stood in the middle of the room. A second paced beside it, tracking him with hungry eyes.

"Well, now," a man said from the couch, where he'd been sitting so still that Santo hadn't seen him. "If it isn't the reaper."

The voice had a lilting note that Santo recognized from the night of the robbery and shooting. It belonged to the scavenger demon who'd worn the mask when he'd broken into Love's to steal and murder.

The scavenger stood and moved to the center of the room. The two hellhounds turned their ugly heads to watch him. He gave them each a stroke as he passed by.

"Who are you?" Santo asked.

"Gary," he said, holding out a hand to shake, a salesman's smile on his pasty face.

Santo ignored the gesture.

Gary had skin so white it glowed and eyes so pale they resembled the hellhounds' eerie orbs. He wore a black turtleneck that couldn't hide the angry rash blistering the underside of his chin and ringing his hairline. Black pants and heavy boots finished his outfit. His hands looked disconnected as they moved in the dark.

"You need a cape," Santo said, just to irritate him. Not the smartest thing he'd ever done, but he figured he'd already sunk his own ship. If this scavenger demon knew he was here on earth, the end was written.

Outside, the raven laughed at his joke.

The demon smiled thinly. "We have a problem, you and I," he said.

"We have several," Santo agreed.

"I want the woman."

Santo had known it was coming, but the words filled him with a sick rage that he couldn't control.

"That is a problem. You can't have her."

Gary smiled and the two hounds growled and licked

their gruesome chops. A locust hopped across the sliding door track and landed near Santo's bare feet. One of the hounds lunged to snap it up.

"Is the reaper in love?" Gary mocked. "Does the reaper think he can live happily ever after with his new toy?"

"She's not a toy and you can't have her," Santo said coldly.

"Are we role-playing? Have you cast yourself as the hero coming to her rescue? That's beautiful. Really. I might need a tissue."

"You might need a bullet between your eyes."

The scavenger only smiled. "What is your plan, reaper?"

Santo would be damned if he told this scavenger that he didn't have one. "I came to reap her," he said instead.

"And decided to have a quick fuck first?"

His eyes narrowed. "Not your business."

"Oh, I guarantee you it is, reaper." He paused. "I'm sure you've heard of Abaddon?"

"Fuck you."

"Will you show me the same good time you did Roxy?" he asked with another smile.

"Fuck off."

"We need to reach an understanding. You are a reaper. *I* am Abaddon's ambassador."

Santo laughed. "You keep telling yourself that."

"Abaddon is interested in your human."

Santo said nothing. His hand itched for his gun as the need to kill this scavenger swelled within him. The biggest of the hounds gave him a snarling warning, feeling Santo's aggression in the air. The hound wasn't tall enough to look him in the eye, but Santo was unarmed. It could chomp him down to bite-sized pieces and he'd have little defense.

"You think you can kill me, reaper?" the scavenger said in a thin voice. "Do you think a bullet would stop me?"

"I'm willing to give it a try if you are."

The scavenger opened his arms and grinned. "Hit me with your best shot."

Santo didn't want to admit he'd lost his gun, but the scavenger guessed.

"No weapon? What a shame. There goes your only opportunity." He dropped his arms and his expression grew hard. "Now. When do you plan to reap your little human?"

"Again. Not your fucking business."

"You do plan to carry out this reaping, though?"

Santo's throat felt hot. His mouth so dry he could barely swallow.

"Because Abaddon would prefer to see it done soon. And right this time."

"Why does Abaddon care whether Roxanne lives or dies?" Santo asked when he already knew the answer.

"It's nice here. We like it. Abaddon's bags are all packed and he's ready to come join us for a long, long visit."

"It's not a resort, scavenger."

"Then why are you on vacation, reaper? You are here for *one* reason. To reap Roxanne Love. But you've lost your way. I'm going to help you find it."

"Abaddon can't have her."

"Wrong again, reaper. Abaddon can have whatever he fucking wants. Are you hearing me now? This can play two ways. The first, you get what you want. The second, you lose it all."

Another locust hopped in from the balcony. The scavenger ground it into the carpet and wiped his boot. One of the hounds snuffled and licked at the squashed remains. The other kept its eyes on Santo.

"Abaddon wants your human gone. He assumes you have a plan to take her *and* keep her this time. It's been poor work you've done up until this point."

Santo watched him, saying nothing.

"I would like to report back that you have the situation under control. He'll want details, however. Let's not make him ask. What do you intend? Beheading?"

Santo's stomach turned. In the beginning, he'd planned for fire. After Roxanne's fourth death, he'd fully intended to take her body and turn them both to ash, releasing him from his corporeal form and preventing Roxanne from ever returning to hers. The thought of doing that now made his skin grow cold and his heart stutter painfully.

"Fire?" the scavenger said hopefully.

Something in his face gave Santo away. The scavenger smiled.

"Fire is an excellent plan. No ambiguity there. No miracle surgery to put her back together again. Abaddon will approve of the method."

"I don't need Abaddon's approval. It's not going to happen. No one hurts Roxanne."

"Wrong answer, reaper. Two choices, remember? Door number one, you take her. You reap her. You keep her. Easy peasy. But door number two . . . that one is not so great. You see, if you try to save your precious human, Abaddon will strip her from you. He will make her his."

Santo gritted his teeth, refusing to comment. Refusing to give credence to anything the scavenger said.

"No one knows what you've done yet, reaper. No one in the Beyond has missed you yet, insignificant being that you are. But if you defy him, Abaddon will make sure you pay."

Santo stared him down, stoic. Not showing a hint of the fear he felt.

"But it won't be just you who is punished. He will make sure that your human dies and when her soul is free, he will snatch it up and take it unto himself. Do you understand what that means?"

He understood. He wished he didn't, but he couldn't conceal the horror he felt.

"You and Roxanne will still be together for all of eternity, both guests of a prison you'll never escape. You can share in the torture. And make no mistake, it will be torture. Day in, day out."

Santo could face Abaddon by himself. He'd known it waited for him as soon as he heard the ravens speaking in his head. But Roxanne? Sweet, beautiful Roxanne? Imprisoned in a place that made hell seem like paradise?

"So there you have it," the scavenger said. "Reap her yourself or watch her be punished for your cowardice. There are no other choices."

"She's not meant to die again," he said, latching onto the fact with both hands. Her fourth death had come and gone and he had no knowledge of when the fifth death might await her. Perhaps years from now when she was an old woman, asleep in her bed. If he took her out of turn, there'd be repercussions.

A fervent hope lodged in his chest that even Abaddon had to abide by the natural order of life and death. Such rules were policed in the Beyond. If he broke them, he'd be tipping his hand, showing the powers that had imprisoned him that he plotted an escape.

The scavenger seemed to know what Santo was thinking. He shook his head.

"Only a fool would implicate Abaddon."

Or a desperate man.

"Reaping Roxanne before her time would draw attention that even Abaddon couldn't avoid," Santo said with more confidence than he felt.

A great wheel of logic spun in the back of his head, pointing out that the scavenger demon had killed others that night in the kitchen of Love's. Santo didn't understand how he'd gotten away with it, though.

"Killing her will draw attention to *you,* reaper," the scavenger answered. "Only you. It's a risk you'll have to take."

Santo's fingers curled into his fists as he searched for another option. He glanced at the balcony. The locusts had accumulated on the glass, blotting out the fat moon and stars. Through the open door, he saw the raven watching with its humanlike eyes. Anything he did, it would see. If the raven saw it, so would Abaddon.

And then there were the hellhounds. They watched their master with bright, fixated eyes. Santo would never get to the scavenger before the hellhounds got to *him.*

He took a deep breath and tried to settle his thoughts, his fears. Panic wouldn't get him out of this mess. He needed to use his brains and his newfound human instincts.

"It sounds like Roxanne scared him pretty bad," Santo said calmly.

The scavenger narrowed his eyes. "Abaddon does not scare."

"No? Then why is he so worried about her?"

"Can't you guess?"

Yeah. He could. But he'd rather make the scavenger spell it out just in case he had it wrong.

"Abaddon has been looking for a way in. He's found it at last. A way in for all of his creatures. He'll tolerate no roadblocks."

Roxanne was more than a roadblock. She could shut it all down—unless someone took her out of the picture completely.

Why was Abaddon giving Santo the option to do it himself? Why didn't this scavenger do the job right now?

He glanced at the raven again. Had the birds told Abaddon how she'd banished them? Was the scavenger afraid she could do it to him? Did they need Santo to end her life because they were all afraid of her?

And what about her brother? Where did that leave Reece Love?

"What do you plan to do with Reece?" he asked.

"He has his role. It's not complicated."

"Dying? Is that it?"

"Dying without his sister. A detail that can't be ignored," the scavenger confirmed. "So what will you do, reaper? What will *your* role be?"

Santo shook his head, unable to see an out from any of this. If he tried to stop it, if he tried to save Roxanne, Abaddon would find another way to take her, manipulate another human or demon to finish the job. Then he'd torture her soul for all time. The only way to save her from that was to kill her himself and take her back to the darkness with him.

It had been his plan from the start. Only now . . . only now how could he even think of doing it? Of snuffing out the beautiful light that she carried inside her? How could he survive knowing he'd never touch her again? Never hold her, kiss her, listen to the sounds she made when he made love to her?

"This is almost fun," the scavenger said, watching him with amused eyes.

"When does it need to be done?" Santo asked softly.

"Tomorrow." The scavenger looked at the clock glowing on the microwave. "Make that today. A messenger will come and tell you where."

"Why don't you tell me now?"

The scavenger shook his head. "Bring the human. Put an end to her existence. You'll feel better for it. Ignore my warning, and roast in the fires of Abaddon, knowing you've condemned her soul to the same."

He moved to the door, hounds following obediently, and paused to look back. With a smile that turned Santo's blood to ice, the scavenger reached inside his jacket and pulled out a gun.

"Looks like you need this more than I do," he said, holding it out.

Santo stared at the gun, stunned that the scavenger would risk giving it to him.

"You can't kill me," the scavenger said calmly. "I am protected by Abaddon. Feel free to try, though. I promise the doggies won't bite unless I tell them to."

Santo reached for the weapon but the scavenger held it back. "Just remember, you may have reaped a human or two and shot a couple of pooches, but you'll lose if you try to take me on, reaper. It's a verifiable fact."

The scavenger handed Santo the gun and was through the door and gone in an instant.

The dream felt so real that Roxanne wondered if she might actually be awake. Her eyes opened in a dark room. After a disoriented moment, she recognized it. Reece's condo, his spare bedroom. She turned her head, looking for Santo but the pillow beside her was empty.

She sensed herself curled on her side, sleeping, but it felt as if she rose from the bed.

"Santo?" she called—or thought she did. The dream made her voice sound strange.

When no one answered, she found the sweatshirt she'd worn before Santo had stripped her naked and put it on. Her panties were on the floor at the end of the bed. She bent to pull them on, and a flash of red caught her eye. She straightened so quickly that she almost fell.

There at the door stood Manny. Manny, her friend,

the dishwasher she'd last seen sprawled on the floor in a puddle of blood.

They stared at each other, Roxanne braced against the footboard, panties around her ankles. Manny looked embarrassed to have caught her undressed.

"Sorry," he whispered and stepped into the hall.

Roxanne quickly yanked her underwear up and followed. "Manny?" she said softly.

"Over here," Manny said.

She turned to find him standing in the kitchen. Hidden by shadows he looked like a child, his soft, slack features making him appear younger than his thirty years. The rolled-up jeans sagged around his sneakers. His Iron Man T-shirt had a large hole in the middle, and a dark stain spread out from the center where he'd been shot.

As she watched, he seemed to fade.

"Manny?" she whispered.

Her voice brought him back into focus. "Heya, Rossanne."

Rossanne, because he could never pronounce the *x* sound correctly.

"What are you doing here, Manny?"

He tilted his head and gave a small shrug. "Looking for you."

She took a step closer, and Manny became translucent. She stilled and he solidified again. "Where have you been?" she asked cautiously.

"Around. I'm not really sure. Have you seen my mom?"

Roxanne shook her head. "I've been a little busy."

"I know. I saw."

A faint stirring came from behind her. She glanced over her shoulder, and the shadows slithered back and settled contemplatively. When she turned around, Manny stood closer.

"Are you here alone, Manny?" she asked.

He didn't answer. Instead he gave her the sweet smile she'd seen on his face so many times before. "Do you remember my birthday?" he said.

"Which one?"

"When we went to the zoo place."

He meant the Rainforest Café in the mall. They'd taken him there when he turned twenty-six and every year after. He'd delighted in the crazy animated jungle animals and their random activity. For him, the place had been magical with all its fake screeches, canned roars, and hollow trumpeting.

"I remember."

"They're going to tell you to go there."

"Who, Manny?"

"You made them maaad." He drew it out like a naughty little boy.

"Who's they?"

"But they got Reece, so I guess you better go."

"Are you talking about the man who shot you?"

Manny tilted his head and blinked at her.

"Do you remember my birthday?" he repeated.

"Yeah. I remember. We had fun."

"We can have fun again," he said earnestly.

"Sure."

His face went blank as he nodded and Roxanne wanted to weep. A part of her had been holding a tight ball of hope in her chest that Manny and the others would be found. That they would survive this, just as she had. But as she watched Manny's figure fade and warble, she knew that would never happen.

"Manny," she said gently. "Where you are . . . do you see a light?"

For her, the light had always led her away from the darkness and back to life, but she knew that others believed it guided them on to heaven. When she'd been younger, she'd read every account of life after death she could, trying to find the reasons for what happened to her. Most told of similar experiences. In death, they were reunited with loved ones and they saw a light. They knew they should follow it.

Roxanne had never understood why, for her, it had been the opposite.

Manny was the purest of spirits, though. She had to assume that for him there would be a guiding beam waiting to take him to heaven.

"I saw *your* light," he said happily. "You scared the birds, didn't you, Rossanne?"

Startled, she said, "You saw that?"

"And the monsters. They were plenty mad about that."

"Who? Who is this *they* you keep talking about?"

"He's going to send me," Manny said, suddenly serious. Intent. He focused hard and his struggle to impress her with the importance of what he said touched her. It frightened her, too.

"He can kill you," Manny said. "Forever."

Roxanne's throat felt tight. "How do you know?"

"I hear him." Manny's jaw moved as he sought his next words. "He's going to use me. But it's not me."

He shook his head, trying to articulate his thoughts. She'd seen him do it dozens of times before. Grief bubbled up from a steaming well as she realized she'd never see it again.

"It's not *me*," Manny finally said in an angry tone. "It's *not me*."

"It's not you," she repeated, her voice thick.

The words seemed to echo and her dream world clouded. Manny no longer stood in front of her.

Roxanne opened her eyes. She was alone in bed, in the spare room at Reece's condo. A glimmer of light shone through the pulled shades. Dawn.

She let out a shaky breath and ran her fingers through her hair, trying to slow her heart and ease the ache inside it. Nightmare or vision? Which had it been?

She climbed out of bed, pulled on her clothes, and stepped into the hall, where a cold wind whisked down the corridor and sent chills through her. Surprised, she padded down to the front of the condo.

Santo stood in front of the open sliding door wearing his faded jeans and the weight of the world on his bunched shoulders. She could see it in the way he braced his hands against the door frame, in the way his head hung low as he stared at his feet. A gun stuck out of his pants, resting against the hollow of his back. Where had he found it? His muscles flexed slowly as he gripped and eased his hold on the door.

"Santo?" she said softly.

He turned so quickly, she jumped. His eyes were red-rimmed and desperate.

"What's going on?" she asked. "What are you doing?"

He gave her his back again. "Watching the sunrise," he said.

She came to his side so she could see, too, feeling the tension radiating off him. On the horizon, a froth of pink and orange reached across the sky, poking fingers at the underbelly of a thin overcast.

She slipped her arms around Santo and pressed close. "You're freezing. How long have you been out here?"

He said nothing, his eyes deep and troubled as he looked down at her. "We need to talk," he said.

The sound of a key at the front door interrupted before she could agree. They both turned and Santo grabbed Roxanne's hand, pulling her after him. He paused long enough to snatch a throw pillow off the couch, before tucking himself and Roxanne behind the front door just as it opened.

"Where'd you find your gun?" she asked.

"Later," he said.

Once again, he used his body to shield her from whatever came through it. She peered around his shoulder, watching a shadow stretch across the foyer floor as a man stepped inside.

Even if he hadn't been dressed in jeans, rolled at the cuffs, and an Iron Man T-shirt, she would have known it was Manny by the way he stood so uncertainly on the tile entryway, by the way his head cocked to the side like a curious bird, by the way his words from the dream echoed in her head.

It's not me.

He turned and spotted her and Santo behind the door. Santo had his gun in one hand, using the other to hold the pillow around it. The gun was pointed at Manny's head.

Her friend frowned at it, trying to muster a shy smile. His eyes were shadowed, his face dirty and splattered with blood. He'd been crying. Tear tracks streaked his cheeks and his lashes had a stiff, salted look. He took a halting step toward them, and she saw the desire to run into her arms in his expression. Fear of the man beside her stopped him.

"Rossanne," he said. "It's me. Manny."

Like she hadn't recognized him. Why else would she stay where she was and not greet him? She saw the questions in his eyes.

He had a gap between his front teeth that he poked with his tongue when he was agitated. He did that now, looking so much like the young man she'd called friend, the one she'd worked with for years, that she had to believe the dream had been wrong.

This *was* Manny, no matter what subconscious message her dream had delivered.

Her relief made her knees shake. She started to push past Santo so she could reach her friend, but Santo blocked her with his body.

"It's not him," he said.

"Of course it is."

Santo didn't let her get by.

"It's not Manny. It's a scavenger, Roxanne."

Manny was shaking his head, his eyes round and confused. "What's he mean, Rossanne?"

"I mean you're a fucking demon."

Santo took aim at Manny's head. Roxanne could scarcely believe it. She didn't understand why he thought *Manny* of all people could be a demon. Yet the dream circled in her head. Manny had said they planned to use him.

"He's a demon, Roxanne," Santo repeated.

And then, before she could think, before she realized that he meant to do more than threaten, Santo pulled the trigger and blew a hole through Manny's head.

(28)

Reece paced the small bedroom—*cell*—he'd been allotted. What else could he do? Everything April had told him clotted in his head like an aneurism just waiting to make its move. He'd been used. Bad enough on its own. But he'd been used for something so horrific he couldn't even bring it into focus. When Gary had explained that demons had arrived ready for bear, Reece had resisted. After he'd seen them firsthand, it had been easier to believe.

But demons using Reece's death as a secret passageway? No way the old head would wrap around that one. Yet . . . He could still remember the cold waters of Canyon Lake, where he'd drowned when he was ten. Dad had taken the boat out and the four kids had been swimming, having a day like normal kids instead of being little slaves at the restaurant. He and Roxanne had been playing mermaid—a girl game that she'd loved, so he'd agreed. He'd been the shark, of course.

They'd been laughing when the current had pulled them down. Only it hadn't felt like a current. It had felt like hands, wrapping around his ankles and dragging him into the darkest place he'd ever known.

They'd been resuscitated, obviously, but Reece had never been the same after. He didn't know why, but somewhere in his bottled-up memories, he figured something bad had happened down there. Something worse than dying.

Roxanne had come back serene. He heard Ryan tell Ruby she'd been talking about a friend who'd waited for her. Reece hadn't talked for days.

"Knock, knock."

He spun to find Karen at his door. He remembered thinking her hot the first time he'd met her. Now it was as if he could see what lurked beneath her skin. Not a pretty sight.

And speaking of skin, the rash that April called a symptom of the body's rejection of its captor had made an appearance, darkening Karen's temples and the area beneath her chin. She scratched self-consciously.

"Gary was wondering if you had a minute for him?" she said, like it was really a request.

Reece had something for Gary, all right. But he hoped it would be more permanent than a minute.

"Sure."

He followed Karen down the hall, pausing outside that door marked *Chancellor*, recalling how freaked out he'd been the first time he'd stood there. Turns out he'd had the right of it. He wished he had one of the weapons they'd given him for the dawn battle, but they were locked up again.

"Go on in," Karen said. "Gary will be there in a minute."

Just like the asshole to make him wait.

Reece went in, taking note of the battered desk and weathered bookcase behind it. The surface of the desk was neat and orderly. An in basket with a few receipts in it—Home Depot, Walgreens, and one from a place called The Meat Shop. Reece picked it up and studied the order for beef. He tried not to think about why Gary had need of such large quantities of raw meat.

He glanced at the door before checking the drawers. All locked. On the bookshelf behind him he found a Bible sandwiched between copies of the Book of the Dead and the Book of Mormon. Others teetered or fell on top of one another for the entire length of the shelf. Most of them were in languages Reece didn't understand, but a few had English translations. Something called the Hindu Tantras leaned against the Golden Verses of Pythagoras, and the New Testament shared space with the Book of Invasions. He'd only heard of a handful of the titles he saw, but he could deduce. Sometimes, he even got it right. Gary had himself a collection of religious texts lined up cover to cover with no rhyme or reason Reece could see. Odds were good that Gary had them for all the wrong reasons.

Gary still hadn't come, so Reece kept looking. A computer older than God sat on the desk. Reece shook the mouse, and something in its guts began to grind and wake up. After interminable seconds, the monitor came on with a password prompt. Reece couldn't begin to guess what someone like Gary might use to access his files. He tried *demon* and *twins* and his name and Roxanne's before giving up.

Frustrated, he looked under the giant blotter and tried the drawers again, when he noticed the calendar. It was one of those old ones that came installed in a little tray that looked like a book. Each day had a miniature month depicted at the top and a place on the opposing page for appointments. Like pay phones, they were a thing of another age.

The pages hadn't been turned for a couple of days. Reece stared at a big circle around the date Gary had robbed Love's and shot Reece and the others. He tried to make out the scrawl beneath it but couldn't.

He and Gary had planned the robbery for that night, but now he knew that Gary had had more than that in mind all along. A math equation was in the corner, and listed on the side were the names of his victims. Someone had made little checkmarks next to his,

Jim's, Sal's, and Manny's names. But Roxanne's had a big circle around it and exclamation marks.

"Reece," Gary boomed from the doorway. "How are you today, my friend?"

Rage simmered in Reece's gut, but he forced himself to keep it together. "What's this?" Reece asked, pointing at the calendar page.

"Accounting. What else?"

"Keeping tabs on your victims?"

"I told you, no victims. Look here."

Gary came around the desk, then gripped the back of Reece's neck in a friendly but persistent manner and led him to the window. Outside, training was going on. Gary pointed to the left. Jim and Sal stood opposite Shrek, listening while the other man gave them tactical lessons.

"I told you no one had been hurt," Gary said. "I sent your dishwasher on an errand. Manny, right? He should be back soon."

Reece didn't say anything, but if April had told him the truth—and he believed she had—that really wasn't Sal or Jim out there. It was some fucking demon in their skin. Manny had suffered the same fate.

"Why did you want to see me?"

"You were good this morning. You protected the compound."

Bile rose in Reece's throat, but he forced himself to

ask, "What were those things that we fought? I mean, I know they were demons. I believe you now."

Gary beamed. The effect was terrifying. "So you're on board?"

"Hell, yes. I just want to know when we go for my sister. I can't stand it that she's out there with one of *them*."

"Wise decision, my friend. I'm glad to hear you say it."

The smile didn't falter but it didn't lessen the threat in his tone either. Gary trusted Reece just as much as Reece trusted Gary.

"Those were hellhounds we fought," Gary went on. "Creatures from the bowels of the demon world. Your sister's captor thought they'd destroy us. But he didn't count on you getting in his way, did he?"

"I'm going to make that demon see God," Reece agreed, thinking of Gary when he said it.

Gary laughed. "That's my boy. I have a plan, you'll be glad to know."

"Which is?"

"Your sister has been showing some spunk."

Reece caught himself before he smiled. "She's been accused of that before."

Gary's eyes narrowed. "We've heard rumors that Abaddon has sent his ravens for her."

Ice formed in Reece's gut. "Abaddon? Is that like the devil?"

"No," Gary replied with a merry laugh. "But there

are things in the demon world to fear just as much. Abaddon is the king of such things. He sent the demon that has your sister."

"And now he's sent ravens?" Reece asked. Lost, as usual, in the twists and turns of Gary's conversation.

"And she sent them back."

Reece frowned. "I don't follow."

"There is only one way into this world," Gary said patiently.

"Through this mysterious door my sister and I open and close," Reece said in a bored tone. But that's not how he felt.

"Yes. And Abaddon's ravens were among the first to come through. They've been here years. Years, Reece."

"How many years?" he asked, but he didn't need Gary to tell him the exact date. He could do the math.

"Fifteen."

Fifteen years ago, he and Roxanne had been fished out of a lake and miraculously revived.

"They are sentries. Messengers."

Gary scowled down at his feet, brooding. And suddenly Reece had a moment of understanding, and he thought he grasped what had happened.

Reece didn't even know what this mysterious door was. He had no clue how he opened it by dying and less of an idea about how Roxanne managed to shut it again. But somehow his sister had worked it out. And she'd sent those ravens back to meet their maker.

"So Roxanne figured out how to kick them out. That's good, right?" Reece said, pulling Gary's attention from the floor. Pretending for all he was worth that he and Gary were on the same team.

"Yes, yes. A victory we needed. And now we need to press our advantage."

Reece's face was going to break from the stress of smiling when inside dread roiled and ripped. "Great. What are we going to do?"

"Your sister has shown an exceptional ability. But we need to help her now. We need to give her the chance to work her magic on a bigger scale."

"And how are we going to do that?"

"We have messengers of our own. And we've sent one with an invitation she won't refuse. We've baited our trap, and now we just need to bring the rest of Abaddon's servants to your sister so she can . . . dispose of them in the same way."

For the first time since this conversation began, Reece felt a moment of relief. Yes. That's exactly what they needed to do. But all he'd learned, all he'd realized had brought him to another point, one that settled low inside him and felt . . . *right*.

Roxanne could close the door . . . but what good would that do if he just kept opening it again? Before his sister *worked her magic,* Reece needed to find a way to destroy the only key.

(29)

S anto felt numb, like he'd been encased in an insu-lated sleeve that made everything seem to happen in the distance. He watched the scavenger Roxanne thought was her friend hit the ground, blood splatter-ing everywhere. The gunshot had been muted by the pillow and he hoped it hadn't been heard, but quiet or not, the bullet had done its job. At his side, Roxanne stifled a scream, but the terror in her gasp clenched in-side him.

He closed the door quickly, ignoring her. He couldn't let himself feel her pain. He couldn't let him-self feel anything.

Keeping the pillow wrapped around the gun, he put three more bullets in the scavenger's head, one after an-other until there was nothing left of the young man's skull. A dark shadow oozed out with the blood and scurried across the floor and through the open back door.

Roxanne made a tight, horrified sound, muffled by the hand she'd clapped over her mouth. Without pausing, Santo moved to the bedroom, yanked a blanket off the bed, and came back to cover up the corpse. It didn't do much good. The bloody mess would be burned on his retinas long after he left the human world behind and no longer had eyes with which to see.

Roxanne watched Santo like she would a wild animal suddenly loose at the zoo. The hurt and fear in her eyes nearly destroyed him. He wanted to hand her the gun, to tell her to do the same thing to him. Put a bullet in his head. It's what the real Santo had wanted all along. The reaper had been foolish to think he could play this game of human. He knew that now. But the game was near an end.

He stalked over to Roxanne, grabbed her arm, and took her outside on the balcony, away from the body. It was the only respite he could give her.

"Why did you shoot him?" she demanded.

"Manny was already dead. A demon killed him two nights ago so it could use his body."

The hard, cold fact of it drained the blood from her face. She gave a small "Oh" and swallowed hard, accepting what he said without further questions. Some part of him rejoiced in the simple show of trust. Some part of him raged in fury.

"I didn't know they could do that," she whispered,

covering her face. "I didn't put it together but it explains so much. The missing bodies." Her voice cracked and her shoulders shook. "They would have done the same to me if you hadn't been there, wouldn't they? Use my body like a change of clothes."

She looked at him with big eyes made wet by tears and Santo felt something inside him shut down. He couldn't do it anymore. Wouldn't do it. He refused to keep lying.

"I wasn't there to save you from them," he said harshly, the words like acid in his throat.

"What?"

"I'm not your guardian," he said. "I'm not your angel. I didn't come to save you. Not to protect you. Not to help."

Her breath hitched and her stormy eyes held so much hurt and confusion, it turned him inside out. She shook her head and took a step back. She couldn't go very far, not on the small balcony, but each inch she put between them felt like a blade sliding beneath his ribs.

Last night she'd given herself to him, let him touch that part of her she kept hidden away, and no matter how he wished it different, she'd changed him. Santo Castillo had been under his skin from the first moment. But Roxanne, she'd been growing in his heart for longer than that. He didn't know when or how she'd become so vital to him. He'd told himself that his only reason for coming to this world was to reap her.

He almost laughed now, but the sound would have been bitter. He'd come because in his own twisted and depraved way, he'd loved her from the start. And before Santo had taught him what love really meant, he'd thought that it gave him the right to own her. To take her. To steal her soul and make it his.

But the moments of time with Roxanne, the hours spent living in Santo's skin, had exposed his selfish desire and changed it. Changed him.

"I'm not Santo Castillo," he said at last.

She blinked with surprise and he wondered what she'd been expecting him to say. "Then who are you?" she asked.

"Not who. What."

She still didn't understand. A frown puckered the skin between her brows. She shook her head.

He went on relentlessly. "I chose Santo because he was on the brink, ready to commit suicide. I took him before he killed himself."

"You *took* him?" she said, her voice still tangled in confusion and pain. Was it only yesterday that he'd gazed into her eyes and thought her empathy a weakness? His pain had been hers when he'd spoken of Santo's dead wife.

Now the tables had turned and her pain became his. Sadly, he welcomed it.

"I reaped him, Roxanne. Just as I intended to reap you. That's why I'm here."

"You what? You *reaped him*?"

Her eyes were wide, her lashes spiky from her tears. He kept talking, fighting the emotions inside that made him want to take the words back and spin them another way.

"I came in person to make sure you didn't cheat me again."

Her lips moved silently before she spoke. "You came to kill me?" she asked, her expression bewildered. "Is that what you mean?"

It broke the heart he'd never wanted.

"I'm a reaper. I don't kill. I take."

She glanced over her shoulder at Manny's body laid out on the floor beneath the blanket, her question clear. Blood had already begun to soak through. He'd certainly killed her friend.

"*That* wasn't human," he said dismissively. "It didn't have a soul to reap."

She was still shaking her head, unwilling to believe what he told her.

"You said you were an angel."

"No. *You* said it."

Her chin came up, indignant. "You let me believe it."

"It served my purpose for you to believe that I had your best interest in mind."

She flinched but the dull hurt in her eyes began to burn away as anger filled them. "My best interest?"

She backed up until she hit the railing, watching

him with narrowed eyes. "You killed Santo Castillo?" she said. "Why?"

Was there a way to sugarcoat it? If there was, he didn't know it and it was too late for that anyway.

"I *reaped* him, Roxanne, so I could pretend to be him."

Her recoil nearly brought him to his knees. Only the hand braced on the railing kept him upright. Roxanne swiped her tears from her eyes and glared at him.

More than anything, he wished he could make the truth something other than it was. Not lie, but do it over. Be on the right side of this horrible wrong. She wanted it, too. He could see the plea in her eyes. But he stood at a crossroads that even a reaper could see. If he lied to her now and denied what he was, it would prove to her that she *couldn't* trust him. If he told her the truth, it would be her decision whether or not she *would* trust him. At least there'd be hope that she might. Slim hope, but he held on to it.

"You murdered Santo so you could steal his soul and his body," she said slowly.

"Take."

"*Steal,*" she insisted. "If it was yours to take, we wouldn't be having this conversation."

Leave it to Roxanne to cut to the quick.

Santo said, "He planned to kill himself. He had a gun in his mouth and he was pulling the trigger. I stepped in just before he blew his brains out."

"But he might have stopped on his own. He might have changed his mind."

"He wanted to die. He wasn't going to stop until he succeeded. I was there to reap him, one way or another."

"One way or another," she murmured.

She shook her head, and something dawned in her expression, an answer to a riddle she'd been puzzling, a dark clue to a desperate crime.

"That means . . . You're just like *them,* aren't you? The one that took Manny and turned him into . . ."

She couldn't finish, and the loathing he saw on her face made him want to turn away in shame. He forced himself to face her revulsion and bear the weight of it.

She thought he was like the scavenger demon. He saw now how close to the truth she'd come. He'd fooled himself into thinking his purpose made him better. But when boiled down, his sins were no less. His choices just as wrong.

"And what was last night?" Roxanne demanded. "An added bonus to your game of pretend? Fuck like a human?"

He couldn't hold her gaze or stop the heat that suffused his face. "I know you don't believe that, *angelita.*"

"Don't call me that!" she shouted, her voice loud in the quiet dawn.

Santo looked around warily. Maybe the gunshot hadn't been heard but coupled with screaming, someone was bound to investigate. He took her arm and hauled her inside, closing the door behind them. Manny's body on the floor scorned him, so he pulled her down the hall, avoiding the bedroom and its memories in favor of the bathroom. He shut the door behind them.

Roxanne shook him off and took a step away. Her voice trembling with anger, she said, "You reaped an innocent man so you could steal his body. You *killed him* because it was convenient."

"Convenient?" he repeated bitterly. He'd had no idea he'd be stepping into such a fucked-up lost cause, or that the human could possibly touch him, impact him. *Change* him. "It's like riding a roller coaster, all the feelings. There was nothing convenient about it."

"How can I believe anything you say?"

"Because I *hate* saying it. Because I hate *you* hearing it. If telling you another lie would fix this problem, I'd be doing that right now. But it won't. All that's left is the truth."

"Everything you told me about your wife. About how lost you felt. It wasn't even you. You never even *knew* her."

"I knew her," he said.

"Why? Did you *reap* her, too?"

At his wince she cried, "You did? You killed her and her *baby*. Did you do it to make Santo miserable so you could use his body?"

"I knew her because Santo knew her," he said grimly.

"It doesn't work that way. You don't get his life by associat—"

"It does work that way," he said sharply, slamming his hand on the counter, suddenly so angry he could hardly speak. "I didn't know it at the time, but it does. It bleeds over. The way he talked. His thoughts. His memories." He looked into her eyes. "The way it feels to be in his skin. I might have begun separate, but that part is long gone."

"And what does that make you?" she asked.

Mouth dry, he shook his head and looked away. "Fucked."

She studied him, those eyes lit with anger and intelligence, shadowed with hurt and shock.

"You thought you'd be stronger than him," she breathed.

"Yeah. I did."

She leaned her hip against the counter and contemplated that.

"I can close my eyes and see the places he went," he said in a rough voice. "Smell the air. Picture the people we loved."

"We."

"I feel what he feels. He wants what I want."

"And what is that?"

You. It burned through him like a flash fire, urging

him to reach out *now*. To touch her while his senses burned, *now*. To light her up with the same inferno *right now*.

He swallowed hard and lowered his eyes, but instead of a distraction, his gaze caught on the soft rise and fall of her chest, the way the big sweatshirt clung to the curve of her breasts.

"So all this was—what you did to Santo—it was all because of the door thing? The door I didn't even know about? You came here, stole another man's identity, and wrecked my life because of that? Why didn't you just kill me like you did him?"

He met her eyes again, not letting her look away. "Before the other night, you'd died three times, Roxanne. Who do you think was waiting for you on the other side?"

She stilled and her breath caught. His answer had shaken her. Good. She'd been rattling his cage from the start. He couldn't see her when she came to him in the darkness, but he could feel her. Her life, her light. For those brief moments in time, he'd been able to imagine what it might feel like to stand in the sun and bask in its warmth.

"That was you?" she whispered.

He nodded.

Her eyes widened and color rushed to her face. "But you weren't there the last time," she blurted.

"That time, I was here. Still waiting," he said simply. *Always* waiting.

"It was me waiting for you in the darkness, but every time you just slipped away," he said huskily. "Finally, I couldn't bear it anymore. I came to see for myself why you were able to cheat death. To cheat me."

"So that's it?" she asked in a wounded voice. "I bruised your enormous ego so you decided to make me *pay*?"

"You know it was more than that."

"I don't know anything about you except you stole someone's body like you were hot-wiring a car."

"I know," he said. He took a step forward, encouraged when she didn't retreat. "I understand that now. I swear to you, Santo *was* ready to die. I'm in here with him. I know. I'm not excusing what I did, Roxanne. It was wrong. But I'm not sorry. I did us both a favor."

She grew quiet again. Thinking. More than anything, he wished he could pry into that head of hers and find the secret decoder to her thoughts. But she remained a mystery to him. An enigma he longed to understand.

"All I knew," he said, putting it on the line, "was that I had to come for you. It just took me a while to figure it out."

She blinked those beautiful eyes, but she didn't hide them as her silence called him a fool.

"And no matter what happens next, I'd do it again."

Her breath hitched softly. "When did you reach that decision?"

"The moment you opened that pretty mouth and made me question everything I thought I knew."

Her color deepened. "Is that the truth?" she asked.

"As God is my witness."

She turned her back on him, staring at the white knuckled fingers gripping the sink. "So what now? Should I *put my affairs in order* so you can take me back to the darkness with you?"

"No."

"You don't want my soul anymore?"

"No," he whispered.

"Then what *do* you want, Santo?"

As much as he wished for it, the question didn't dance with innuendo. It came at him straight on and fast. She wanted an answer, and he would never get what he truly desired without first giving it.

"You," he said simply. "A life with you. How did you put it? I want to be like everyone else. And I want that with you."

The deep throb of emotion in the words rattled his precarious sense of self, but he met her gaze in the mirror and didn't look away. He didn't let her look away either.

She stared back, her eyes shadowed but no longer hard. He could see the battle going on inside her. She'd been pretending to be normal her entire life, and now a reaper—a reaper who'd come to hunt her, who'd stayed to protect her, who'd *fallen in love with her*—asked that

she embrace something so far from normal that it boggled the mind.

"I've been living alone in death for far too long. I
want to stay."

And there it was. That elusive idea that he'd been
sidestepping and evading from the start. It had been
lurking like a creeping shadow since that very first moment when he'd been galvanized by the storm of Roxanne's eyes.

"You want to stay," she murmured.

"Yes."

But it went so much deeper than that, and the idea
that she knew it, that she understood, tugged at him
like an anchor giving way. He felt the soft suction of his
hold dislodging, and the dizzying *whir* of being towed
up. Up. To an unknown he couldn't grasp.

He followed it nonetheless, taking another step
closer to Roxanne, breathing in her intoxicating scent,
yearning for so much more. He turned her to face him.

"How will you do that?" she asked. "Are you allowed to stay?"

"No," he answered.

Her lashes lifted, her eyes flashed, striking a chord
within him that zinged through every cell in his body.
If he kissed her now, she wouldn't stop him. He saw
that in the golds and grays. But he wanted more than
compliance. He wanted it all.

He braced his hands on either side of her and waited.

She caught her bottom lip with her teeth, but she made no attempt to escape his loosely constructed cage.

"I'm sorry I lied to you," he said. "I won't do it again."

She nodded uncertainly.

"Even though I want to."

"Why?" she asked.

He took a deep breath and slowly let it out. "The scavenger demon who shot you, the one with the mask . . . he was here while you were asleep. He told me he'd be sending a messenger. I knew when Manny walked through the door what he was."

He could see the questions forming in her mind.

"I knew he was a demon the same way Manny knew *I* wasn't human."

She swallowed hard and nodded for him to continue.

"You rattled Abaddon's cage when you sent back his birds, Roxanne. Now he's scared."

"Of *me*?"

"That you'll mess up his plans to take over the world."

She snorted.

"I'm not joking. He confirmed my theory. Each time your brother has died, demons have found a way in. Each time you die, they find a closed door. The only way to keep you from closing the door that Reece opens is to destroy you—no coming back. Without you, they can keep it open forever."

She sagged, her hands braced on the edge of the sink all that kept her upright. Santo lifted her and set her on the counter, moving to stand between her legs, hands on her thighs, making it clear that he wouldn't let her go.

Without looking at him, she asked, "Why am I still alive, then? Why didn't that demon kill me in my sleep? Did you stop him?"

"Not exactly."

He'd started down this path armed with anger, thinking he might goad himself into carrying out the deed and have it done with before there was time to regret. Now he knew he couldn't. Wouldn't. Ever.

"When they let us go the night they broke into your restaurant, I had the idea that they didn't know what I was or what you could do. The scavenger shot you, intending to rip out your soul and leave it to wander aimlessly for all of time. He meant for your body to be occupied. By a demon. That was the fate that your friends endured."

She caught her bottom lip and bit down hard.

"But I was there and I screwed their plan by saving you. Now that they know what we both are, they're afraid. Especially after you sent Abaddon's ravens back to the Beyond. They don't know how you did it."

"I don't know how I did it. It was your voice that guided me. I kept hearing you telling me to come back to you and I knew if I didn't get rid of the birds, I wouldn't be able to."

Her soft words wrapped around his heart and squeezed. He cupped her face and kissed her. He couldn't stop himself.

"Maybe that's all you need to know," he said against her lips. "That I'll always be waiting for you. You're not alone in this, *angelita*. Maybe we do it together."

She caught her breath and leaned forward, resting her forehead on his shoulder. The gesture held exhaustion and defeat, but it held something else as well. Hope. He felt it in the air between them. It filled him up and made him strong.

"They still want you dead. They want me to reap you and clear the way for their invasion. They gave me a choice," he said, pulling on her shoulders until she sat back and looked into his eyes. "I can take you myself and bring you back to the darkness as mine. Or we try to fight and risk burning forever in the fires of Abaddon."

She stared at him as she digested that. "There's no door number three?"

"Earlier, I would have said no. But now I'm not so sure."

She waited for him to go on, that hope growing in her gaze.

"When someone is going to die, a reaper knows,"

he said in a low voice. "They feel it, a stirring. A calling. And they answer it."

He waited, so afraid she'd turn away. So afraid he would see fear in her eyes. Or revulsion. It would break him.

"The reaper moves between the Beyond and earth at will. There's no door, no passageway. It is intended, the reaper's presence at death. It violates no rules. Do you understand?"

She nodded, though he wasn't certain she did.

"I've reaped a million souls in my existence, yet I only remember you. I held you in my arms for your first breath and I was changed."

"What are you saying?"

"All these years I've thought you cheated me. But, Roxanne, what if it was *my* doing? What if I sent you back?"

A tear spilled over her lashes. "Why would you do that?"

Santo smiled, his heart so full he couldn't contain it.

"So I could follow you," he said in an unsteady voice. "So I could follow."

(30)

Santo's words washed over Roxanne, as warm as the darkness where he'd waited for her so many times. How could she distrust what she saw in his eyes when it spoke to her on every level? He'd saved her, challenged her, and now he claimed he'd re-created himself, just for her.

"Roxanne," he said softly, "I would die for you."

And there it was, a declaration that could have been written in blood. In the space of a few days, Santo had gone from stranger to angel to lover to reaper who'd held her heart for every second of death, every moment of life.

What did she do with this man who told her he'd defied the laws of the Beyond to be with her—*to reap her*—now that he didn't mean to reap her anymore?

Santo's eyes were so full that she was drowning in everything she saw there. She cupped his face with her hands, needing to feel him with more than her heart.

"I could never hurt you," he said. "You have to believe that. Even when I thought I'd come to take you, I knew deep inside that I could never put out that beautiful light that shines inside you."

Her tears blurred her vision and clogged her throat, making it impossible to speak.

"Don't leave me, *angelita*," he said. "Please don't leave me."

His plea broke the bonds that held her back. Leave him? She couldn't imagine life without him now that she'd had him beside her, at her back. Protecting her. Loving her.

You cried when you left it the last time, Ryan had said. She believed him.

She knew a side of Santo that he didn't know himself. The presence that had touched her soul and made it stronger. He gave a piece of himself each time he let her go. And he did let her go.

Because she wouldn't have left him if he'd fought for her. Even then, he must have known he wanted more, and to get it, he had to set her free.

So I could follow.

Come back to me.

"I won't leave you," Roxanne told him now. "I won't leave you again."

He grabbed her up in his arms and held her tight against his chest. She felt his tears as he buried his face in the crook between her neck and shoulder. Her own tears streamed down her cheeks.

When Santo kissed her, he tasted of salt and reprieve, a man who'd seen everything he cared for slipping away and had only just realized he need only tighten his grip to keep it. She pressed her nose to his chest and breathed in the scent of him, holding it in her lungs, in her heart. He gave her his kiss like he gave her his life. A pledge, an act, a moment shared for all of eternity.

Every kind of horror imaginable waited outside their closed door, but right now there was only Santo, his arms holding her, his mouth soft against hers. Opening the door meant letting in reality. They kept it closed and made love right there on the bathroom counter. Santo with his pants at his knees, Roxanne with her underwear discarded on the floor.

But when he joined his body with hers, time stood still and all that existed was this man she'd fallen in love with while running for her life. He'd risked the fires of Abaddon to find her.

She was willing to risk more to keep him.

Roxanne resisted facing the world outside their small sanctuary for as long as possible, but finally, with obvious reluctance, Santo led her out. Reality and a future that included demons awaited, no matter how much she wanted to pretend they didn't.

Before they left Reece's condo, Santo insisted on damage control.

"There's a small chance we might get out of this," he told her. "The less we leave behind, the better."

He used bleach to wipe down all surfaces, including the gun that the scavenger had given him. After it was clean, he left it on the blanket covering Manny. She could tell he hated leaving it behind, but as they'd acknowledged too many times, bullets would not win this showdown, and keeping the gun would tie him to what the police would see as the cold-blooded murder of an innocent, disabled victim.

Roxanne washed the bedding in the spare room, using more bleach at his insistence. While they waited for the sheets to dry, Santo told her about Gary's visit and explained the deal he'd offered in more detail.

"I knew when I heard the key in the door that it was the messenger he promised," Santo told her. "I didn't want to give Manny the chance to say where the meeting would be. I was too afraid. I knew you'd want to go if you thought there was a chance your brother would be there."

"It doesn't matter," Roxanne said. "Remember in your hotel when I thought I saw Manny sitting in the corner?"

He nodded.

"It was his spirit. He never moved on to heaven."

"He won't either. The demons made sure of that."

Roxanne swallowed hard, unbearably sad to think of her friend lost between worlds.

"Manny came to me in a dream," Roxanne went on, explaining what Manny had said to her while she was sleeping. "I should have known when he walked in the door that he couldn't be the Manny I knew, but I wanted to believe he was still alive."

Santo pulled her against his chest and pressed his lips to her temple.

"They're going to be at the mall," she said in a small voice.

"The mall?" Santo repeated, surprised. "Why there?"

"I don't know. I guess if Gary intended for Manny to be my guide, he had to pick a place I'd believe. There's a restaurant there that Manny always loved. We took him to it for his birthday every year. If Manny were alive and asked to go to his favorite place in the world, it would be there."

Santo nodded gravely. "So what now, *angelita*? Is that where we should go?"

"Gary thinks his message was delivered. He'll be expecting us."

"Not really. You saw the shade—the demon inside

Manny. It left him when his body couldn't be used any-more. I'd wager the scavenger knows that his messenger is dead."

Roxanne took a deep breath. "Manny said Reece would be there."

The look Santo gave her made her want to cry. There was so much sympathy in it that she knew his next words would hurt.

"If Reece has been with the demons all this time . . . he might not be Reece anymore."

"No. I would feel it."

"How?"

"You asked me once if I felt Reece with me in the darkness. I told you, I sense him. And I sense him in life, too. Two halves, one whole. Twins, remember?"

"Good and evil?"

"A little of both in each. I won't leave my brother to fight this battle alone, Santo."

He nodded. "Then we go."

Arizona Mills mall, where the Rainforest Café was located, sat squarely on a mile of property bordering the college district on one side and the weirdly "old Mexico" town of Guadalupe on the other. One of the last indoor malls to be built before the dawning of the boutique-style outdoor shopping center, the Mills consisted of over one hundred eighty shops and restaurants in one climate-controlled location.

In short, chaos confined.

Over the years, it had become a favorite of teenagers, gangbangers, and a seedy element that followed bargains in a herd. Roxanne remembered that it had always been crowded, and today was no exception.

When they'd pulled into the lot, only a few clouds had covered the autumn sky. Since then, more had gathered, and now they blocked out the sun, leaving everything below bathed in an aggressive gloom that made Roxanne feel unsettled and skittish.

"I don't like this," Santo said for the second time.

In truth, Roxanne didn't either.

But if there was a chance Reece would be here, she couldn't ignore it. She needed to talk to him, tell him what he was dealing with. And if he already knew, well then, she needed to talk him back to sanity.

They'd arrived just as the mall opened, and now they waited in Jorge's truck, eyeing the entrance to Manny's favorite restaurant from a distance. With Halloween just a few days away and the holiday season bearing down on them, the parking lot was already full, and more cars seemed to be arriving by the minute.

"Is it always like this?" Santo asked.

"It's always crowded, but I don't think I've ever seen it this packed."

A minivan pulled up to the curb and emptied its cargo of screaming, giggling girls. Behind it, another did the same. Roxanne saw a pack of adolescents trudging up from one of the far lots, and as she turned in her seat, she took note of a dozen more making their chattering, laughing, squealing way inside. She rolled down her window and leaned out.

"Excuse me," she called. "Can you tell me what's going on today?"

"Justin Bieber!" two of them screamed at once and burst into excited laughter.

"Here?" Roxanne said, surprised. "At the mall?"

The girls squealed and shrieked at her question, then they all started talking at once. Roxanne was able to glean that he'd announced a surprise visit just that morning and he'd be signing autographs and taking pictures with fans. No concert, but who cared, if they got to meet him? *See* him *in person!*

While Roxanne's unease ratcheted up a notch or two, the teenagers screamed some more, jumping up and down like four-year-olds at Disneyland. They moved on, talking so fast that she wondered how they understood each other.

Santo looked at her with raised brows.

She said, "Would you feel better if we were waiting for Reece in a dark alley? At least we know what we're getting into. We know he'll be here. We know it's a ploy. So now we just have to figure out how to keep from getting trapped."

He let out a deep breath, eyeing yet another carload of teenagers. "I don't like it. What if they've found another way to get to you? A way to destroy you that won't link your death back to them?"

"Well, that's not really going to work for me," she said with a lame smile.

She surprised a laugh out of him. "I can't say I'm on

board with it either." He drummed his fingers on the dash. "There's just too much we don't know."

Yeah. Like how to fight back.

"In and out, Santo. That's what we agreed to. I only need a few minutes with Reece. I have to know what's going on before we leave."

If they were able to leave. Neither said it, though.

He sighed. "All right. So what now? Sit here all day, or go in?"

"Go in."

He gave a short nod and reached for the door. "Just stay with me, okay? No running off."

"I'm not thirteen, Santo. I'm not going to see Justin Bieber and race across the mall to tackle him."

He didn't even smile at that. Worry pulled at his brows and tightened his lips.

"There are at least a thousand people here today, Santo. What can they do in such a public place?"

This time the look he gave her actually spoke. They could do a million things. She knew the truth of it even if she chose not to acknowledge it.

Anxiously, she scanned the faces of the other people walking toward the mall. A part of her feared she and Santo wouldn't find her brother. That something horrible would happen to him before she came close. And a part of her feared that what they'd find wouldn't resemble her brother anymore—just like Santo had warned.

Either way, Roxanne had to believe that Reece

didn't know what he'd gotten himself into with the scavengers.

Or at least, not until it was too late.

A long trailer with a radio station logo on its side was parked at an angle near the mall entrance. A table had been set up out front, and two DJs wearing head-phones broadcasted live. A crowd had gathered, shout-ing, putting hands in the air to catch the T-shirts they shot out of a big tube. Music blared out of king-sized speakers.

"That's right," one of the DJs announced. "You heard it exclusively here. Bieber Fever at Arizona Mills!" The screams nearly ruptured Roxanne's eardrums.

The café that Manny loved could only be accessed from inside the mall. Roxanne and Santo circled to the left and came in by the movie theaters and the food court, where the scent of caramel corn and french fries mingled with hot pretzels, corn dogs, and pizza. The shoppers all buzzed with excitement, teenaged girls bouncing in anticipation of Justin's arrival and their male counterparts trying not to look equally excited. Santo took Roxanne's hand as they moved through the press of people. Halloween decorations grinned from windows, glowered from planters, and lurked in every nook and cranny.

They skirted the café, staying close to the walls. A stage had been set up in the open area outside the restaurant, and already people gathered in front of it, waiting for a "pre-Justin" show to begin. Stadium seating had been assembled in the corridors branching off, where more fans sat shoulder to shoulder. Like a moat around a stronghold, others waited on foot, standing ten to fifteen deep in a circle that completely encompassed the center and effectively blocked the exits. The music played at deafening volumes.

A dark thought filled Roxanne's head. If something bad were to happen, it would be a nightmare for anyone to get out.

Something bad? a voice jeered in her head. *What else did you expect?*

A host of entertainers worked the crowd, dressed in skeleton costumes that covered them from hood to hem. They carried crates of balloons and delighted even the coolest of the cool with an assortment of animals and shapes—some questionably lewd, others blatantly so. But even the mothers who'd accompanied their adolescents took it in stride, channeling the vibe of excitement.

"Wish we'd thought of costumes," Roxanne muttered, thinking how much easier it would have been to move around without fearing they'd be recognized as wanted criminals.

"This feels wrong, Roxanne," Santo said.

He tugged her hand and eased her away. Casually, he put his arm around her and tucked her close to the heat of his body.

They waited almost forty minutes before she saw

Reece enter the mall beside a woman she didn't know. Her brother wore jeans and an old gray sweatshirt with the hood pulled up. The woman wore a jean jacket with a baggy University of North Dakota T-shirt and yoga pants. Petite and dark-skinned, she contrasted perfectly with Roxanne's tall, fair brother. The couple walked apart, fingers brushing but not clinging, yet there seemed to be an intimacy in their deliberate distance.

Reece gave the crowds a casual scan, his gaze narrowing on the stage and the frantic fans in front of it. Frowning, he leaned close and said something to the woman.

The pair kept moving at an unhurried pace, pausing to window-shop. Only someone watching them would notice the studied attention they gave their surroundings. From across the wide corridor, Reece's disinterested gaze passed over Roxanne and then snapped back.

She saw his lips form the words *Fuck, no.*

Santo echoed the statement behind her, grabbed her arm, and turned her around the way they'd come.

"What are you doing?"

"Look at his face, Roxanne. He's afraid for you."

She glanced back. Reece lounged against a wall near where she'd last seen him with the woman by his side. Just a couple of young lovers at the mall. But he looked shaken as he watched them over the woman's head.

"Santo, stop. Listen to me."

"Not until I get you someplace safe."

"And where is that? Where, Santo?"

He made an angry sound, glanced around, and pulled her off to the side. People still poured in the doors, but she could see police cars pulling up out front and officers directing traffic away from the entrances. Through the open doors, they heard the DJ say, "Folks, if you're headed down to Arizona Mills, you're too late. Police have blocked the entrances, and the mall is at ca-*paci*-tee. No joke, you'll be turned away."

"Where will I be safe?" she insisted, looking Santo in the eye. "Outside? Inside? He knows who I am. He knows how to find me. There's a reason he hasn't taken me. You said that yourself. I don't think it has anything to do with *where* I am. If I can stop what's happening, then I can't run away just because I'm scared."

Santo scowled. "The woman Reece is with? She's a scavenger."

"How do you know?"

He raised his brows.

"Okay, she's a scavenger. She's a small one though. We can take her."

He rolled his eyes but almost smiled. Roxanne leaned in and brushed his lips with hers. "I know you don't like it. But you're going to have to trust me just a little while longer," she said.

"I haven't trusted you yet," he answered. But he took her hand and faced Reece again.

She started across the jostling walkway and Santo

followed right behind her, as she'd known he would. She shot him a grateful look over her shoulder and surprised an expression of such naked dread on his face that it slowed her steps.

"Have a little faith," she said.

As they approached, Reece pushed away from the wall and ushered his girlfriend into a sunglasses shop without glancing at them. Roxanne and Santo followed them inside a few moments later. Two young men in matching polo shirts and khaki pants stood at the door, watching the mall action.

"Help you?" one of the clerks asked as they entered.

"Just looking," Roxanne said.

The man turned back to the unfolding excitement without another word. Reece moved from the rack where he and the woman had been trying on glasses and, with a quick glance at the clerks, ducked behind the counter and into the back room. Roxanne and Santo did the same, following Reece straight through to a door that opened onto a tunnel-like corridor.

"Come on," Reece said and led them down the dim passage. They'd barely turned the corner before they heard a door open behind them and a voice say, "I don't know where the hell they went. Did they steal anything?"

"Shit, I don't kn—"

The door closed and Reece turned on her.

"What the fuck are you doing here?" he demanded.

"I saw Manny last night. He told me you'd be here."

"Manny's not who you think he is, Roxanne."

"I know. I saw his . . . spirit. And I saw what he'd become."

"Did he hurt you?"

She shook her head.

Reece pulled her into a tight hug. "Christ, Roxanne. I've been so worried about you. I'm sorry I got you into this."

"It's not your fault," she answered.

Reece gave a harsh laugh, still holding her. "You always say that."

He stepped away, his eyes dry but red, and waved for the woman he was with to come forward. "This is April," he said.

Roxanne and April gave each other guarded nods. Roxanne introduced Santo, then they all stood awkwardly, caught in a social nicety that had no place in this gloomy tunnel.

April crossed her arms beneath her breasts and Roxanne noticed an ugly rash covering her elbows, as well as an outbreak at her temples. Up close it looked berry-red and angry against the white patches of skin.

"Roxanne, I've got about five minutes," Reece said. "But you need to get the hell out of here."

"Why? What's going to happen?"

"You remember the robbery? The missing people?"

"Of course I remember—"

"They still haven't found them. They never will. Those bodies are walking around, Roxanne. But it's not Jim and Sal anymore. Their bodies are occupied. They're *here*."

After the scavengers had hunted her, after the hellhounds, after the ravens, *occupied* sounded innocuous enough. But she'd seen Manny. She knew exactly what *occupied* meant.

Reece went on. "They're called scavengers, and they like it here. They want to set up shop, and today they're out to harvest."

He stopped, turning his face away.

"I know what they are," Roxanne said. "I know what they want. And this is *not* your fault."

"You don't know what you're talking about."

"I promise you I do."

"Then you know that I'm the key. I'm the fucking key that lets them in."

Roxanne started to say something, but Santo gave her hand a squeeze, stopping her, and sent a meaningful glance April's way.

"You can talk in front of her," Reece said, taking April's hand. "She's not like them."

Santo asked, "How?"

"None of your fucking business how," Reece answered.

The bang of a door opening somewhere out of sight and voices carrying through the tunnel distracted them. "They went this way?" someone asked.

"I don't know, man. They didn't come out the front, and they're not in the shop. That's all I know."

"Shit," Reece said. "We need to go."

They started walking away from the voices. Reece said in a low tone, "All these people, it's a trap for them. Bieber isn't coming. Gary leaked the news in order to pack the mall. None of them are getting out alive if things go down the way he wants. And if you get caught here, neither will you. And I mean permanently this time. No coming back from it, Roxanne."

"What about you?"

"Didn't you hear me? I'm the fucking *key*. The golden ticket. The buddy pass for all of their friends. They're keeping me around forever."

"What are you going to do?"

They reached an exit door. Reece hit the bar and it swung open to murky daylight.

"Go, Roxanne. For once in your damn life, listen to me and go."

"But what are *you* going to do?"

He let out a deep breath. "I'm going to stop it."

"How?"

"Don't worry about it. It's handled." He started to shut the door, then hesitated. "Are you sure you can trust this guy?" he asked, looking at Santo.

"I'm sure," Roxanne said vehemently.

April gave her a hard look. "It's not going to be pretty," she said. "When it starts."

Roxanne stared back, confused. Of course it wouldn't be pretty. The scavengers planned to kill. To steal the bodies of innocent people.

"I'm talking about the decay," April clarified, nodding at Santo.

Beside her, Roxanne felt Santo tense. April shifted her attention to him and said, "You didn't think you'd get to keep it forever, did you, reaper?"

Seeing Roxanne's frown, Reece said, "The body. It rejects them." With a look of sadness, he gently touched the rash on April's arm.

Seeing Roxanne's bewilderment, April said, "The Beyond and earth were never meant to meet in this way. The scavengers found a way in, but that doesn't mean they've figured out how to sustain it. We deteriorate."

"I'm sorry?"

"Like Reece said, our bodies reject the demon that's inside them. We can't maintain. We begin to erode. It's why most of us look like ghosts. White skin. Even the eyes go white in the end. Eventually, all semblance of humanity is leached out of us. Isn't that ironic?"

The girl looked very human in that moment, and Roxanne had a hard time reconciling how she could be one of *them*.

It was Santo who gave the answer. "You took her

before she died," he said in that husky voice that betrayed his emotions.

The sorrow in her eyes said it all, and Roxanne saw a message pass between April and Santo. An understanding that made her uneasy.

"You need to tell her," April said, nodding at Roxanne. "Don't make her guess."

Reece gave Roxanne a tight hug before she could say anything else. "Get out of here." He looked over her head at Santo. "You hear me? Get her out of here."

With that, the two ducked back into the passageway, closing the door behind them, locking Roxanne and Santo out.

(32)

Santo felt like he'd swallowed glass. He'd suspected that the rash was a symptom of deterioration occurring with the scavengers. When Gary had visited in the hours before dawn, Santo had thought his eyes resembled the hellhounds'.

But Santo hadn't fully grasped what it meant. What it meant for *him*.

"What was she talking about?" Roxanne demanded as soon as the door closed. "Does she think that's going to happen to you?"

"We'll talk about it later," Santo said, eyeing the delivery bay where they'd come out. A long ramp led up to a sliding door where merchandise could be unloaded. Tucked against the far wall stood five trash bins, lids open.

He took her hand and moved them away from the door, strolling casually. As if they weren't afraid. As if they had no goal.

Roxanne tugged on his hand and stopped him. "I thought we were past secrets."

He let out a deep breath and acknowledged her point. As much as he didn't want to tell her what April meant, she had the right to know.

Walking again, anxious to get out of the open, Santo said, "She's telling the truth. If it happens to them, it could happen to me."

Roxanne said nothing, but he could feel her runaway thoughts. He could feel her worry as she tried to find a solution to a problem that wasn't her own.

The police had the main accesses blocked off, but they hadn't made it to all the store entrances yet. Roxanne and Santo circled around from the delivery bay until they found one that was unmanned.

"Did you know?" she asked in a hurt voice.

"No, but I should have suspected."

"Why?"

"The hellhounds," he said bluntly. "They haven't been heard of in the Beyond for so long that we thought them a myth. But when I saw the scavengers in the hotel parking lot and the hellhounds appeared right after them, something clicked in my head. I realized the hellhounds hadn't come through from the Beyond—

not like the scavengers. Not like me. They'd evolved. Or, I guess, the opposite."

Roxanne stared at him, her brows puckering the flesh between them. She didn't want to understand. But there weren't a lot of ways she could misinterpret what he'd said.

"My guess is the rash is just the beginning," Santo went on. "After that . . . like April said, it won't be pretty."

"And you didn't think it was worth mentioning?"

"We covered a lot of territory in a short amount of time, *angelita*. It didn't seem like something I should bring up when I wasn't certain."

"Have you seen signs yourself?"

He didn't answer.

"Have you?"

Reluctantly, he shoved up his sleeve and showed her the small eruption at the crook of his arm.

"When?"

"This morning."

He shook his sleeve down again and waited until she met his eyes. "I'm sorry. I didn't want it to be true either."

"I won't accept this. Do you hear me? I *won't*. I'm in love with you, Santo. I'm not going to let go."

He'd waited for those words for so long that he wanted to weep at their beauty. He vowed that he would hear them again. That he would find the moment to give them back.

But this was not the time or place.

"I'm trying to hang on to that faith, *angelita*. You keep hold of yours."

She looked so beautiful. So fierce. He remembered the despair that Santo had fought over his dead wife. If he had to give up Roxanne, his anguish would surpass anything Santo had endured. Becoming a mindless beast might be a blessing.

"I'm not giving up," she said, kissing him. "Don't you either."

B ack inside the mall, Roxanne and Santo made their way to the impromptu stage in front of the restaurant. The number of costumed performers had grown in the short time they'd been gone, and now it seemed they were everywhere.

Standing on the stage were a few other people wearing an officious air but no costumes. The noise level dropped from deafening to a loud rumble as one of them moved to the microphone and began to speak. Tall and pasty, he wore a black long-sleeved shirt and black pants. The collar was buttoned up to his chin, but Roxanne could see the fine shadow of a rash just below his ears and at his hairline. He wore dark sunglasses, so she couldn't see his eyes, but she didn't have to see them. She knew who he was.

"That's Gary, isn't it," she murmured.

Santo nodded grimly.

"Just a little while longer," the man shouted into the microphone. "While we wait, your entertainment committee has some fun planned."

From speakers located everywhere music blasted out and the crowd began to sing and dance along.

In her mind, Roxanne kept replaying her conversation with Reece. She leaned against Santo so he could hear her.

"What do you think Reece has planned?"

Santo shook his head. "I've given up on guessing what any of you will do."

"There's only one way he could stop it," she told him. "He said he's their key. Their *buddy pass*. The only way he quits being that is by not coming back. By dying for good."

She could tell by Santo's expression that he'd figured that out already.

"Roxanne," he said gently. "Maybe it's the way it should be."

"No. I can't believe that."

"You won't believe it."

"That, too."

"Behold," the man onstage exclaimed over the din, making every syllable sound theatric.

He stepped back, and others dressed in skeleton costumes came to the front and stood in a line. A movement at the edge of the stage distracted Roxanne, and she craned her neck to see six shadowy figures waiting behind the performers, like dancers preparing to do some elaborate number. Not so odd, except there was something about them that struck Roxanne wrong. At first she thought it was the street clothes they were wearing when everyone else had on costumes, but then . . . She frowned, inching over to get a better view. They had a strangely *ethereal* look to them. Like Manny had last night in the dream.

The performers began to move, waving their hands and motioning for the audience to join in. Each time one of them took a step, the spirits behind followed, as if bound. They made a gruesome, *ghostly* synchronized dance parody. Souls trapped here so their deaths wouldn't be noted in the Beyond.

The injustice, the horror of it, made her sick.

Roxanne slowly looked from one of the jostling people around them to another. She saw more souls emerge in the audience, appearing like an illusion as her gaze touched on them. There was Jim Little and Sal Espinoza, from the bar. Even Manny's spirit stood at the far edge of the gathering in his rolled up jeans and Iron Man shirt. He smiled at her.

Onstage, the skeletons performed, riling the spectators into a shrieking frenzy. Someone dimmed the lights, and the skull and bones costumes began to glow. The happy, playful antics they'd been performing slowed with the music. It throbbed over the agitated bodies. That didn't sound like Justin's music any longer.

People blocked the walkways and spilled out of the stores, swaying to the deep beat. They stared at the performers with expressions of rapture, no longer talking or screaming as the music lulled them into silence.

Then the man with the microphone looked up, right into Roxanne's eyes. He smiled.

She heard a loud shriek as the ravens flocked down from the ceiling. At the same time, locusts swarmed and buzzed at their feet. The screams bounced off the walls and came back tenfold as people began to flail wildly, fighting the talons above as they reeled away from the bugs clinging to their legs below.

The crowd lurched to the side and Santo's grip on her hand broke. Before she could call his name, a big hand covered her mouth and someone jerked her off her feet.

The lights went out, plunging them into darkness as the screams rebounded with terror.

(34)

Santo had never realized how completely a life could change in just a second. That's all it had taken. He'd glanced away and then she was gone.

He spun, looking in every direction, but the lights had been doused, and only the doors offered a dubious, overcast glimmer. He shouted Roxanne's name, but she could have been right beside him and not heard it over the panic. The ravens swooped, the locusts swarmed. People on the risers tried to get down, people on the floor tried to push through the circle of spectators surrounding them, and the outer ring fought back, trying to get closer because they had no idea what had happened. They thought Justin Whoever had shown up.

On the ceiling, the Black Tides of Abaddon washed ashore. A sharp report of gunfire cut through the madness and chunks of plaster rained down on them all, inciting more wild-eyed terror. Santo pushed his way against the surge of people, heading for the stage. The scavenger no longer stood there, but others did, and someone had to know where they'd taken her.

From the corner of his eye, he caught sight of the mall doors. They'd been locked, and as the first crush of panicked people tried to exit, they found themselves flattened against the glass or trampled in the commotion. From outside, police officers attempted to pry the doors open, but to no avail. They'd been sealed.

Fear swelled like rising floodwaters, and the reaper inside him tasted it against his will. In that moment he understood the reason for this elaborate ruse, the crowds . . . trapping them here. The rampant terror was like a drug for the scavengers. An exciting jolt of the most forbidden pleasure. Fighting his own dark cravings, he pushed people aside and gained access to the stage.

It was deserted now, but from his vantage point he could look over the sea of humanity spread out all around him. The pandemonium defied description.

Scavengers stood among the pushing, frightened people, showing fleeting glimpses of their real faces, adding to the terror. The shriek of ravens as they scratched and pecked made even Santo afraid.

After that, people began to die.

(35)

They'd commandeered the Rainforest Café. Reece stood inside the dark jungle of decorations and tried not to look nervous, but every time the fake elephant or animated monkeys switched on, they startled him. He and April had been over and over the plan, and in the quiet of his room, it had seemed feasible, logical, the right thing to do.

But now it seemed stupid and impossible to execute.

He pulled the flask from his jacket and turned to April. "Ready?"

She nodded.

Somberly, Reece splashed her with kerosene and then stood still while she did the same to him. It wouldn't take much to make them flammable.

"Are you sure about this?" she asked as she handed the empty flask back.

But she knew the answer.

Gary and his scavengers intended to open the door for Abaddon today. Reece knew what his role in that horrible event would be, but only because April had told him.

The version Gary had shared of how things would go down did not include Reece being sacrificed over and over until the tunnel they created became big enough, stable enough for Abaddon. But that's how it would play out.

It wasn't until just before they'd left that Gary had given him the details of the clever trap he'd set. His expression serious and concerned, he'd said, "We've found a way to put a stop to all the evil. The reaper who has your sister won't be able to resist the trap we've set, and once we have him, we'll win this war."

"What trap?" Reece asked.

"Terror. It's like an aphrodisiac to reapers. We're going to put a big pot of honey out and lure him in. Trust me, he won't be able to stay away."

"What about my sister?"

"We'll make sure he comes alone. We want her safe, just like you do."

He'd been glad to give Reece the details. The faked celebrity appearance. The packed mall. The bolted doors. April had already told Reece about the security guards the scavengers had "liberated," but Gary made it sound like security had been part of their team all along.

"Once we catch the reaper, we can find the source of evil. We can lock it out of God's sweet world, Reece. Are you in? Are you one of us?"

Hooray.

"I'm in. Hell, yes, I'm in."

Gary had been smugly pleased, but he didn't have a clue what Reece was in for. Only April did.

Still, Reece hadn't understood how they meant to keep the door open if Roxanne could close it, but seeing her today with the reaper had been an answer.

"They mean for him to reap her before they kill you," April said.

And that meant Reece and April needed to turn themselves into human torches before that happened. If Reece died first, Roxanne could seal the passageway. It was their only hope of getting rid of this demon infestation.

Reece had always understood that in some way, he was not meant for this world. The feeling had shadowed him his entire life. When he was younger, it had emerged in random acts of violence that had shamed him even as they'd consumed him. There was a reason why his family had never had pets, even though Ruby had begged for a puppy for years.

That shamed him, too.

And once the dying began . . . a part of him had

always felt he deserved the misery and disappointment of knowing that nothing waited in the afterlife but pain. The world would be a better place without him. Literally. And he was ready to face that reality.

He and April had a plan. One in which they would end their pain together and, in doing so, he hoped, lock the door to Abaddon for all of eternity.

(36)

Roxanne fought, but they'd pulled something over her head and she couldn't see. She struggled blindly, kicking and squirming. That big hand was still over her mouth. She tried to bite it through the bag or mask or whatever it was that covered her face, but her efforts only earned a hard shake that snapped her head back. The arms holding her squeezed so tight they forced the breath from her lungs.

She sensed they'd entered somewhere new, quieter than the screaming echo chamber of the mall. But it wasn't until she heard the shriek of monkeys that she knew just where they'd taken her. The café. An unlikely place for whatever they had planned, she thought, picturing it in her head.

Someone manhandled her into a chair, then ripped

the bag off her head. She sat in the deserted dining room of Manny's favorite restaurant. All around her were pseudo jungle vines and strategically placed artificial rock formations with gurgling waterfalls. A small pack of animatronic elephants stood in one corner; a group of monkeys watched from another, and on the far side a jaguar twitched its tale lazily. Overhead a huge moss-dripping kapok tree spanned the ceiling, complete with a gigantic snake in its branches. The ceiling had been painted black, and twinkling lights peeped through the foliage like a star-spangled sky.

But as she watched, a black ooze crept over it and blotted out the stars. She recognized the Black Tides of Abaddon and the plunging dread that accompanied it.

Perched among the fake leaves sat a dozen ravens, black as a spreading plague. Their sharp beaks clacked in the quiet. Down below, locusts skittered and rubbed their legs in a horrible song.

The tables and chairs had been pushed back from the center. A handful of men stood in a half circle around their leader. Ice formed in her belly as she met the eyes of the pale man who'd shot her without hesitation. *Gary.* She knew what they meant to do with her, and now it seemed almost fitting, the location. Tucked against the stones of a man-made waterfall stood a carved totem—a demigod that glared down, waiting for its sacrifice.

Gary smiled benignly before giving a low whistle.

Two of the massive beasts that had tried to kill Roxanne and Santo at the hotel trotted out from a camouflaged door set behind the waterfall.

They padded to her chair and sat one to each side, watching her with nervous eyes. The one on the left made a high, whining sound and inched back just a bit. Not enough to draw Gary's attention, but Roxanne saw it. They looked hungry and mean . . . and abnormally wary. Roxanne felt something tighten beneath her breastbone and squeeze past her fear.

"Well, then," Gary said. "I think introductions are in order. I'm Gary Knolls, the man who's going to rip your soul from your body before I remove your head and feed it to my doggies."

He lifted a wicked-edged blade from the table and faced Roxanne. Too long to be called a knife but not quite a machete, it looked like it would cut through flesh and bone without effort.

"Sad that your reaper didn't save us the trouble, but there's always Plan B."

Terror made her limbs stiff, but she forced her eyes away from the knife and stared Gary in the face like she wasn't frightened to death.

"Why here?" she challenged calmly.

Gary raised a brow. "You don't like the service?"

"I don't like you. And it strikes me as odd that you would wait for your little circus to do me in. You came for a visit last night. Why the delay? Why didn't you just kill me then and there? You could have done it easily enough."

"My. You have a lot of questions."

"I've heard that before."

He smiled, cold eyes glittering. "Insurance," he said at last, fingering the handle of his blade. "I wanted you here, today, as insurance."

"Against?"

"For. As long as you're alive and in my custody, I have your brother's cooperation."

"And the part where you rip out my soul and chop off my head?"

"After I get it."

"Wow. *That's* your big play?"

Gary's mouth opened with surprise. Roxanne looked down at the hounds again and stared into the biggest one's eyes. It began to growl just as two diseased-looking scavengers hauled Santo through the door. Both of the big hounds stood excitedly, ready to move over to the new victim. Gary snapped his fingers and they settled again. But they didn't like sitting so close to Roxanne. Not a bit.

Helplessly, she watched them heft Santo onto an empty chair. His head hung limply and his feet trailed behind him. Blood poured from a wound at his temple and his eyes were shut, but she saw his chest move with an inhalation. He was alive.

"This one belongs to you, I believe," Gary said.

Roxanne didn't answer. She watched anxiously as they shoved him onto the seat.

"Do you know what happens to a reaper when he dies?" Gary asked.

"Reapers don't die," Roxanne said, hoping she sounded more certain than she felt.

"Unless they're reapers who have stolen a human's body."

She gave Gary a cold look.

"You don't want to ask," he chided. "But you want to know. I can see it in your eyes. If he were to die now—say, here, for example, before Reece *volunteers* his services—your reaper will be trapped. Not part of your world. Not part of mine."

"The same would be true of you, then."

"Oh, no. I'm here on orders, Roxanne. I will be called home."

Gary moved over to Santo's unconscious body and ran his fingers through Santo's hair. Roxanne turned her focus on the hounds, glaring at the big one until its hackles rose and it growled deeply. It backed up again, and the smaller one followed.

Gary turned with a frown just as Roxanne caught sight of someone moving quickly from the front doors, through the cavernlike entry to just behind Gary.

Reece.

She forced herself to keep her focus on the dogs, recklessly challenging the big one with her eyes. Did it sense something inside her, as Abaddon's ravens had? She remembered the night at the hotel and how one of the hounds had sniffed the air. At the time she'd thought Santo had caused it to recoil. Now she wondered.

Reece came up behind Gary fast and sure. Her brother's knife was much smaller, but it looked no less lethal as Reece pressed it to the demon's jugular. The others in the room looked startled, as if it had never occurred to them that a threat could invade their sanctuary.

Roxanne tried to stand, but the big dog wasn't intimidated enough to let her move. It snarled and snapped and kept her in her seat.

"Tell Shrek to drop his guns. The knife, too," Reece said, pricking the skin of Gary's throat. Blood trickled down. "Tell him."

"Dave," Gary said, cutting his gaze to an ugly, hulking man.

Roxanne heard something clatter to the floor. Reece kicked it away, and April materialized from the shadows to scoop it up. Gary flashed her a look of loathing.

"This won't end well for you," he snarled.

"But it will end," she answered coolly.

"The rest of them, too," Reece ordered. "Do it, Gary, or I swear to God, Abaddon will be the least of your worries."

Gary gave his men a speaking glance, and more weapons clattered to the floor. When they'd been kicked out of reach, Gary said, "This is quite an impasse we have."

"I don't see it that way. I see a bunch of demons who are about to get sent back where they belong."

"Where we will await your return to us. It seems like a long way to go to end up in the same place."

April moved closer, a gun in her hand. Reece met Roxanne's eyes and looked quickly away, but in that one fleeting glance, she saw it all. She knew exactly what her brother meant to do, and killing Gary was only the beginning.

"Don't be stupid, Reece," Gary said.

Roxanne didn't like the way Gary kept using her brother's name. Like they were old buddies. Confidants.

Reece gave Gary a dismissive glance and said, "You keep talking like you're still in charge. But guess what? You're not. I'll tell you what's going to happen, asshole. You're not going to hurt my sister. You're not going to hurt any more of those people out there. And you're not going to be bringing any more fucking demons to earth. I know what you are."

"You go against me and you go against Abaddon."

"Yeah? Fuck Abaddon. I know what waits for you here on earth," Reece said. "Decay. Day by day, a little more of you will rot off until you don't even know what you've become. I don't have to kill you. I could lock you up in a cage and watch you turn."

The threat worked. Gary's snide expression couldn't hide the panicked look he sent the hellhounds. From the corner of her eye, Roxanne saw Santo's head move and his lashes flutter. He was waking up.

Roxanne turned all of her focus on the hounds and pushed with her mind, pushed with that hot light she felt building inside her, hoping to keep them distracted from Santo. The ravens scattered. Even the locusts scuttled out of her radius.

As if sensing a threat they couldn't see, the hounds turned on one another with furious snarls, tearing at flesh as they fought. Gary tried to shout, but Reece held the knife too tight. The pale, icy eyes narrowed as he twisted, trying to get a better look at what Roxanne was doing.

Roxanne's heart felt like a jackhammer. She kept her hands clenched in her lap so Gary wouldn't see their shaking. It took all of her will not to glance at Santo again. Not to give anything away.

"What are you doing?" Gary demanded.

Roxanne tossed her head fearlessly. "I'm not just going to shut your door, Gary. I'm going to shove you through it and seal it tight."

Gary said nothing for a full count, and then he laughed. The sound agitated the ravens and sent the locusts whirring. The hounds paused, jaws bloody, eyes wild. Gary snapped his fingers and they broke apart, subdued but not quite back under his command.

She could feel the tension running through the others in the room but no one moved. The echoes of screams from the mall came at them in waves—sickening, terror-filled bursts that made her want to jump to her feet and run.

Roxanne risked trying to stand again. In the same instant, Santo came up and around, taking out the man standing behind him with a quick elbow to the face. He scooped a rifle from the floor and fired point-blank, swung it and took down two more of the demons, while Reece made Gary hiss with pain.

The elephants trumpeted the victory, swinging their heads back and forth and flapping their ears. Before they grew quiet, the monkeys started up followed by the jaguar, until they all roared and groaned, growled and screeched in a deafening cacophony. Santo turned the gun on Gary, who was still pinned by Reece's knife.

"What's your play, Reece?" Santo asked.

"End it."

What happened next came in halted jerks. Roxanne saw more scavengers rush in from the door. Santo spun to stop them just as Gary snapped his fingers and spoke a sharp command that Roxanne didn't understand until the hellhounds attacked.

The big one flew at Roxanne's throat, and the smaller one caught her shoulder and jerked. She screamed. Reece cried out, slicing Gary's throat with a deep, fatal gash. Santo had turned at the sound of her pain and as the hounds took her down, she saw him charging into the fray. A loud gunshot boomed an instant before red blossomed over his chest. Another shot, another hole, and then a third. Santo hit his knees and fell beside her, eyes open but dazed.

She was screaming inside, screaming as the hounds ripped at her flesh. Fear tried to make Roxanne its victim, but she refused. She gathered her thoughts, remembering what he'd told her. They do this together. *Together.* She called Santo's name as she focused and felt the power swell within her just as it had before.

It worked. The hounds recoiled.

She had a moment to breathe. She reached out for Santo but he was sprawled beside her, his eyes glassy and fixed. She couldn't find a pulse. Frantically, she searched, calling his name, crying.

"Roxanne!" Reece shouted.

She looked up to see her brother standing with Gary's body clutched in his arms, the other man's head hanging gruesomely. Reece held a lighter in his hand. It took her less than an instant to understand what he meant to do. April was on the other side of the room, trying to fight off the demons who'd come in. She gave Reece a desperate glance as he turned the wheel on the lighter.

"It's what I want," Reece said.

She thought of what Santo had told her about the man whose life he'd taken. *Santo was ready to die. I did us both a favor.*

Just like Reece was ready. The thought came before she could stop it.

In Reece's eyes, she saw despair and mixed with it, determination. While every instinct urged her to stop him, she felt the finality of the moment weld her to the spot and understood there wasn't a damn thing she could do to reverse his tragic decision.

Reece held the lighter to his sweatshirt and it caught. He went up like a bonfire in a whoosh of heat and flame that engulfed both him and Gary. Roxanne screamed again, and April shouted Reece's name as she tried to get free of the demons that held her.

Roxanne searched through the pain for that kernel of fury that had grown so bright when the ravens had come to Louisa's. She watched her brother scream in agony and felt the last of Santo's lifeblood drain away.

She'd lost them both. Grief filled her in a painful rush.

It felt as if she moved through a thick gel that kept her from hearing, from feeling. One of the demons raised a gun and fired at her. The bullet plowed through her chest and out the other side. She looked down at the blood and thought, *Yes. It's how it should be.*

She teetered on the edge of consciousness, aware of Santo's skin already beginning to chill. Hearing Gary's words . . . had he told the truth? Would Santo be stuck between worlds?

I'll always be waiting for you.

Suddenly, she was in the dark again. But she wasn't alone. She sensed Santo with her, though she couldn't see his familiar shape, his beloved face. "What will you do now, *angelita*?" he asked in that husky voice she loved so much.

"Shine," she whispered.

She felt the smile she couldn't see. Found comfort in the embrace she couldn't quite feel.

She looked down, and there was the dining room of the deserted restaurant below. Reece, a burned husk wrapped around the blackened shape of Gary. Their bodies still burned and smoked. The emergency sprinklers had activated, but they'd been no match for the accelerant and inferno that had burned her brother and the scavenger demon to ash and husk. Dead scavengers littered the floor and their shadows lurked in the room, looking for the way out.

To her right was the chaos that reigned in the mall. Here, the scavengers had yet to sense the turn of the tide. They killed with glee, and lost souls wandered the carnage with shocked eyes and hopeless expressions. Roxanne stared in horror, and the tight ball of her fury became a rush of energy that lit up the spot where she and Santo lay in death. The souls of the humans who'd been murdered by the demons turned with interest to see it.

A great pressure built against her eardrums until the pain became excruciating and a blinding light appeared above her. Bright. Hard. Warm. It coalesced, drowning out all sound. Roxanne felt like she was trapped between two spotlights, the one that shone from her own body and the other that could only be the Beyond.

The lost souls turned their faces up and Roxanne understood. The Beyond beckoned them. It beckoned *her*. Never before had it opened this way. Never had she felt its pull. Did that mean this time would be the last? Would her fifth death bring the finality that the others had lacked?

She watched as the souls began to climb the rays of light, finding the home the demons had denied them. She saw Manny, felt the brush of him as he passed her by. Jim and Sal followed right behind. After them came the others. So many others.

The light kept shining even after the last soul had entered and Roxanne knew it waited for her.

She turned in the darkness to let Santo know she wouldn't go, but he was gone and she was alone.

Come back to me. I will always be waiting.

That's what he'd said, but he wasn't there anymore.

Below, the light that surrounded their bodies began to fade and Roxanne fought it. She would not give up. Not on life. Not on Santo. Not on the love they hadn't had a chance to share. He didn't believe he had a soul, but she knew better. His soul was a mate to her own and she would not leave him in limbo. She wouldn't abandon him to a fate he didn't deserve. Four times he'd saved *her*. *He* was the reason why she'd survived in the past. Now she would do the same for him.

She focused everything, keeping his words in her head, in her heart.

Come back to me. I will always be waiting.

No, Santo!

You come back to *me*.

The light to the Beyond vanished with a flicker and all that remained was the glow below. *Her* light. The one that Santo had fallen in love with. The one he'd cherished and protected.

All around her the darkness began to crumble and Roxanne shouted Santo's name, reaching out with all that she had, all that she was, until she found him and then she held on. He belonged to her. She belonged to him.

There would be no more waiting.

She gripped Santo as tight as she could while a feeling inside her swelled like a great tidal wave, rising up and up until she could no longer see over it. And with it came pain—excruciating. Worse than dying. Worse than anything she'd ever imagined. She cried out as she plummeted down and slammed through the barriers of the Beyond and back to the world she knew.

The moment burned so hot that she feared the fires of Abaddon had followed her, but the Beyond had closed. Why, then, were there still scavengers, ravens, and shades lurking in the corners? Locusts scurrying about?

Beside her, Santo groaned but she saw a pulse beating at his throat. "Santo," she breathed, pressing her fingers to it.

A great rumbling came from all around. It shook the floor and cracked the ceiling. The black ooze that had covered the stars shrank back. The scavengers whimpered.

"What is it?" she whispered.

"The souls," Santo said, his voice weak. "The souls have arrived in the Beyond. They know."

She had only a moment to understand who he meant by *they*. The powers of the Beyond. Santo had told her that life and death were monitored there. It appeared that the tally sheet had been reviewed.

She felt a huge wind sweep down and howl through the walls. It opened like a tunnel leading into a dark that smelled rotten and dank. Within it came a blast of heat that singed her lashes and burned her throat. The wind twisted and turned, sucking up the debris of scavengers and hurling them into a glowing furnace that waited at the end. The fires of Abaddon. Instinctively, she knew it. Feared it. Desperately, she gripped Santo's hand and held on tight as the punishing wind whipped around them.

"It will take me, *angelita*," he said softly. "There's no fighting it. It's where I belong."

"No. You belong with *me*."

All around, scavengers shrieked in fear as their dark

shadows were wrenched free of their bodies and spun into that burning tunnel. She saw her brother, eyes terrified yet determined to face whatever came next. Gary's dark shadow wrapped itself around Reece's soul in a strangling grip as the wind towed them both into the jetsam. In her mind's eye, Roxanne caught her brother and held him as she'd done so many times before, but she couldn't win, not when Gary's grasp was stronger, not when Reece fought so hard against her.

For one horrid moment Reece hung between them. Then he was gone. She felt the wind circle Santo, tug . . . and release. And suddenly it was over. The tunnel was gone.

The scavengers were gone.

But Santo was still there.

(37)

Santo faded in and out but finally the sound of crying brought him around. Certain that when he opened his eyes, he'd find the raging heat and the Black Tides of Abaddon awaiting him, he lay still. It didn't smell like Abaddon, though. It smelled like . . . caramel corn. French fries. Roasted meat. A shrill scream joined his dawning awareness, a sound so unique it could only be a siren.

He was still on earth. Still in the human world.

At last he opened his eyes and saw the woman he loved sobbing beside him. He tried to speak, but no words would come out. He managed to lift his hand and settle it on her thigh. Roxanne gasped and turned her wet, tearstained face to him.

She threw her arms around him, and her hot tears splashed against his throat. She kissed him, crying all the while. Santo didn't care. He didn't understand what had happened. He only knew that he was here. With her.

"Are you hurt?" he asked, carefully easing up to sit. The floor beneath him was wet and filled with blood and ash. His chest ached and he had a fuzzy, painful memory of being shot, of feeling the life drain out of him.

"I'm not hurt," Roxanne said. "Well, a little but . . . I'll live."

She laughed and cried at the same time. Santo felt his lips curl into a smile. "Yeah. Me, too, I guess."

He looked around at the carnage of the dining room. The bodies that had been used and abused by the scavengers lay in pools of blood throughout the room. Dead, already stiffening. He looked closer. But human. The rash that had marred their faces had gone with the wretched occupants.

Yet he was still here. It made no sense.

"Roxanne, how am I alive? What did you do?"

"I held on. We've waited for each other forever. I wasn't about to let you go now. I promised you I wouldn't leave you. Remember?"

Tears burned his eyes as he pressed his mouth to her palm. "I remember," he said.

"I saw the Beyond, Santo. I felt it calling me. But I chose you. My *soul* chose you."

The beauty of her words settled deep inside what

could only be *his* soul. A soul he shouldn't have. A soul he could no longer deny. Humbled by what he saw in Roxanne's eyes when she looked at him, Santo knew that he was no longer *other* . . . reaper . . . imposter. He'd become one with his human form. One with the heart that drove this human race.

And he was glad of it.

Proud of it.

In *love* with it, as he was in love with this woman who'd believed in him and fought to save him.

He looked at the charred bodies of Roxanne's brother and the scavenger who'd started it all. April sat beside Reece, weeping silently.

Santo still didn't understand. The punishing wind had taken all the demons with it. It should have taken him, too, when it swept up everything else that didn't belong.

But it had left both Santo and April. Why?

As if hearing his question, April turned her tearstained face his way. "It found us human," she said.

She pulled back her hair, showing him her face where the rash had blistered her skin just hours before. Now the rash was gone, the skin clear and unblemished. "The winds tested us and judged us to be human." She gave a bitter laugh. "Can you believe it?"

Amazed, Santo looked at Roxanne and she threw her arms around him. "We were meant to be together, Santo. And now nothing can ever drive us apart."

From the first time he'd touched her soul, he'd fallen in love. He'd thought she'd cheated him, when all along he'd been praying she would save him. And now she had. She'd given him more than a second chance. She'd given him life.

He cupped her face in his hands. "I love you, Roxanne."

She smiled at him, her eyes so beautiful he would gladly stare into them every day of his gifted life.

As he took her in his arms, he murmured, "I never thought I'd want to grow old. But Roxanne, with you anything is possible."

She laughed and cried as she declared her love and each word from her soft lips made that nebulous part of him stronger. His *soul*.

"I feel the same way, Santo. But let's see if we can take things a little slower in the future. Less running and bleeding this time."

He smiled. "And more making love."

She wiped her tears and kissed him. "Yes. A lifetime of making love."

Read on for a sneak peek of
Erin Quinn's next novel of the Beyond

THE THREE FATES OF RYAN LOVE

Coming from Pocket Books in 2014!

Ryan Love stared at the wide-open door to his apartment with something that felt a lot like dread. He'd locked it before going on his nightly run, no doubt about it. He lived too close to Arizona State University to be careless. So why did it stand gaping now?

He scowled, wincing as it pulled the tender skin around his black eye, and took a step closer. At his feet, his German shepherd cocked her head, watchful but not whining or agitated. A small reassurance. She'd know before he did if someone was inside, attempting to rob him or lying in wait.

He paused on the threshold of his own home, unsure. It wasn't like him, this hesitancy. At six-two and two-twenty, Ryan didn't scare easily. But in the last few weeks, he'd had his beliefs scrambled in too many ways not to be rattled now.

Add to that, yesterday had started with the lights going on and off relentlessly for fifteen minutes. No loose bulbs, no blown fuses. Just flickering lights that followed him from bedroom to kitchen to bathroom and back. Then last night he'd been downstairs closing up Love's—the pub he owned with his brother and sisters—when he'd heard footsteps racing overhead. He'd charged up to his apartment only to find his dog, Adrian, sitting all alone inside with her ears pinned and her tail tucked. No sign of a break-in. Nothing missing.

This morning, his cell phone started ringing—not his ringtone—and when he answered, no one was there. Empty text messages sent by no one came next. They continued even after he'd taken out the battery.

And tonight his front door stood open.

Quietly, Ryan pushed the door back all the way, dropping Adrian's leash as he fisted his hands, ready.

The door swung open soundlessly, revealing the spacious apartment that sat above Love's. He hadn't closed the shutters before his run and now the floor-to-ceiling windows gave an unequaled view of sleeping Mill Avenue and a spangled sky. Beside him, Adrian paused and sniffed the air.

Ryan's gaze moved over the room, taking in the hulking couch and the sixty-inch HD TV in front of it. Off to the side sat a leather chair and his guitar, propped upright on a stand. A seven-foot Japanese screen divided his bedroom from the rest of the room.

With the big windows, there always seemed to be movement in the loft. Shadows shifting, light dancing on the walls, dust particles floating in bright sun- or moonlight. But tonight, everything seemed . . . rigid. Frozen. *Off.*

He couldn't explain it. And he didn't like it. As he scanned the stillness, Adrian's ears swiveled vigilantly. She felt it, too.

A loud creak turned his head. In the corner his punching bag began to sway. Too thick and too heavy to be manipulated by the breeze from the open door, it rocked back and forth for no obvious reason. Ryan searched for the cause while he slowly bent down and unhooked Adrian's dragging leash. The dog gave him a perplexed look and stayed by his side.

"Chicken," he breathed.

Adrian whined, unamused.

The stillness began to grate on his nerves as his awareness of that swinging bag in the corner grew. He strode across the room and caught the bag in midrotation, fighting its momentum until it stopped. For one disturbing moment there was calm, and then a woman's scream shattered the quiet.

Without stopping to think, Ryan charged out the door, taking the stairs two at a time. Adrian raced ahead of him, her bark sharp and fierce, and Ryan nearly tripped over the excited dog as he jumped to the landing, burst through the door to a small parking lot out back, and paused, searching for the source of that terrified shriek.

Overhead lights illuminated the blacktop and the few cars still parked there. Not even a wind whispered across the asphalt or shivered through the hushed night. Wary, Ryan stepped out, checking to make sure he had his keys before he let the door slam behind him.

He found the woman huddled in the corner between the cinder-block barrier that housed the dumpsters and the south wall of Love's. She had her knees pulled up and her arms wrapped around them, head down. Long, dark hair gleamed under the bright streetlights, spilling over her shoulders and hiding her face. He frowned. Her skin had an alabaster sheen—and there was a lot of it. She was naked.

Signaling for Adrian to sit, Ryan approached the woman cautiously.

"Hey," he said in a soft voice, hunkering down beside her. "Are you okay?"

She looked up and his labored breath skittered to a halt. She had wide, clear eyes as blue as a desert sky. Even in the dark the color was vivid and they shimmered with something he couldn't begin to define. Long lashes the same rich sable as her hair framed them and accented their luminescent glow. They tilted at the corners, cat-like. The dark wings of her brows drew the focus to the delicate shape of her face, the smooth line of her nose, the dusting of freckles that covered it. Her lips were full, her mouth wide. He didn't see any bruises or blood, but her scream still echoed in his mind and her nudity set off alarms he didn't even want to think about.

Before he could repeat his question, she whispered, "Ryan?"

The sound of her voice stood the hairs on his neck on end as a chill that had nothing to do with the cool night crept disquieting fingertips down his spine. He'd never seen this woman before, or at least he didn't think so. So how did she know his name?

He nodded and she sighed, a tiny smile catching the corners of her mouth. As he watched, a shiver went through her body and goose bumps rose on her arms. Quickly, he reached over his head, wincing as strained muscles protested, and pulled off his shirt.

"Here, put this on," he said, handing it to her.

She fingered the soft fabric and pressed it to her face, smelling it. The action was so surprising that at first all he could think to do was mumble, "Sorry, it's all I have," while hot embarrassment flooded his face.

"It has your scent," she said, that mystifying smile still on her lips.

There was something so intimate in the comment that it made him swallow hard and look away as she tugged the shirt on. The shoulders dropped to her elbows and the long sleeves hid her hands.

Her gaze never left his face, lingering on the cut over his nose, the puffy skin of his black eye, and his swollen jaw. He could almost feel the quicksilver stare on his bare chest and battered ribs. He must look like a big ugly thug to her.

He realized, suddenly, that there *was* something familiar about her, but he couldn't pinpoint it. He didn't think they'd ever met—he knew himself enough to know he'd have remembered her. Still . . .

He shook his head. It didn't matter. Something had happened to this woman and helping her was his first priority.

"Are you hurt?" he asked as he scanned the deserted parking lot for signs of trouble. Adrian's watchful silence told him that there was no one else here, but he was too shaken by the woman's appearance, her vulnerable position, to take chances. He hadn't seen any wounds, but that didn't mean she wasn't injured.

She hadn't answered him yet. He returned his attention to her face and gently asked again, "Are you hurt?"

She blinked at him, seeming to ponder the question. He could almost see her taking inventory. Her toes wiggled, her knees contracted slightly, then her spine stiffened and her hands flexed around her legs.

"Not permanently," she told him in a calm voice.

Not sure exactly what that meant, what *un*permanent things might ail her, he tried again.

"Did someone attack you?'

"No," she said with a definitive shake of her head.

"Why did you scream?"

"I didn't expect it to be painful."

Frustrated by her cryptic response, he said, "You didn't expect *what* to be painful?"

She shrugged. "Coming here."

Thoroughly confused, he opened his mouth to ask what had happened to her that would cause her to be in this parking lot, naked, but Adrian interrupted with a small questioning sound and the woman peered around Ryan's shoulders to look at the dog. Her eyes widened with a flash of what he'd swear was wonder and delight before she masked it.

Uneasy, he said, "Who are you?"

"Sibelle," she replied matter-of-factly, still watching Adrian.

He glanced back to see his dog down on her belly, inching closer in the most unthreatening manner a ninety-five pound German shepherd could manage.

Eyes narrowed, he turned back to the woman. "Where are your clothes, Sybil?" he asked.

She shook her head, pulling her gaze from Adrian to look him in the eye. "S'*belle*," she corrected. "Not Sybil."

"S'belle," he pronounced carefully. "Why are you naked?"

A hot flush turned her skin pink a second before she lied. "I don't remember."

She shifted with agitation and Adrian made a sound low in her throat. Not aggressive. Consoling. The dog had managed to army-crawl close enough to put her nose on the woman's foot. Sibelle's lips parted as she settled her fingers on Adrian's silky black ear. Adrian squirmed closer and laid her big fluffy head on Sibelle's lap.

"Okay," Ryan murmured, way out of his depth. "I need to call the police."

"No," she said, her voice suddenly urgent. "No police. What time is it?"

"I don't know. One? Two in the morning?"

Her eyes rounded and she scrambled to get her feet under her. "So late already? We need to leave here. Now, Ryan."

She stood, long legs protruding from his big shirt. Her hair brushed her shoulders and impatiently she swiped it back as she eyed the shadows anxiously.

Ryan stood as well, reaching in his pocket for his phone. "Calm down. You're safe now, but you seem a little disoriented. I don't know what happened but maybe the police can help you get it worked out."

"No police."

With a determined look, she turned and moved to the door he'd banged out of just moments before.

"Wait," he said. "Sibelle Whoever-You-Are. Wait."

She seemed more alert, more focused, but there was still a dazed air about her that worried him. He followed as she gingerly picked her way through the glass and gravel of the parking lot, ignoring him until she stepped on something sharp and gasped.

"Hold up. Would you stop?" he said, exasperated. "Let me help you."

She was tall but light as he lifted her in his arms and carried her to the door. Adrian escorted them like a devoted admirer, her wet nose brushing Sibelle's feet whenever the dog could reach them. Inexplicably nervous about letting her in, Ryan jockeyed her weight as he fumbled his key in the lock. Sibelle wrapped her arms around him, pressing all those soft curves against him as he tried valiantly not to notice.

Once inside he set her on her feet again, but she continued to hold on, staring into his face as if to memorize his features. She lifted one fine-boned hand and brushed her fingertips over the bruise on his cheek. He winced and she stilled.

"It hurts," she said.

"Yes."

"Why do you do it, then?"

Fight, she meant. *Why did he fight?* Some people inherited fortunes. Ryan had inherited a mean right hook, a keen sense of body language, and a failing pub he was desperate to keep afloat. But that wasn't any of her business.

Ignoring her questions, he took her shoulders in his hands to set her away from him. He felt the loss of her heat instantly and decided then and there that he needed to keep this strange, unsettling woman at a distance.

Adrian raced up the stairs ahead of them and waited on the landing. Ryan followed Sibelle, eyes averted from the long, silky legs and the hem of his shirt, which twitched with each step she took.

He didn't know who she was, how she had gotten here, or what had happened to her, but he knew he needed to get her help. She didn't act injured or even afraid, but shock affected people in different ways.

The front door stood open and Sibelle entered without waiting to be asked. She padded past the breakfast bar, trailing fingers over the back of the couch as she took in her surroundings. The microwave's clock read 1:30. He saw her note it with a deep breath and a nod. She said something in a low voice that sounded like "there's still time," but he couldn't be sure.

"Sibelle?" he said, drawing the startled blue gaze. "What happened? Why were you in the parking lot"—*naked*—"in the middle of the night?"

Adrian sat at her feet and leaned into her legs. Sibelle's fingers moved aimlessly over the dog's head as she gave him an unwavering look.

"I was sent, Ryan."

"By who?"

"It doesn't matter."

It did if that person was the reason she'd screamed.

"What happened to your clothes? Why weren't you wearing any?"

"They didn't travel with me," she said. "It makes sense, but I didn't think of it."

Ryan shook his head. "Back up. Start from the beginning. How did you get here?"

"I was sent to save you."

"*Me?*"

A dozen questions populated that one syllable. Like, who had sent her? Why? Save him from what? Was she off her meds? How could this slip of a woman save him from anything?

But he couldn't get any other words out because playing in the back of his head like a booming overture was the memory of the last couple of days. The lights. The cell phone. The front door gaping open, the swinging punching bag . . . her scream so close on the heels of all of it.

Sibelle glanced at the clock again and said, "I don't have time to explain things to you. But we need to leave this place. Quickly."

"I'm not going anywhere."

"Then you will die and I will have failed."

Ryan blinked in surprise.

She went on before he could speak. "Are you listening? You have twenty-two minutes to live if that clock is set correctly."

He cut his eyes to the clock and back to Sibelle.

"Did you hit your head?" he asked.

Ryan had always had an uncanny ability to hear a lie, and for all her crazy talk, she spoke with conviction. Still, he knew this woman had been traumatized. Her perceptions couldn't be trusted.

"You know I'm telling the truth. I can see it in your eyes."

"I know you believe you're telling the truth," he countered. "Not the same thing."

She moved to his guitar and pointed. "You'll need this."

"That's a guitar," he said. "Why would I need it?"

"Because it helps you think. And later, you'll want to do that."

She was right. Playing cleared his head and helped him organize his thoughts. He could use a few minutes alone with it right now, actually. But how could she know that?

"The money you have stashed under the floorboards. You'll need that, too. You won't be able to use your credit cards."

His mouth fell open.

"Clothes, of course. And Adrian. We'll need her."

"We?"

She gave him a frustrated look. "Eighteen minutes. That's all you've got. Unless you want to die?"

"Listen, I don't know where you came—"

"You don't need to know. The fact is I'm here. To help you. To save you. You can stand there and argue with me, or you can cooperate."

She moved into his bedroom. Dumbfounded, Ryan followed, watching her open his closet. Yanking his duffel off the top shelf, she began to stuff clothes in it. She rifled through his belongings with a familiarity that stunned him. Her fingers unerringly selected his favorites. She pulled a pair of basketball shorts from his dresser and stepped into them without asking.

"Can I borrow some shoes?" she inquired calmly, then spotted a pair of flip-flops on the floor of the closet and put them on before he had the chance to respond. They looked huge on her, but she didn't seem to care.

"Get the money, Ryan."

"You think you're going to rob me?"

The irritation in his voice finally penetrated her focus. She faced him.

"I know this probably seems—"

"Crazy?"

"Surreal. But why not humor me? There's no way I can hurt you. I'm not armed. I'm wearing *your* clothes and nothing else. Are you afraid I'm going to overcome you?"

He almost laughed. "No."

"Humor me, Ryan," she repeated and smiled in a cajoling way that did little to reassure him.

"Get your money, grab the guitar and your dog, and wait it out on the sidewalk with me. If nothing's happened by two thirty, you can call your police and be done with me."

"Or I could do that now and save myself the trouble."

She crossed to him and settled her hands on his arms,

locking those baby blues on him. "Please. You're going to die if you don't trust me."

She was all in when it came to her belief in what she said. The elfin face was earnest, the eyes determined. And incredibly, he felt his skepticism waver. He couldn't even imagine any type of threat this woman might save *him* from. He knew she must be nuts. That meant the only lurking danger was the one she might put herself in while she acted out her delusions.

And yet . . .

"Ryan, this isn't the kind of danger you can fight your way out of, no matter how big and strong you are," she said, as if reading his thoughts. Her warm hands gripped his bare arms tightly. "This danger you can't dodge."

Frowning, he said, "So what makes you think I can run from it?"

"I don't think that. You have one hope, Ryan."

"And I suppose that would be you?"

She shook her head. "Your fate has been measured, cut, and woven. The only hope you have is to change it."

"Lost me again, sweetheart."

She moved back to his duffel, zipped it up, and dropped it at his feet. "My fate is tied to yours now. Either we both die in the next few minutes or we live. It's your choice. Our fate is in your hands."

"I don't believe in fate," he said, turning away.

Sibelle stopped him with a touch.

"That doesn't matter. Fate doesn't require your belief, Ryan Love. Only your life."